Praise for Jennifer Erin Valent

"The first book in this series was a gem. The second a sparkler. But with *Catching Moondrops*, Valent closes out her series with a glistening jewel of a book. This is an author coming into her full talent, telling honest stories about love and conviction."

—Sibella Giorello, Christy Award–winning author of
The Clouds Roll Away

"An immensely satisfying conclusion to a beloved series, *Catching Moondrops* is a can't-put-down read that will open your eyes as much as your heart. With vivid characters and snappy dialogue, Valent brings the pre–civil rights South to life."

—C. J. Darlington, award-winning author of
Thicker than Blood

"Valent is a gifted author with a promising future."

—*Romantic Times* on *Cottonwood Whispers*

"Valent's debut is both heartwarming and hand-wringing . . . [and] the cast of characters is rich."

—*Publishers Weekly*, starred review of *Fireflies in December*

"Valent has created a darkly evocative historical novel that boldly explores the divisive effects of unreasoning hatred, greed, and fear on a community."

—*Booklist* on *Fireflies in December*

"With expressive descriptions and credible characters . . . Valent shines an awareness on the racial tensions in the South in the 1930s and its impact on innocent children."

"I found [*Fireflies in December*] difficult to put down, and it stayed in my heart well after reading the last page."

"A tight, finely crafted novel that challenges us to root out any hint of prejudice in our own hearts."

"Jennifer Erin Valent's debut novel is as sweet and salty as the South itself."

"*Fireflies in December* is an extraordinary first novel— a pure joy to read."

"I love this book! And I cannot wait to see what comes next from Jennifer Erin Valent!"

Catching Moondrops

CATCHING

MOONDROPS

Jennifer Erin Valent

AWARD-WINNING AUTHOR

TYNDALE HOUSE PUBLISHERS, INC.

Carol Stream, Illinois

Visit Tyndale's exciting Web site at www.tyndale.com.

Visit Jennifer Erin Valent's Web site at www.jennifervalent.com.

TYNDALE and Tyndale's quill logo are registered trademarks of Tyndale House Publishers, Inc.

Catching Moondrops

Designed by Jennifer Ghionzoli

Edited by Sarah Mason

Published in association with the Books & Such Literary Agency, 52 Mission Circle, Suite 122, PMB 170, Santa Rosa, CA 95409-5370, www.booksandsuch.biz.

This novel is a work of fiction. Names, characters, places, and incidents either are the product of the author's imagination or are used fictitiously. Any resemblance to actual events, locales, organizations, or persons living or dead is entirely coincidental and beyond the intent of either the author or the publisher.

Library of Congress Cataloging-in-Publication Data

Valent, Jennifer Erin.
  Catching moondrops / Jennifer Erin Valent.
    p. cm.
  ISBN 978-1-4143-3327-4 (sc)
  1. Race relations—Fiction. 2. Virginia—Fiction. 3. Domestic fiction. I. Title.
PS3622.A4257C38 2010
  813'.6—dc22   2010022909

Printed in the United States of America

16 15 14 13 12 11 10
7   6   5   4   3   2   1

To my uncle Jim Corrie, and to our Savior,
who has welcomed him home.

Acknowledgments

With every book, I stew over this part. Who to thank? There really are too many people. I've been blessed with a wonderful family and group of friends—people who have supported me, encouraged me, and walked this crazy journey with me. You all know who you are, you know what you mean to me, and you know how thankful I am to have you in my life.

Most particularly, I'm immensely grateful to my parents, who have always and forever had my back. Mom and Dad, I love you with all my heart!

To my Tyndale family—I owe you *all* an enormous thank-you! I'm learning as I go along just how many members of the Tyndale staff have had a hand in the wonderful production of my books, and I'm honored to have each and every one of you on my team. Stephanie Broene, Maggie Rowe, Babette Rea, Sarah Mason—I've had the opportunity to work closely with each of you, and I'm honored to have you by my side during this process. Thanks for all the coaching and support!

To all my readers who have taken time out of their lives to read what I write—thank you, thank you, thank you! I truly hope you've enjoyed every page.

Above all, I owe everything to my Lord and Savior, Jesus Christ. Lord, help me to use each step of this journey to glorify You—my amazing God!

Chapter 1

There's nothing in this whole world like the sight of a man swinging by his neck.

Folks in my parts like to call it *lynching*, as if by calling it another word they can keep from feeling like murderers. Sometimes when they string a man up, they gather around like vultures looking for the next meal, staring at the cockeyed neck, the sagging limbs, their lips turning up at the corners when they should be turning down. For some people, time has a way of blurring the good and the bad, spitting out that thing called conscience and replacing it with a twisted sort of logic that makes right out of wrong.

Our small town of Calloway, Virginia, had that sort of logic in spades—after the trouble it had caused my family over the years, I knew so better than most. But the violence had long since faded away, and my best friend, Gemma, would often tell me that made it okay—her being kept separate from white folks. "Long as my bein' with your family don't bring danger down on your heads, I'll keep my peace and be thankful," she'd say.

But I didn't feel so calm about it all as Gemma did. Part of that was my stubborn temperament, but most of it was my intuition. I'd been eyeball-to-eyeball with pure hate more than once in my eighteen years, and I could smell it, like rotting flesh. Hate is a type of blindness that divides a man from his good sense. I'd seen it in the eyes of a Klansman the day he tried to choke the life out of me and in the eyes of the men who hunted down a dear friend who'd been wrongly accused of murder.

And at times, I'd caught glimpses of it in my own heart.

The passage of time had done nothing to lessen its stench. And despite the relative peace, I knew full well that hearts poisoned by hateful thinking can simmer for only so long before boiling over.

In May of that year, 1938, the pot started bubbling.

I was on the front porch shucking corn when I saw three colored men turn up our walk, all linked up in a row like the Three Musketeers. I stood, let the corn silk slip from my apron, and called over my shoulder, "Gemma! Come on out here."

She must have been nearby because the screen door squealed open almost two seconds after my last words drifted inside. "What is it?"

"Company. Only don't look too good." I walked to the top of the steps and shielded my eyes from the sun. "Malachi Jarvis! You got yourself into trouble again?"

The man in the middle, propped up like a scarecrow, lifted his chin wearily but managed to flash a smile that revealed bloodied teeth. "Depends on how you define *trouble*."

Gemma gasped at the sight of him and flew down the steps, letting the door slam so loud the porch boards shook. "What in the name of all goodness have you been up to? You got some sort of death wish?"

A man I'd never seen before had his arm wound tightly beneath Malachi's arms, blood smeared across his shirtfront. Malachi's younger brother, Noah, was on his other side, struggling against the weight, and Gemma came in between them to help.

"He ain't got the good sense to keep his mouth shut, is all," Noah said breathlessly.

I went inside to grab Momma's first aid box, and by the time I got back out, Gemma had Malachi seated in the rocker.

Gemma gave him the once-over and shook her head so hard I thought it might fly off. "I swear, if you ain't a one to push a body into an early grave. Your poor momma's gonna lose her ever-lovin' mind."

Along with his younger brother and sister, Malachi lived down by the tracks with his widowed momma—as the man of the house, so to speak. He'd taken up being friends with Luke Talley some two years back when they'd both worked for the tobacco plant, and they'd remained close even though Luke had struck out on his own building furniture. Malachi was never one to keep his peace, a fact Gemma had no patience for, and she made it good and clear many a time. Today would be no exception.

"Goin' around stirrin' up trouble every which way," she murmured as she pulled fixings out of the first aid box. "It's one thing to pick fights with your own kind. Can't say as though you wouldn't benefit by a poundin' or two every now and again. But this foolin' around with white folks'll get you into more'n you're bargainin' for."

The man who'd helped Noah shoulder the burden of Malachi reached out to take the gauze from Gemma. "Why don't you let me get that?"

Gemma didn't much like being told what to do, and she glared at him. "I can clean up cuts and scrapes. I worked for a doctor past two years."

Malachi nodded toward the man. "This here man *is* a doctor, Gemma."

I was putting iodine on a piece of cotton, and I near about dropped it on the floor when I heard that. Never in all my born days had I seen a colored man claiming to be a doctor. Neither had Gemma, by the looks of her.

"A doctor?" she murmured. "You sure?"

He laughed and extended his hand to her. "Last I checked. Tal Pritchett. Just got into town yesterday. Gonna set up shop down by the tracks."

Still dumbfounded, Gemma handed the gauze to him.

"What d'you think about that?" Malachi grinned and then grimaced when his split lip made its presence known. "A colored doc in Calloway. Shoo-wee. There's gonna be talk about this!"

The doctor went to work cleaning up Malachi's wounds. "I ain't here to start no revolution. I'm just aimin' to help the colored folks get the help they deserve."

"Well, you're goin' to start a revolution whether you want to or not." Malachi shut his eyes and gritted his teeth the minute the iodine set to burning. "Folks in these parts don't much like colored folk settin' themselves up as smart or nothin'."

Gemma watched Tal Pritchett like she was analyzing his every move, finding out for herself if he was a doctor or not. I stood by and let her assist him as she'd been accustomed to doing for Doc Mabley until he passed on two months ago. After Tal had bandaged up Malachi's right hand, she seemed satisfied that he was who he said.

Noah slumped into the other rocker and watched. "It's one thing to get yourself an education and stand for your right to make somethin' of yourself. It's another to go stirrin' up trouble for the sake of stirrin' up trouble."

"I ain't doin' it for the sake of stirrin' up trouble. I done told you that!" Malachi flexed his left hand to test how well his swollen fingers moved. "Ain't no colored man ever gonna be free in this here county . . . in this here state . . . in this here *world* unless somebody starts fightin' for freedom."

"Slaves was freed decades ago," Noah said sharply. "We ain't in shackles no more."

"But we ain't free to live our lives as we choose, neither. You think colored people are ever gonna be more'n house help and field help so long as we let ourselves be treated like less than white people? No sir. We're less than human to them white folks. They don't think nothin' about killin' so long as who they're killin' is colored."

"Don't you go bunchin' all white people together, Malachi Jarvis," I argued. "Ain't all white folk got bad feelin's about coloreds."

Malachi waved me off in exasperation. "You know I ain't talkin' about you, Jessilyn."

Noah had his hands tightly knotted in his lap and was staring at them like they held all the answers to the world's problems. "All's you're doin' is gettin' yourself kicked around." He looked up at me pleadingly. "This here's the second time in a week he's come home banged up."

I put a hand on Noah's shoulder and set my eyes on Malachi. "Who did it?"

He put his bandaged right hand into the air, palm up. "Who knows? Some white boys. You get surrounded by enough of 'em, they all just blend in together like a vanilla milk shake."

"How's it you didn't see them? They jump you or somethin'?"

"Don't ask me, Jessie. I was just mindin' my own business in town, and then on my way home, they start hasslin' me."

"What he was doin'," Noah corrected, "was tryin' to get into the whites-only bar."

Gemma sniffed in disgust. "Shouldn't have been in no bar in the first place. There's your first mistake."

"Whites-only, too." Noah kicked his foot against the porch rail and then looked at me quickly. "Sorry."

I smiled at him and turned my attention back to

Malachi. "It's a good thing Luke ain't here to see this. He don't like you drinkin', and you know it."

Malachi's eyeballs rolled between swollen lids. "I don't know why he gets his trousers in a knot over it anyhow. Ain't like there's Prohibition no more. And he's been known to take a swig or two himself."

"Luke says you're a nasty drunk."

"He is." Noah knotted his hands back in his lap. "And he's been at the bottle more often than not of late."

"Quit tellin' tales!" his brother barked.

"I ain't tellin' tales; I'm tellin' truth. They can ask anybody at home how late you come in, and how you come in all topsy-turvy. He comes home in the middle of the mornin' and sleeps in till all hours the next day."

"What about your job at the plant?" Gemma asked.

Malachi closed his eyes and waved her off, but his brother provided the answer for him. "Lost it!" He loosened his grip on his hands and snapped his fingers. "Like that. There goes his income."

"I said I'll get another job."

"Oh, like there's jobs aplenty around these parts for colored folk. And anyways, if you find one, how you gonna keep that one?"

Gemma had her hands on her hips, and I knew what that meant. I leaned back against the house and waited for the lecture to commence.

"You talk a fine talk about colored folks needin' to stand up for equality, but you ain't doin' it in any way that's right and good. You're goin' about town gettin' people's goat and tryin' to get in where you ain't wanted and gettin' yourself all liquored up and useless. Now your family ain't got the money they depend on you for, and why? Because you walk around livin' like you ain't got to do nothin' for nobody but yourself."

"I'm standin' up for the rights of colored folks everywhere." Malachi was angry now, pink patches spreading on his busted-up cheeks. "You see anyone else in this town willin' to go toe-to-toe with the white boys in this county?"

"Don't put a noble face on bein' an upstart."

Malachi pushed Tal's hand away and sat up tall. "You call standin' up to white folks bein' an upstart?"

Doc Pritchett tried to dress the wound on Malachi's temple, but Malachi pushed his hand away again. That was when the doctor had enough; he smacked his hands on his thighs and stood up straight and determined in front of Malachi. "I ain't Abraham Lincoln. I'm just Doc Pritchett, tryin' to fix up an ornery patient, and I ain't got all day to do it. So I'm goin' to settle this argument once and for all." He pointed at Gemma. "She's right. There ain't no fightin' nonsense with more nonsense, and all's you're doin' by gettin' in the faces of white folks with your smart attitude is bein' as bad as they're bein'." Then he pointed at Malachi. "And he's right too. There ain't never a change brought about that *should* be brought about without people standin' up for such change. And sometimes that means bein' willin' to fight for what's right."

Gemma swallowed hard and didn't even try to argue. My eyes bugged out of my head at the sight of her being tamed so easily.

"Now, I'm all for civil uprisin'," Tal continued. "I don't see nothin' wrong with colored folk sayin' they won't be walked on no more. I don't see nothin' wrong with wantin' to use the same bathroom as white folks or sit in the same chairs as white folks. Way I see it, none of that's goin' to change unless someone says it has to." He squatted in front of Malachi again and stared him down nose to nose. "But all this hotshottin' and showboatin' ain't goin' to do nothin' but get your rear end kicked. Or worse. You aim to stand tall for somethin'? Fine. Stand tall for it. But don't you go around thinkin' these battle scars say somethin' for you. You ain't got them by bein' noble; you got them by bein' stupid. All's these scars say is you're an idiot."

It was one of the best speeches I'd heard from anyone outside my daddy, and if I'd ever thought for two seconds put together to see a colored man run for governor, I figured Tal Pritchett would be the man for the job. As it was, I knew he was the best man for the job he had now. Sure enough, being a colored doc in Calloway would be a challenge. But I figured he was up for it.

Regardless, he shut Malachi up, and for the next five minutes we all watched him finish his job with skill and finesse. When he'd fixed the last of Malachi's face, he stood and clapped his hands. "Suppose that should do it. Don't see need for any stitchin' up today. Let's hope there's no cause for it in future." Then he looked at me. "You got someplace out here where I can wash up?"

I held my hand toward the front door. "Bathroom's upstairs."

He hesitated. "I'd just as soon wash up out here."

I caught the reason for his hesitation but didn't know what to say. As usual, Gemma did.

"I done lived in this here house for six years now, and I'm just as brown as you. You can feel free to go on up to the bathroom, you hear?"

He looked from Gemma to me, then back to Gemma before nodding. "Yes'm." And then he disappeared inside.

"'Ma'am,'" Gemma muttered under her breath. "Ain't old enough to be called ma'am, least of all by a man no more'n a few years older'n me."

"You know what happens once you start gettin' them crow's-feet . . ."

Gemma whirled about and gave Malachi the evil eye. "Don't go thinkin' I won't hurt you just because you're all bandaged up."

Noah got up and paced the porch until Tal came back outside. "Doc, you have any problem gettin' your schoolin'?"

Tal shrugged and leaned against the porch rail. "No more'n most, I guess. There's a lot to learn. Why? You thinkin' about goin' to college?"

You could have heard a pin drop on that front porch. Never, and I mean never, in all the days Calloway had been on the map, had there ever been a single person, white or black, to step foot at a college. The very idea of that mark being made by a colored boy was a surefire way to start war.

And Noah knew it.

He looked at his feet and kicked the heel of one shoe against the toe of another. "Ain't possible. I was just wonderin' aloud, is all."

"What do you mean it ain't possible? All's you've got to do is work hard. You can get scholarships and things."

But Noah took a look at his brother, whose face was hard and tight-lipped, and nodded toward the road.

"Nah, there ain't no use talkin' over it. We'd best get home, anyhow."

Tal didn't push the subject. He just picked his hat up off the porch swing and plopped it on his head. "Miss Jessie, Miss Gemma, it was a fine pleasure to meet you and a kindness for you to give us a hand."

"You should stop by sometime and meet my parents," I said. "They're off visitin', but I'm sure they'd be right happy to know you."

"I'm sure I'd be right happy to know them, too." He turned his attention to Gemma. "You said you worked for a doctor?"

"I worked for Doc Mabley. He was a white doctor. Died some two months ago."

"He let you assist?"

"Only with the colored patients. Doc Mabley was kind enough to help some of them out when they needed it. Otherwise I kept his records, kept up his stock."

"Well, I'll tell you, Miss Gemma, I could sure use some help if you'd be obliged. An assistant would be a good set of extra hands, and I could use someone known around here to make my introductions."

Gemma eyed him before slowly nodding. "Reckon I could."

"Wouldn't be much pay now, you know. Ain't likely

to get much in the way of fees from the patients I'll be treatin'."

"Don't matter so long as I have good work to put my hands to."

"That it would be. My office is right across the street from the Jarvis house."

Malachi snorted. "*Shack's* more like it."

"Room enough for me," Tal said. Then to Gemma, "You think you could stop in sometime this week to talk it over?"

"I can come day after tomorrow if that suits."

"Nine o'clock too early?"

"No, sir. I've kept farm hours all my life."

He grinned at her. "Nine o'clock then?"

"Nine o'clock."

Malachi watched the two of them with his swollen eyes, a look of disgust growing more evident on his face. He'd made no secret over the past year about his admiration for Gemma, and the unmistakable attraction that was growing between her and Tal was clearly turning his stomach.

"Mind if we go home?" he muttered. "Before I fall down dead or somethin'?"

Gemma tore her eyes away from Tal to roll them at Malachi. "Would serve you right if you did."

"And on that cheery note–" Malachi groaned on

his way down the steps—"I'll bid you ladies a fine evenin'."

I gave Noah a playful whack to the head, but he ducked, so I only clipped the top. "Luke will be back home tomorrow evenin'. He'll be itchin' to see you, I'm sure."

"I'm itchin' to see him." He took the steps in one leap, tossing dust up when he landed. "You tell him to come on by and see us real soon."

"And tell him to bring his cards," Malachi added. "He owes me a poker rematch."

I squinted at him suspiciously. "Only if you play for beans."

"I hate beans."

Malachi leaned on Tal for support, and Noah scurried to catch up and help. I watched them go, but I wasn't thinking much about them. I was thinking about Luke. It had been two months since he'd left to collect customers for his furniture-making business, and every day had seemed like an eternity.

The very thought of him got my stomach butterflies to fluttering, but one look at Gemma told me it was another man who had stolen her attention. "That Doc Pritchett's a fine man." I smirked at her. "Looks about twenty-five or so."

"So?"

"Good marryin' age."

She crossed her arms defiantly. "Jessilyn Lassiter, what's that got to do with anythin'?"

"Only what I said. I'm only statin' fact."

"Mm-hm. I hear ya. You'd be better off keepin' your facts to yourself."

She grabbed the first aid box and headed inside, but the sound of that door slamming told me I'd got to her.

It told me Tal Pritchett had got to her too.

Chapter 2

We'd had all sorts of troubles in Calloway. We'd had violence, hate, sickness, and death. We'd seen droughts and floods, lost crops, and run out of money. But this late May day in 1938 wasn't a day I wanted to think about past pains or wonder about future ones. Today was the day I'd see Luke Talley for the first time in months, and there wasn't any room in my mind for sadness.

Which is why I scowled extra hard at the leaflet Gemma had found stuck to our porch rail with a thumbtack. Scrawled across the top was a ridiculous cartoon depicting a colored man reading the Constitution upside down. The text below read:

> Meeting to discuss the potential uprising of Negroes in Calloway County. June 15 at seven in the evening. Cole Mundy's barn.

"Cole Mundy's barn!" I balled the paper up tight and threw it onto the table beside the rocker where Gemma sat. "Ain't nothin' but evil goes on in Cole Mundy's barn, you ask me. I wouldn't step foot there for all the world. It'd be like steppin' off into hell."

Gemma clucked her tongue at me for saying *hell*, but I just rolled my eyes.

"Anyways, what sort of confounded idiot goes tackin' somethin' like that up to our house, of all places? Makin' colored men out to be dim-witted morons. Daddy sees that, he'll be on a manhunt."

"Then he best not see it." She reached over to snatch the paper, but Daddy came out of the house and beat her to it.

"You got somethin' I should know about, Gemma?" He stood there and looked from one of us to the other. "Reckon a man ought to decide for himself what he should and should not see."

I looked at Gemma and shrugged. "Maybe it's best he does see it."

She put her hand protectively over the paper for about five seconds, but that was all it took for her to figure she wouldn't win any sort of argument with my daddy. She sighed and handed him the wrinkled-up paper. "If you want, but it ain't nothin' but drivel."

Daddy unfolded it, and I watched his face for a

reaction. It didn't take long for his cheeks to light up, for his jaw to start doing that little dance it does whenever he's riled. But he didn't say a word. He took one good, deep breath, puffed his cheeks, and then let it out with a long sigh. The paper got squished into a tight ball again. "I ain't goin' to dignify this with a remark" was all he said. "Where'd you get it?"

I nodded to the post I was leaning on. "It was tacked up to the porch."

He didn't say anything, just retreated into the house, threw the leaflet into the fireplace, and struck a match.

I watched through the window as he leaned against the fireplace and stared until every speck of paper transformed into black ash. Then he slammed his fist into the mantel so hard that Momma's candlesticks shook.

Gemma and I jumped at the noise of it, and Gemma turned around in her seat to look inside. "What in the world . . . ?"

Daddy stomped off into the kitchen, where I could hear him giving Momma a whispered earful. I stopped staring through the window and slid into the other rocker. "That was Daddy takin' his frustrations out on the fireplace."

"I knew it'd be best if he didn't see it."

"No, you knew he'd get upset about it; that don't mean it weren't best. A man ought to know what sort of nonsense is goin' on about him. How else can he protect his family from it?"

"The more we stay out of it, the better he'll be able to protect us."

"That's a coward's way, Gemma Teague."

She flashed me one of her angry momma looks that always made me feel pity for her future children. "Call me a coward, call me crazy, call me whatever you want, but one thing you can't call me is a pot stirrer. I ain't out there just itchin' to get white people mad at me. I know my place, and I keep it."

"Oh, and your place is livin' with a white family like kin?"

She put her head back down to study her needlework, but I wasn't letting up.

"You think you'd have had a good home after your momma and daddy died if we hadn't decided you belonged with us no matter what people thought? You wish we'd decided you should 'keep your place' then?"

We didn't say anything for a few minutes until she dropped her needlework in her lap and sighed. "Won't they ever just go away?"

"Who? Men who hate colored folk? Klan? Not unless someone makes them go away. There ain't no reason, Gemma, why a couple dozen men should be able to say what's what when there's a couple thousand able-bodied people out there who could come together against them."

"There ain't a couple thousand hereabouts who'd fight for colored folks."

"All right, a couple hundred. Any which way, they ain't got the right to spread this sort of nonsense on our property. You see what they're tryin' to do, don't you? They ain't never wanted nothin' but to tell colored people what they can and cannot do, and now that there's some talk stirrin' about colored people havin' more rights, they aim to shut 'em down right off."

I pointed through the den window in the direction of the charred remains of the leaflet. "That thing there weren't no gentlemanly invitation. That was a threat. You think they thought in a month of Sundays we'd show up there? All they're doin' is bein' heavy-handed with us, mockin' us, and Daddy won't stand for it."

She shook her head. "I done told those boys they were askin' for trouble, tryin' to get into whites-only places and whatnot. Malachi and his lot . . . they should've known better."

"Gemma Teague!" My whisper came out sharp between clenched teeth. "Them boys is just tryin' to get somethin' more out of life."

"Oh, they'll get it, all right. They'll get it at the end of a gun barrel . . . or a rope."

"And what about Doc Pritchett? You're plannin' on workin' for that colored doc, and you know good and well folks in this town don't take kindly to what they see as a colored man goin' above his proper station."

She didn't look at me, so I knew I had her. "That's different."

"Ain't different nohow."

Gemma couldn't say much back. She couldn't argue with me once I made it personal.

I stood up and remembered why I was out here waiting on the porch in the first place, then went back to pacing the whitewashed floorboards just like Momma always does when she's anxious. It didn't escape my notice how much I became like her as I grew older, but Lord knows I didn't model her in all ways, and Gemma was first to say it.

"I swear you're the edgiest woman I ever done seen. Why can't you be more calm and peaceful like your momma?" She glared at me from her post on the rocker. "You got to do that? You're makin' the porch shake."

I didn't pause or reply. I just dug my eyes into hers as I paced in her direction, then spun around and headed back, nearly tripping over Duke, our ages-old basset hound. Years earlier, he would have scurried under the porch to escape my worrisome mood, but now it was all he could do to lift his eyes and glance at me.

"That dog may as well be nailed to the floor." I looked down the road both ways. "You sure there weren't any calls?"

"Would've told you if there were." She had her needle-point in her hands, her face so close to it I was surprised she wasn't cross-eyed. "You ain't gone nowhere all day, anyhow. Think you would've heard if the phone rang."

I studied her face with squinty eyes, hands balled up on my hips. "You need spectacles. You can't see a thing two feet in front of your face."

Gemma rubbed the space between her eyes, though I guessed it was more in exasperation than eye fatigue. "You ain't got to boss me, Jessilyn. They're my eyes. I ought to know when they need fixin'."

"You know full well they need fixin'; I ain't arguin' that. It's just you won't admit to it. You worried about lookin' funny around Tal Pritchett?"

"I ain't so vain as that, Jessie."

I backed away from the fiery stare, worried she might prick me with her needle. "Then you're worried about money." I tapped my toe waiting for her to answer, but she ignored me and went back to her needlepoint. "I'm full aware why a colored doctor won't be able to pay much, but I already told you I'd help buy you some spectacles. I been workin' for Miss Cleta more and more, and she's as generous as the day is long. I got me more than I need."

Her pointed focus on that needlework got under my skin, and after a good minute of silence broken only by the squeak of the rocker, my nerves were so raw my palms itched. But I was determined to play at nonchalance.

"Fine, then. Let yourself go blind. Next thing you know, you'll be sewin' your fingers together with that there needle. I reckon you'll think twice then."

A tuneful whistle off in the distance broke through our quarrel, and I nearly jumped out of my new shoes. I tipped a finger under Gemma's chin and made her look at me. "How do I look? Is my hair still put up nice?" I pulled my skirt out by the sides and inspected it. "My dress wrinkled?"

Gemma sighed and set her needlework on the table beside her. "It's only Luke, Jessie. Ain't like he's a stranger now. Don't get so riled up. You look right nice."

"I ain't seen him in two months," I managed to murmur even though my voice gave out halfway through. "Leastways, he ain't seen me in two months neither. What if he don't think I'm much to look at?"

"What d'you think's changed so much in two months? You stopped growin' two years ago, you ain't changed your weight none, and your hair's still long and golden brown like ever."

"But I'm wearin' it different." I lifted one finger and

ran it across my forehead. "I added five more freckles, too. Before you know it, I'll be nothin' but freckles."

"Age sure has made you vain."

"I got to worry about my looks now. I'm runnin' out of time to make Luke notice."

"You're not even nineteen years old, Jessie Lassiter. Time ain't runnin' out for nothin'."

"And Luke's twenty-five. How much longer you think I got before some city girl snags him up?" The whistling got louder, but I could barely hear it over my heart-beat. "Luke's gone off all the time, now he's all famous and whatnot. For all I know he's got a sweetheart in every town."

"Luke's a carpenter. He ain't Valentino."

"Everybody within a hundred miles of Calloway knows Luke Talley's furniture," I argued. "Ain't no one works wood better in this whole state."

"I didn't say there was." Gemma looked up the road behind me and reached out to pinch my cheeks twice.

"Ouch!"

"You're pale as a ghost. And he's just about to turn up the walk, so you best get that silly, sour look off your face and put a smile on."

The stupid grin I manufactured was enough to make Gemma have to bite her lip to avoid a laugh, but it was all I could manage without having my mouth quiver.

Gemma gave me a shove and then stepped back into the shadow of the doorway, leaving me and Luke alone and chaperoned all at once.

Luke stopped whistling and walking the minute I managed to make it off the porch and step into the sunshine. There was a good early summer breeze, and it picked his golden hair up and skimmed it across his forehead. He was dressed up like it was a church day, a new hat gripped in his hands. I watched his eyes for any sign of affection; it was all I could do to keep from running down to toss my arms around his neck. I reminded myself that only happened in my daydreams and stood my ground, waiting for him to make up his mind what to do.

He strolled slowly up the walk, a smile building with each step, and when he came within two feet of me, he stopped. "Jessilyn, you're a sight for sore eyes." Then he tossed his hat on the porch step behind me and pulled me close.

Even though his arms didn't embrace me in the kind of way I wished for, there was no better place to be in all the world, and I wanted to stay there for the rest of my life. Even at five feet seven and in my pretty new shoes, I had to stand on tiptoe to reach his neck.

"It's been two long months," I whispered in his ear.

He pulled away from me to look at my face, and for

one flickering moment I saw the brotherly smile slip from his eyes to be replaced by something far more to my liking. "Two *days* is too long."

Ten seconds of bliss dissolved the minute the clomp of my daddy's shoes rang off the new boards he'd nailed into the porch floor last week, and Luke let me go like I'd burnt his fingertips.

"You plannin' on keepin' the boy to yourself, Jessilyn?" Daddy asked, a glint of protectiveness brightening his eyes. He took Luke by the arm and nearly dragged him up the steps. "Come on in the house, son. Sadie's itchin' to see you, but she's up to her elbows in supper fixin's."

Luke and I shared one last glance before he skittered off alongside Daddy, stopping only to grab his hat from the steps. "There ain't no need for her to go makin' somethin' special."

Gemma stepped out of the shadows, and Luke stopped and shook his head at her. "I swear, Gemma, you get prettier every day." Then he swooped her up in a hug that looked far too much like the one he'd given me.

And he'd never said a thing about me being pretty.

A frown tugged at the corners of my mouth, but I gritted my teeth to keep from letting it have its way.

Gemma patted Luke's back and chided him. "You talk a good line, Luke Talley. I ain't changed one bit since you lit out of here a couple months ago." She nodded in my direction. "Jessie . . . now, she's the one doin' the prettyin' up. I swear her hair gets more like the wheat fields all the time."

I felt a tug at my heart over her doing that, and the frown let go of its hold in time for me to turn up one corner of my mouth.

"Sure enough it does." Luke looked back at me and let his eyes linger just long enough for Daddy to get antsy.

"Come on inside, boy. We got us some catchin' up to do." He pulled Luke's arm so hard, Luke nearly tripped over the threshold, and as annoyed as I was about having him torn away from me, I couldn't stifle a giggle.

"Same old, same old," Gemma murmured once they'd disappeared inside with Daddy hollering, "Sadie, look what the cat drug in." She held a hand out to get me to come up on the porch. "Your daddy won't be restin' this summer, I can tell you that. He'll be watchin' you two like a hawk."

"I don't suppose there's much to worry about," I said. "Luke hugged you just the same as he did me. Either he thinks of me like his sister, or he's got a crush on you."

"Oh, it ain't neither, and you know it. He's got eyes for only you, Jessie, so stop your worryin'. He'll figure it out soon enough."

"Don't see how you can say things like that when he looks at me no different than he looks at a chicken leg."

Gemma dug an elbow into my ribs, making me bend over and pull away from her side. "The way he feels about food, you should take that as a compliment."

My halfway smile gave out into a full one, and I wrapped my arm around her waist as we made our way inside to the smell of Momma's cooking.

"Jessie made the corn fritters," Momma was saying when we came into the kitchen. "You should just see her in the kitchen, Luke. She's becomin' a real fine cook."

"Yes'm, I know. She made me some tarts for my trip, and I ate 'em all up before I made it ten miles down the road."

Gemma gave my side a pinch, and I nudged her with my hip.

Momma had put Daddy to work carving the roast, and as she talked up my cooking to Luke, the knife hit the cutting board a little more loudly with each slice.

As I set the table, I kept letting my eyes peer out their corners, checking to see what Luke was up to. I'd never seen him look more like a real man, and I hoped he was thinking that I finally looked like a woman. I'd pinned my hair up, but there was never a day I could put it up without little wisps falling out, and those strands kept sticking to the gloss I'd patted on my lips. There was always a fight between my tomboy side and my womanly side, and I felt awkwardly trapped in between.

"You ain't got to worry about neither, Jessilyn," Momma'd said when I told her so one day. "You just let you show. Ain't nothin' better'n that."

But I felt all mismatched despite her words, and it was all I could do to swallow each bite of food at supper. Between snatching glances at Luke and battling my self-consciousness, I was too busy to think about food.

Daddy took my bad appetite as proof I was lovesick, so he dominated the conversation, leaving me and Luke with no chance to talk. I pushed my peas around with my fork and cleared my throat several times to get Momma's attention. It was clear by her face that she felt my pain, but even Momma's well-practiced artistry handling Daddy couldn't change the situation.

Gemma had plenty of sideways looks for me, and I knew she felt sorry for me.

I felt sorry for me too. I wondered if there'd ever be a day that Daddy would see me as a full-grown woman. After all these months of not seeing Luke, it was killing me to have to sit by so quiet and uncomfortable, and I was growing angrier with my daddy by the minute.

The only good thing to happen came with dessert, when Luke's knee met mine beneath the table. That was no uncommon occurrence at our tiny table, but it made a difference to me that he didn't move it, and the cobbler I'd made tasted even better than usual that night.

After supper, I grabbed an apron from the hook on the wall, resigned to an evening that didn't measure up even close to the one I'd imagined.

"Don't you go helpin' me," Momma whispered when I started to put it on. "You get on out and talk to Luke."

"Ain't no point in it, Momma. Daddy won't let me do no talkin'."

Momma planted her hands on her hips and sighed. "That man . . ."

"He ain't ever goin' to see me for nothin' more than his baby girl."

She cupped my cheek with her hand. "Yes, he will, honey. Don't you worry none about that. It'll come right; you'll see."

Gemma snatched the apron from my hand and pushed me toward the doorway. "Go on. I'll help clean up."

"You both go on," Momma said, grabbing the apron from Gemma. "I'll call your daddy in to help, and you three can go on the porch. It'll soothe things a bit if you're there, Gemma."

Momma walked on ahead into the hall and called for Daddy. "Harley, on second thought, why don't you come on and help me clean up so those girls can have a break. They did most of the precookin' since I got home late from town."

I made Gemma look at me close. "My hair okay?"

"It's fine. You look pretty and natural, like a real lady." She tucked a loose strand behind my ear. "Ain't no man who wouldn't say so, neither."

Daddy was staring at Momma with a furrowed brow when Gemma and I came into the den. He'd already lit his pipe, and the smoke was fairly floating up in question marks. "Can't you leave them dishes till later?"

"Only if I want to spend an hour scrapin' dried-up grease from them. Why don't you give me a hand now so we can all sit together in a bit?"

There weren't many times my daddy didn't oblige my momma's requests, and this wasn't one of them. He put his pipe down on the tray next to his favorite chair and got up with a long sigh. I could hear him whispering something to Momma as they retreated into the kitchen, but I didn't much care what it was now that I had Luke to myself . . . and Gemma.

"Why don't we go outside?" I offered like the perfect hostess. "There's a nice breeze this evenin'."

Luke hopped up from the sofa and opened the door for me and Gemma, but once we were outside, Gemma retreated to the rocking chair, leaving the swing for me and Luke.

I made extra certain to be ladylike when I sat down on the swing, tucking my skirt beneath me with grace, crossing my ankles perfectly. Luke took his seat next to me and got us swinging with one push off the floor.

"Was there any trouble on your trip home?" I asked, breaking a few moments of silence.

"Train left a little late, that's all."

"Business go fine?"

"Seems so." He squinted and pointed off into the front yard. "What happened to that old maple?"

"Came down in a storm. You should've heard Momma yelp."

"Good thing it didn't come down on the house." He tapped his foot to keep us moving. "Ain't got your tree swing no more, then?"

"Oh, it made it out alive. It's just stuck in the shed, is all. Figure there ain't no need for a tree swing now we're all grown-up."

"Seems all wrong not seein' it swayin' in the breeze." He put his arms behind his head and grinned. "I can remember you swingin' on that thing like it was yesterday, your ponytail floppin' every which way."

"I loved that swing. I watched Daddy make it when I was four years old. He helped me carve my initials into the bottom, too."

"Time sure does fly."

A good five minutes of silence passed before I finally suggested we take a walk. "We could go see the new garden Gemma planted. She's got some fine flowers there."

"I didn't know Gemma liked playin' with flowers enough to keep a garden."

"She took it up of late. Says it relaxes her. Don't you, Gemma?"

But Gemma was asleep in her chair, her head tipped to the side. I didn't buy it for a second, but I knew better than to question her. She was just doing what any good friend would by letting me and Luke wander off for a bit of time alone.

I looked at him and shrugged. "She's had a busy day."

He smiled and held out his arm for me to take, and I walked down the steps beside him like I was walking down the aisle.

The sun was just starting to say good night, and the crickets and frogs were celebrating loudly. The breeze stirred up my hair, and I could feel even more strands start to drift down around my face. But I didn't care if my hairpins all fell out in a heap. All I wanted was to listen to Luke breathing beside me.

By the time we reached the garden, I was feeling a bit more at ease in his presence, like being silent together made me remember some of what we'd been to each other for the past six years. But that relationship had changed as I'd become more woman than girl, and there was still a difference between us that we hadn't quite learned to cope with.

Luke was the first to speak when we reached the garden. "Looks like Gemma's been busy."

I walked away from him to finger a carnation. "Gemma says there's a meanin' to every flower she's got in here. I like the daisies the best." The rhododendron beside me rustled, playing into the spell between the two of us, and I kept my gaze on the plants rather than on Luke. "Did you meet anyone interestin' while you were away?"

"Just city folk. Can't say I met anyone who made me forget what I left behind."

I stood a little taller and let my eyes wander over to him. "Oh? Don't you like city folk?"

"They ain't Lassiters, is all."

A few more strands of hair dropped in front of my eyes, and I peered meekly through them.

Luke reached into his pocket and held out a small box tied with ribbon. "Brought you somethin' back."

I was pretty sure my feet came off the grass, but I steadied myself and did everything I could to keep from showing my excitement. "You didn't need to do that."

"I know I didn't." He sauntered up in front of me, stopping just beside the pink rosebush. "I *wanted* to."

I eagerly took the box from him and tried to untie the

35

ribbon without letting my fingers shake. When I managed to fish the top off, I gasped at the necklace inside, a perfect pendant with one sparkling green stone in the center. My words got caught in my throat, but I managed to whisper, "It's beautiful."

"Ain't a real gem or nothin' . . ." Luke pulled it from the box and turned me around by the shoulders. "Let's see how it looks on you." He fumbled with the clasp, but once he'd secured it, he turned me back around and stared at me solemnly. A swatch of hair blew in front of my left eye and stayed there, impeding my view of his face. He reached up and brushed it away, tucking it behind my ear. "It matches your eyes."

His hand lingered against my face a few moments, and while we stood there together, the sky lit up pink, casting color all around us. It was a moment to be stored away in memory for years, and I avoided breathing for fear of breaking the spell. But just as quickly as the last bit of sun dropped out of sight, so did the moment between us, and he stepped away as though some forgotten thought had suddenly crept into his brain.

I bristled at the change. It seemed it wasn't only Daddy who had trouble noticing I'd grown up. The past two years had been endless days of the same: Luke giving me ideas that he had feelings for me and then pushing me away. The only way I'd found to cope was by purposely torturing him, mocking his discomfort; and necklace or no necklace, it was still the only way I could see my way out of the moment.

I fingered his gift and watched the remnants of the setting sun glint off the stone. "Sure is a pretty thing." I walked toward him and held the pendant next to my eye. "You think it matches, you say?"

"That's right."

"You must spend a lot of time admirin' my eyes if you could remember just how they look after two months without seein' them."

He looked away. "I've seen them for six years now, Jessie. I ain't color-blind, after all."

I stepped up in front of him and smiled. "So there weren't no city girl with green eyes that modeled for you or nothin'?"

He was blushing right to the tips of his ears as he always did when I taunted him, but he looked at me seriously. "Ain't nobody with eyes like yours, Jessilyn."

And there it was, the truth I always managed to pull out of him with my taunts. I could feel the fire in my own cheeks, and I stepped back to hide them. But as we watched the pink and orange sky together, side by side for the first time in months, that small bit of truth was enough to tide me over.

For now.

Chapter 3

Gemma stood in the middle of Tal Pritchett's office, her hair pinned up in a kerchief, an apron wrapped around her middle.

I dug my fists into my hips and sighed. "You belong on a pancake box."

"Don't you go makin' fun of colored folk, Jessilyn."

"I ain't makin' fun of colored folk. I'm makin' fun of you. First time a fine, eligible man comes around here for you, and you go dressin' up like you're ready to pick cotton."

"Well, it suits the occasion, and that's all there is to it. And besides, he ain't here."

"Right now he ain't. But he and Luke will be here soon with the supplies, and he's gonna wonder when Gemma left and Aunt Jemima walked in."

"Oh, shush!" She grabbed a feather duster and ran it across one of the shelves that lined the back wall of Tal's tiny office, spattering the air with dust that lit up like sparks in the sunlight. "Sakes alive!" she sputtered, then bent over in a coughing spell. "This place is filthy."

"And ain't we lucky we get to clean it?" I pulled my shirt up over my nose to keep from inhaling the dust and went to open one of the windows, but it was stuck tight. I pounded my fist on the four corners and tried again. "Stuck good," I murmured. I pounded again and managed to get the window to move, but once it came unstuck, it slid up so fast it hit the top of the opening and shattered.

I heard someone outside whistle in dismay, and I stuck my head out, careful to avoid the shards that threatened to stab me. Luke was standing there with a toolbox in his hand, his hat tipped back on his head so I could see how high his eyebrows were.

"You wouldn't happen to have some glass in that there toolbox?" I queried.

"Fresh out."

Tal came up behind him and surveyed the damage, his arms full of paint supplies. "You girls mad at me for somethin'?"

I rolled my eyes. "I didn't do it on purpose, for heaven's sake. It slipped."

"Whatever you say, Jessilyn." Luke smiled that mischievous smile of his that made my heart flutter every time. It had happened so many times by now, I was surprised my heart could still take it.

"Would you stop bein' ornery and come in here? This place is so rickety, I swear it might buckle under and cave right on in. Hope you can work some miracles with those nails."

Tal rounded the corner and stepped in ahead of Luke, who had to duck under the low doorway.

Luke set his toolbox down and gave Tal a nudge with his elbow. "You sure you ain't better off just takin' this place down and puttin' up a tent?"

Tal didn't say much at first, only gave the dusty, decrepit building a once-over. Cobwebs hung on the ceiling two layers thick, floorboards poked up like molehills, and a trail of ants followed a straight line across the floor, up the wall, and around the one unbroken window. There wasn't much about the place that said *doctor's office.*

"It's what the Lord provided." He sighed. "Reckon I won't be seein' many people in here, anyways. I'll mostly be goin' door-to-door."

"Well, if it's what the Lord provided, there ain't nothin' but good to come of it, then," Gemma said. "The Lord always works out good for those who love Him."

"Looks more like a closet than anythin'." Luke took off his hat and scratched his head thoughtfully. "Ain't space for much more'n a table and chair."

"Well, since when did Calloway ever have nice places to accommodate colored folks?" Gemma swirled her duster and filled the air again. "Ain't like colored folks get the pick of the land hereabouts."

Luke's eyes traveled up the structure and along the ceiling, where bits and pieces of plaster had fallen away. "Tal, you plan on treatin' your patients for free after the ceilin' falls off and hits them in the head?"

Gemma clucked her tongue at him. "Oh, it ain't goin' to do no such thing."

"If you say so."

"Well, this is a fine mess. Just one more thing to take care of." I crouched down and picked up one of the jagged pieces of glass, tossing it into a wastebasket, and then I grabbed the broom and dustpan. "Honestly, Tal, I wasn't tryin' to bust your window out."

He smiled and took the broom away from me to finish up. "Leastways we got plenty of fresh air, Miss Jessie. Lord knows, we'll need it."

Turned out we needed much more than that broken window could provide. With four of us in that small space, all hot and tired and dusty, bumping into each other at every turn, a whole wall of windows wouldn't have given us even half the clean air we needed. By the time we stopped work for a late afternoon lunch, I was about ready to pitch my dust rag in the woods and never look back.

We had cleaned, sanded trim, and painted surfaces for hours, so I gratefully walked outside with the basket of food Momma had insisted on packing for us, my spirits lifting the second I presented my face to the soft breeze.

There weren't many words exchanged while we ate, but it didn't take any words for me to see that there was something stirring between Gemma and Tal Pritchett right there on that hot, sticky workday. The looks that passed between those two could have come off a movie screen.

Tal would look at Gemma, but Gemma wouldn't look back. Then Gemma would look at Tal, but he wouldn't look back. It was the silliest and sweetest thing I'd ever seen. And it continued on even as we worked. Several times throughout the day I felt Luke looking at me, and when I glanced over, he'd nod at Gemma and Tal almost imperceptibly, then smile or wink.

Neither Luke nor I said a single word. We kept our peace and behaved ourselves, but we couldn't help but take note of all the times Tal offered help to Gemma or all the cups of sweet tea Gemma offered to Tal.

It didn't take a genius to figure out that we were see-ing the start of something big.

Around four o'clock I noticed the light that had streamed through the windows all day was beginning to fade, and before too long I was having to put my face closer to the window frame I was painting to get my strokes right. It wasn't long before a rumble of thunder sounded in the distance. I looked at Gemma out of sheer habit.

Her whole body tensed as it always did when she heard that sound, and then I saw her peer around at our rickety shelter. I figured just as she did that this wasn't the sturdiest place to ride out a summer storm, and I knew without a doubt that the confinement of this space, with its broken window and porous ceiling, wouldn't even come close to making Gemma feel safe.

Tal noticed the change too. "Gemma," he said softly. "Miss Gemma, you okay?"

But Gemma didn't answer. Another round of thunder, this one closer than before, had stolen her attention away.

Tal looked at me for help.

"Gemma's not too keen on thunderstorms," I told him softly. I leaned in to whisper, "It's what took her momma and daddy all them years ago."

Concern flared in Tal's eyes, and he tossed his hammer to the floor and went to Gemma's side. "Miss Gemma," he said with such ease a body would never have guessed he was a bit flustered. "Why don't we get on in my truck and get you home before this storm hits? This place is all leaks and open windows, and I won't have you gettin' all wet and soggy."

I could see Gemma's face relax the second he suggested they hightail it out of there, but she attempted a protest. "We still got work to do."

"And it can be done another day. It's more than kind of you to do what you've done, and I'd feel sore at myself if I had to take you home drenched. No, you'd be doin' me a favor if you'd come on with me just now." He threw a few tools into his toolbox and tucked it under one arm, holding the other out to Gemma. "Luke and Jessilyn, that's enough for everybody today, I think. Can't thank you enough."

"You go on ahead," I told him. "We'll finish gathering these things and follow behind you in Luke's truck."

Tal looked at Luke, who nodded and said, "We'll only be a few minutes behind."

As soon as they left, I went to the broken window to watch them drive away. Tal was as gentle as a man could be as he helped Gemma into his old, beat-up truck, and I felt a peace inside because of it. "He's a good man, that one," I murmured. "I can feel it in my bones."

"Sure enough." Luke tossed his hammer and a bag of nails into his own toolbox and whistled between his teeth. "And darned if he ain't got stars in his eyes for our Gemma."

I gave him a cockeyed grin and folded my arms in front of me. "What makes you such an expert?"

"I know a trick or two about such things, Jessilyn. Don't you go underestimatin' me."

The thunder grumbled louder now, and the clouds that had coasted in suffocated the landscape with gloom. The wind through the broken window tossed Luke's hair across his forehead, and I stepped forward to sweep it away. "I ain't never underestimated you over nothin', Luke Talley."

His expression grew serious as it always did when a moment like this crossed our path—one of those moments when we couldn't help but acknowledge the depth of feeling between us. He slipped one finger beneath my chin and opened his mouth to say something, but I never found out what it was. An abrupt crash sounded through the tiny structure, and Luke shoved me to the ground beneath a shower of glass.

We stayed there on the floor until the shards stopped falling from the last good window in the place. Finally Luke whispered in my ear. "You okay?"

I was more stunned than anything, and it took me a

second before I managed to nod. He carefully pushed himself away from me and brushed aside some pieces of the glass before crawling to the doorway.

I rose to my knees but kept my head down. A large rock lay off to my right, and I leaned over to retrieve it, running my thumb across its smooth surface. I held it up for Luke to see. "One thing we know: this didn't get blown in here from the storm."

He peered at me over his shoulder and scowled. "Stay down! Same people who threw that in here can try it again. Or worse."

I crawled across to where he was. "See anythin'?"

"Nothin'."

He stood up slowly and scoured the landscape under the moody black sky. I followed his lead, but he put one arm out to guide me behind him. Someone had thrown that rock, someone who could still be here, watching us, preying on us like coyotes. We gingerly made our way around the side of Tal's office until we reached the back of the building and saw what had been done to it.

There, scrawled in red paint, was the word *nigger*.

Anger and fear coursed through me all at once. From behind Luke, I slipped my arm beneath his and gripped the front of his shirt as though if I hung on to him tightly enough, everything would be all right.

He put his hand over mine but didn't say a word, still scanning the trees for whoever had done this.

And then we both found him.

A flash of white shot out in front of us like a ghost coming out of hiding. I cried out, but Luke squeezed my hand in reproach. I watched, hardly breathing, unable to take my eyes away from the very thing I'd dreaded ever seeing again.

Memories from my childhood swept across my mind, thundering images of ghostly figures, darkness lit by the eerie glimmer of a burning cross.

The figure stood there wordlessly, the edges of his white robe flapping in the breeze. The ominous slits where his eyes should be showed only darkness, the truest reflection of the soul that lingered beneath.

I couldn't breathe. It was as though the mute apparition before me had sucked the air from my lungs. My fingernails dug into Luke's chest, but he didn't budge. No one moved; no one said a word. After several seconds that seemed more like hours, the man in white lifted one arm in our direction. He pointed a finger toward us and cocked it back once, twice, like a boy playing gunfighter. And then he disappeared into the woods.

My knees were shaking, my heart pounding so violently I could hear it over the wind and thunder.

Luke stepped backward so he was beside me and

slipped an arm around my waist. "Let's get on home," he said softly.

"But the office," I whispered. "Look what they did."

He didn't look back at it; he just sighed. "Creative, ain't they? But we ain't waitin' around while they're out there. We'll deal with it another time."

"It's gonna kill Gemma to see this." I stared off into the woods where the Klansman had disappeared. "I never thought to have to run across them again."

I waited for Luke to reassure me that we never would, that this was the last time, but he didn't say a word. I suppose he couldn't. Who is there on this earth that can promise evil won't ever touch your life again?

He just rushed me around to the front of the office, loaded our things in the truck, and swept us away from there without a word. When we pulled up at the house, Momma and Daddy were on the porch, and they shot down into the yard like cannon fire the minute they saw us coming. They could smell our fear without a word, and before I could count five, Daddy was between us, nearly dragging us up to the porch and inside the house.

When we got inside, I saw Tal and Gemma standing in the middle of the den. Gemma ran to me and took me by the arms. "What's wrong? I told them somethin' had happened to keep you. I had a bad feelin' in me."

Daddy locked the door behind us. "What's goin' on?"

"Klan," I murmured breathlessly. "They're at it again."

At the mention of the Klan, Momma's hands shot to her mouth, and I could hear her whispering a prayer to Jesus.

"Who said they ever moved out?" Daddy paced the floor with loud, angry clomps. "Jessilyn, you sure it was Klan?"

"Oh, it was Klan all right," Luke answered for me. "Only saw one, but he did enough damage. Put a rock through your other window, Tal. Looks like you got cross-ventilation now."

Gemma slid down to the sofa and tucked her hands tightly between her knees. I knew well enough she was doing it to keep them from shaking. I sat beside her and put my arm around her shoulders.

Tal walked over to the fireplace and leaned on the mantel, his back to us. "They do anythin' else?"

Luke shifted his weight and cleared his throat. "Left a little note for you, is all."

"I reckon it didn't have nothin' to do with welcomin' me to town."

"Reckon not."

"Harley," Momma gasped, "I thought the law took care of this years ago."

Daddy leaned back against the doorjamb and sighed loud and long. "Honey, the law may have shut down the local Klan back then, but they weren't able to clean up people's hearts none. It was only a matter of time."

Gemma finally found her tongue and interrupted Daddy with a shaky voice. "And what with Malachi and his like goin' about town talkin' nonsense, there ain't no wonder they's started up again." She slumped back into the sofa and hugged her arms around her waist. "I knew he'd stir things up round here."

"No, ma'am. It ain't just Malachi. It's me, too." Tal crossed the room and knelt in front of Gemma. "They ain't goin' to take kindly to no colored man claimin' to be smart enough to doctor folks around here, even if them folks is colored. You best think about that long and hard, Miss Gemma, 'cause if you're thinkin' to work side by side with me in this here town, you're like to be caught right up in this with me."

"They ain't got call to go after you. You ain't done nothin'."

"Most folks they go after ain't done nothin' except be born colored. Makes it worse, them thinkin' I'm bein' uppity. I got me a target on my back, and I won't have you gettin' hurt because of that."

Gemma scowled at him. "Don't you go tellin' me what to do, Tal Pritchett! If I want to work for a colored doctor,

I'll work for a colored doctor. I ain't ever had no Klan tell me what to do, and I won't have you doin' it, neither."

Despite the fact that my knees were still shaking, I couldn't help but smile. If Tal Pritchett hadn't gotten a good taste of what Gemma Teague was made of, he certainly was getting one now.

Tal sat back on his heels, slipped his hat off, and smiled. "Well, Miss Gemma, I ain't a man to go fightin' a woman who knows her mind. I reckon a body's got the right to do what a body feels the need to." He took one of her quivering hands in his. "All I ask is you give this another day or two thought; put your mind to prayer over it. It'll make me feel a right bit better about the whole thing."

Gemma pursed her lips and nodded firmly. "I reckon that's the best way to do anythin'."

Meanwhile, the whole scene of those two hand in hand and face-to-face had brought my momma and daddy to a standstill. They had met Tal Pritchett the same day Gemma and I did. Tal had come back by our house that evening to ask Daddy if he'd be all right with Gemma coming to work for him. The way I figured it, he couldn't have done much better than that to impress my daddy, but I don't think either Momma or Daddy had bargained on seeing Gemma and Tal get to know each other quite so quickly.

But the second Momma noticed what was up between the two of them, her fear melted away like candle wax, and she clapped her hands together in front of her face. "Well, I reckon the best medicine here is some fried chicken. Y'all are stayin' for supper, right?"

Tal let Gemma's hand slip away from his and stood up. "Mrs. Lassiter, that's right kind, but I don't want to impose."

"You'll be imposin' if you *don't* stay. I always like guests at my table."

"She ain't just bein' polite, neither," Luke told him. "She's had me here most nights for six years, and I've only seen her put out when I say I can't come."

"With all due respect, Mrs. Lassiter, I worry my bein' here might bring y'all trouble."

It was Daddy's turn to speak up this time, and whether he was keen on Tal and Gemma finding friendship so fast or not, I knew the last thing he'd want Tal to think was that he wasn't welcome. He crossed his arms and stood firm in front of the doorway. "Son, we welcomed Gemma into our house all them years ago, and we're better for it. I ain't likely to start changin' now. Them confounded idiots want to run around here with their robes and torches, it won't be nothin' we ain't seen before."

Tal hesitated a second, then walked over to my daddy

and firmly gripped his hand. "Mr. Lassiter, I'd be honored to stay for supper."

Gemma could hardly hold back the ecstatic smile that was trying to burst out all over her face, so I grabbed her hand and pulled her up off the couch. "Let's get on upstairs and clean up. I feel like I've got dust from head to toe."

We rushed through our washing, both of us eager to get back to certain someones but neither of us saying a word about it.

She finished dressing before I did and flopped down onto her bed. "I feel like your momma does. I'd hoped maybe we'd been done with them Klan boys."

"Like Daddy says, evil don't just disappear. Mostly, I guess it hides its head for a while till it seems a good time to pop out again." I did up the last button on my dress and sat beside her. "Just wish it wouldn't pop out at us." I shrugged, then took her hand and squeezed it hard. "Leastways, we still got each other to lean on. I ain't got any plans on lettin' nothin' happen to you."

She looked at me then in a hollow way that sent a chill down my spine, like there was something behind those eyes that spoke of worse things to come. "You can't always protect people, Jessilyn, no matter how hard you try."

I didn't know what to say. Her expression frightened

me more than the ghostly figure in the woods. She took my hand and turned her head to stare silently out the window.

I looked at her brown hand and swallowed hard to keep down the fear that was welling up inside me. If the Klan was rising up again in Calloway, there wasn't one person who could count themselves truly safe.

Especially not the colored ones.

Chapter 4

There's something about an early summer sunset that colors everything a shade of peaceful, even when peace is hard to find, and there was no difference in this one as I sat next to Gemma watching the sky go orange. We had plopped down in an unladylike way right smack in the middle of the meadow, and I knew we'd be picking ticks off each other before bed tonight. But we didn't care about ticks or snakes or any of the other tricks nature had up its sleeves. All we wanted was the best view of the sky, and we'd found it.

Once the sun dipped out of sight, I lay back and studied the clouds that reflected the waning light. "Miss Cleta didn't bake today," I murmured. "I didn't never think to see a day her bakin' would slow, but she's gettin' more and more weary."

"She ain't no spring chicken."

"No. Ain't never been as long as I've known her. But she ain't never been tired enough to keep her fingers out of the flour, neither." I picked a long, fat string of grass and peeled it into little strips. "She barely has the energy to get out of that chair of hers some days. I hope she ain't sick or nothin'."

"Maybe she ought to see a doctor."

"She won't see one now Doc Mabley's died. She calls that new doctor nothin' but 'a schoolboy with fancy knickers.'"

Gemma snorted and rolled onto her side, her head propped up on her elbow so she could look at me. "She's still got enough gumption to be stubborn."

"She'll be stubborn the day she stands at heaven's gates." I turned my head to search Gemma's eyes for concern and found it there. "You think she needs to see a doctor, don't you?"

"Last time I saw her, she looked right poorly around the eyes. Sickness always hits the eyes first, you ask me."

"But she won't see him."

"Maybe we can take her to the hospital."

"There ain't no way you're gettin' Miss Cleta to the hospital unless she's out cold, and I ain't goin' to be the one that bats her over the head." I stared back up at the sky in time to see it switch from orange to pink.

"Nope. We're goin' to have to come up with somethin' else." The crickets and frogs joined up in a boisterous chorus, and I smiled. "That's the sound of summer."

"They're loudest after a particularly nice day, you notice that? My momma used to say they were singin' praises to God for another fine day."

Gemma's voice was touched by that same husky tone of remembrance that always tickled her throat when she talked about her late momma or daddy, and I reached my hand out to take hers. "Then your momma and daddy have the best seat in the house."

She squeezed my hand in reply, and we lay there amid that peaceful buzz until the moon lit a path back home.

Luke had stayed after supper to help Daddy work on his old truck, and when we reached the house, he was still under the hood tinkering with things I couldn't identify and didn't want to. In the lantern light, Daddy was nowhere to be seen, and I took the opportunity to get under Luke's skin.

"Ain't nothin' more attractive to a woman than a man workin' with his shirtsleeves rolled up," I sang out.

Luke stood up so sharply at the sound of my voice, he smacked his head on the hood.

I cringed and ran over to give his head a good rub. "I didn't mean to startle you." Even in the insufficient light, I could see his ears light up pink, but they were tinted for more than my benefit this time.

Out of the corner of my eye, I saw Daddy come around the truck. I turned slowly toward him only to find his eyebrows raised up to his hat.

"Oh . . . there you are, Daddy." With one hand still cuddled up in Luke's hair, I tried to smile, but Daddy's expression was like an antidote to smiling. "Looks like you're workin' hard," I managed to murmur. I looked at Gemma for help and found her struggling to keep the corners of her mouth down. I guess Daddy's face was only withering to me and Luke.

But she came to my rescue no matter how humorous it all seemed to her. My hand was still on Luke's head like it had been glued there, and she took me by the arm, pulling me toward her so it would drop away. "Bet some lemonade would hit the spot right about now. Me and Jessie'll go fetch some."

I tripped along behind her, taking the steps into the house without grace.

"You always got to say things," she whispered as we entered the kitchen.

"Most people do say things, Gemma Teague!"

"Not the things you say. Talkin' flirty to Luke in front of your daddy."

"I didn't know he was there."

"You best stop your teasin', anyhow." She grabbed two glasses from the cabinet and pushed them into my hands. "It makes Luke nervous."

"I'm only playin'."

"You ain't only playin', and you know it. You're fishin' for his feelin's is what you're doin'." She held Momma's best pitcher in her left hand and grabbed my right hand with her own. "Hold the glass steady, for heaven's sake. I'm tryin' to pour."

"Keep your voice down about Luke," I whispered, steadying the glass against the kitchen table. "Momma's in the den."

"Well, you should leave him be, is all I'm sayin'. He'll come around in his own time."

Momma's voice rang out from the hallway. "Who'll come around in his own time?"

I should have known better. My momma had been a momma long enough to hear a whisper better than a shout, and I dropped my head with a sigh.

A bead of lemonade sloshed over the side of the glass, sliding down to rest on my hand. Gemma scolded me for it. "Keep it still, I said."

"Who's that you're talkin' about?" Momma asked again, joining us in the kitchen.

I scanned my mind for anything that would fill in for the truth without really being a lie, but Gemma was too quick for me. "Luke," she said plainly. "Jessie's been teasin' him again, and her daddy heard it."

I scowled at her. She never looked up to catch it, but I knew she felt it.

"You're goin' to wear that boy out." Momma cut up a strawberry and plopped the slices into the glasses. "I never took you for a tease, Jessilyn. I swear, you surprise me more days than not."

"Well, if Luke Talley's goin' to take so long to see me for a woman, I ain't goin' to sit around twiddlin' my thumbs."

Momma poked an elbow into my ribs and nodded toward the kitchen window. "It's open," she whispered.

We all stopped dead still, but Luke's voice floated in on the breeze, and I figured if he was able to talk about carburetors, he hadn't heard any of what we'd been saying.

Momma shook her head and added some cookies to the tray that Gemma had set the lemonade on. "No matter what you say, Jessilyn Lassiter, you ain't all the tomboy you think you are." She handed the tray to me and patted my cheek once her hands were free. "Next time you figure on workin' your womanly charms, you best make sure your daddy's out of earshot."

I gave her a smile in reply and carried the tray out, hoping Daddy had softened a bit. But he wasn't around when I got there, and I wondered why I couldn't have saved my comment for now instead.

Luke was leaning against a tree, one foot propped up on it, wiping his hands on an old cloth.

I peeked under the truck just to be sure. "Where's Daddy?"

"Gone off to the field shed for a tool." He lowered his voice for safety's sake. "You best not go teasin' me like that again. Makes your daddy think I'm takin' liberties or somethin'."

"How would you be takin' liberties when I'm the one doin' the talkin'?"

"Don't matter who's sayin' what. He's bound to think there's somethin' goin' on between us, and you know well and good there ain't."

I looked away from him, the tray starting to shake a bit, more from frustration than nervousness. I set the tray on a nearby stump and walked over to lean against the truck, never letting my eyes drift to his. "Ain't nobody in their right mind who'd ever say there was somethin' between us." The hood was still up, and I turned my back to him and peered inside. "Looks like a bunch of nothin' if you ask me."

I felt him walk up behind me, and those familiar prickles started parading down my spine. "I wasn't tryin' to put you out, Jessie."

"Didn't say you were. You're right. There ain't nothin' between you and me for Daddy to get his back up about. He ought to know you don't see me as much more'n a sister."

He put his hands on my waist and turned me to face him. "You may be a lot of things to me, Jessilyn, but you ain't like no sister."

I didn't get much more than a second to stare at him before Daddy's singing sounded from the back of the house, but it was enough to make the rest of the world fall away. Luke stepped back but held my gaze, and I sauntered slowly backward, smiling at him as a way of saying good night. He returned my smile with a dimpled one of his own, and I turned around and floated into the house. Momma and Gemma were chatting in the den, but one look at my face made them take a break.

"You all right, Jessilyn?" Momma's face spread into a sly grin. "You seem all flushed."

"Ain't nothin', Momma. Just warm outside, is all."

"Uh-huh." Gemma's gaze filtered down to my waist. "That why you got grease prints on your dress?"

I looked down to find perfect fingerprints decorating my sides like a sash. "Oh. I was around the truck and all . . ."

Momma's face showed signs of trying not to laugh, but she managed to nod in the direction of the stairs.

"Best get that off before your daddy figures out where them smudges came from."

"I don't know what you're talkin' about," I murmured without a lick of conviction.

"Well, all the same . . . get on upstairs and put on somethin' fresh."

"Yes'm." I hurried upstairs, but once I got that dress off, I laid it carefully across the bed like it was made of glass. Most times, the first thing I'd do once I'd gotten something on my dress was to soak it, but not this time. Those fingerprints were like a trophy to me. Dressed only in my slip, I slid down onto the window seat to admire the dress, and every time I looked at the dark smudges, I remembered Luke's touch.

Chapter 5

Men like Delmar Custis just aren't satisfied with peace and quiet. Delmar had a cotton farm with a rickety old house plopped in the middle. Most days he did nothing but sit on that run-down porch of his with some kind of liquor in one hand and a cigarette in the other. From what I saw, the only reasons he ever got off his backside were to lay into his wife or one of his hired hands or to head over to the bar in town, where nine times out of ten he ended up making trouble.

My daddy would tell me that men like Delmar argue and fuss so much, there wasn't any use in debating with them. "People who are wantin' a fight will find a way to get one whichever way they can," he'd say. "Don't matter to them who's right."

Well, he was right, I'm sure, like Daddy mostly was.

But I wasn't of any mind to keep from trying to convince somebody they were stupid when I got the chance. I'd been that way from the time I could put words together into sentences, and all the years that had passed didn't do much to change that except I'd learned a whole lot more words to use in my arguments. After all, if a man's a fool, I figure he ought to know about it.

Which is why I stood toe-to-toe with Delmar Custis and Sheriff Clancy that Wednesday afternoon, telling them just what I thought about Klansmen and their plans for backhanded dealings in Cole Mundy's barn.

"You ain't the sheriff in these here parts, Jessilyn Lassiter. Seems you still ain't figured that out."

"I don't need no badge to know evil when I see it."

Miss Cleta had sent me into town in Mr. Stokes's taxi to fetch some groceries for her, and one of the bags started slipping from my hands. Neither man moved to help me; they just watched me use my hip to bump it back up into my arm.

"Sheriff, I didn't call you over to listen to this man run off at the mouth. I called you over here because he was threatenin' me."

Delmar huffed and tobacco juices shot out of his mouth. "I ain't done nothin' to this girl."

"Except step in my way so I couldn't pass."

He swept his hand to the side like he was putting the

whole town on display for me. "This here's a pretty big space for me to take up all by my lonesome. Seems to me I'd be mighty hard-pressed to block your way."

"The way I see it, if a lady's walkin' down the sidewalk and a man sidles up in front of her and doesn't budge, he's goin' out of his way to be threatenin'. And that's just what you done."

"Anybody say you got the right-of-way?"

"Most times what we call *manners* says I have the right-of-way, but then what am I thinkin'? I ain't talkin' to someone who was raised on such things. Men who go around beatin' their womenfolk ain't too likely to be chivalrous."

Delmar drew his hand back like he was planning to whack me with it just like I figured he'd done to his wife a time or ten. I gripped the bags in my arms extra hard like I had some strange notion they would protect me against Delmar's beefy hand, but Sheriff Clancy put his arm in front of Delmar like a barricade.

"Now that's enough of this nonsense," he said. "Jessilyn, I ain't got no reason to arrest Delmar. We best just let this all go now, you hear?"

"I ain't askin' you to arrest the man, Sheriff. I just figured maybe you could let him know he don't own the sidewalk, so he should let a woman pass if she sees fit to."

Delmar shook his head with an expression that implied I was the dumbest woman he ever laid eyes on. "You just can't shut your mouth, can you? I'm tellin' you now, girl, you better back off."

"All right, that's enough." Sheriff Clancy stepped in between us and gave Delmar a little shove. "Everybody needs to move on and let this lie."

I had cold food to get back to Miss Cleta's, and for her sake I might have done just what Sheriff Clancy ordered if things hadn't taken the turn they did. I hiked up my bags, gave Delmar Custis one last look that told him I thought he was less than worthless, and turned to walk away.

Sheriff Clancy lit up a cigarette and sauntered back to the jailhouse, but Delmar stood right where he was. "You best keep an eye out for yourself, girl," I heard him say from behind me. "I don't take too kindly to people talkin' against me."

I stopped and swung around to look at him, but he only gave me a sordid grin.

"You threatenin' me?" I asked.

"Just a friendly warnin'." He glanced at the post office, where a group of young men stood around, apparently having nothing better to do than talk nonsense all day. "Bobby Ray!" Delmar called to his son. "You seen Jessilyn here?"

Bobby Ray flicked his cigarette into the bushes and stood up straight. "Hey there, Jessilyn." His eyes made their way from my head to my shoes in a way that made me feel dirty. "Ain't seen you in a while."

"Best keep an eye on her," Delmar said. "Seems she's gettin' on the wrong side of some folks hereabouts."

Bobby Ray pulled another cigarette from his pocket, lit up, and watched me, squinty-eyed, through the smoke. "Yes'r. Reckon I won't mind keepin' an eye on her at all."

Being around one Custis was enough for any girl to stomach, but being around two got the butterflies working inside me. Delmar smiled at me and winked, then climbed into his truck and drove off. Bobby Ray still stared at me through that veil of cigarette smoke, and I figured I'd best get back to Mr. Stokes's taxi while I could.

That was until I saw Noah Jarvis coming down the street, his head lowered like he wasn't looking for a bit of trouble but expected it anyway. No doubt he'd seen those boys there on the steps and hoped he'd get by without a problem, but I didn't bet on them keeping their peace. They watched Noah the whole way down the street, whispering to each other like they hoped beyond all hope he was heading their direction.

I made my way to meet up with Noah, but he put his

head back down the second he saw me. "Best not come over here, Jessie," he said loud enough that only I could hear. "They won't like it much."

"I don't care what they like."

He looked up at me with an uncharacteristic fire in his eyes. "Maybe you don't, but it ain't you they'll pick a fight with."

I got his meaning good and quick and stopped right there. A car horn alerted me that I was standing in the middle of the road, and I scurried to the sidewalk, watching Noah but not approaching him, knowing with dismay how right he was. Those boys were just waiting for a reason to light into any colored man no matter how peaceful he may be. But I couldn't just walk away, so I made up some reason in my head why I would need to go into the post office and walked right up the steps, Bobby Ray Custis and all.

When I got three steps up, Bobby Ray tipped his filthy hat at me and eyed me like I was on the menu for supper. "Jessilyn, you're lookin' fine today."

"I ain't asked for your opinion, Bobby Ray." He was leaning against a post, his feet out in front so they blocked my path. "You reckon you can get your giant boots out of my way?"

"Not so fast." He leaned forward and flashed a smile that showed teeth I figured hadn't ever met a toothbrush.

"I ain't seen you in a while. You and me, we got some catchin' up to do."

He reached out to grab my arm, but a hand shot around me to catch his instead. I looked over my shoulder to see Luke standing there with a death grip on Bobby Ray's arm. Bobby Ray's face turned bright purple, like the blood had all been pushed up to his cheeks, and he stopped breathing for a second. When Luke let go of his arm, Bobby Ray sucked in so much air, I wasn't sure there'd be any left for the rest of us.

Luke leaned close enough to Bobby Ray that their hat brims touched. "I reckon you're caught up now." Then he took my arm and escorted me into the post office.

I looked back at Bobby Ray with pure satisfaction.

"I swear it ain't safe for women to walk around this town in broad daylight no more," Luke muttered. He took his hat off and whacked at the front as if he needed to clean the stench of Bobby Ray off of it. "Those boys do anythin' to you before I got there?"

"Just bein' ornery, is all."

"You're all right, then?"

"Sure, I'm all right." Of course I was. I was perfect. It isn't every day the love of your life comes in and man-handles a lout on your behalf. I set the bags down and tucked my arm through his. "I'm glad you came along, though."

He looked around the post office. "Well, what'd you need in here? I'll wait for you and walk you back out. I was drivin' by when I saw you, so I can drive you home."

"I didn't need anythin'. I just came up the steps to distract those boys while Noah walked by. They looked rarin' for a fight, and I didn't want him gettin' picked on for it."

"Noah?" Luke walked over to the window and peered outside. He smacked his hat against his thigh and then shoved it back onto his head.

"What?" I rushed over next to him to see Malachi's brown face sticking out from a crowd of white ones. "What's he doin' here?"

"He was with me, helpin' me get a load of lumber. No doubt those boys said somethin' to Noah and he just couldn't help himself."

Heat crept up my neck into my cheeks in two seconds flat. "He's only stickin' up for his brother."

"Only stickin' up for your brother when you're colored means riskin' your life." Luke pulled his gun from his waistband and handed it to me. "If there's a scuffle, I don't want to risk one of them boys gettin' hold of it."

I took it from him reluctantly. "Be careful."

"I'll be fine." He flung the door open but turned back to point at me. "You stay here!"

Once upon a time those words would have whooshed

past my ears and I would have barged on out as I pleased, but I'd done my momma proud in some ways and learned to take heed of good advice when I heard it.

At least sometimes, anyway.

But today I listened, even though I was a nervous wreck, and I watched the brewing riot from that open post office window as though I were watching the first blows of the Civil War.

Dolly Gooch worked there. I could smell that dead roses perfume of hers as she crept up behind me, peering over my shoulder like I was a fence post or something. I'd known Dolly since we were small, and I didn't much like the idea of being in a bad situation with her and her dramatics.

"You reckon there's somethin' brewin'?" she asked with a quiver in her voice. "I'm in charge here, you know, and I don't want to get in no trouble for somethin' happenin' to the buildin'."

I dropped my shoulder so her chin slipped off it. "I ain't rightly concerned about any damage to the buildin' just now, Dolly. Lest you can't tell, men's well-bein' is at stake, and I reckon that's a little more important."

She tried to lay her chin on my shoulder again, but I pulled away and stepped closer to the window.

At first there was so much chatter and shoving and pushing outside that I couldn't make heads nor tails out of any of it, and the chaotic feeling of it all made my nerves so raw I could barely stand still. Malachi was right in the thick of things, his cockeyed, arrogant grin the perfect fuel for the fire, and poor Noah stood at the bottom of the steps wringing his hands and calling for Malachi to let it all alone.

But Malachi and I had one thing in common—stubbornness—and he wasn't about to even think of backing down. I was sure of it.

Bobby Ray let out a shout that got everyone's attention on him and then pushed his way front and center. Luke had wedged in between Bobby Ray and Malachi, but being a good head shorter than Luke, Bobby Ray slipped under his arm like a weasel and stood so close to Malachi, I was surprised he didn't fog up his face. "Boy, you best go on back where you came from before you ain't got legs to carry you there, you hear? You're messin' with the wrong men now."

"Men," I muttered. "Can't believe that boy has the audacity to call himself a man."

Malachi didn't respond to Bobby Ray at first, only grinned that grin that I was sure would be pasted on his face the day he died at a white man's hand, and Bobby Ray gave him a good poke in the chest. "You hear me, boy?"

He'd have to be deaf not to, and Malachi only stood

taller on his toes and pumped a fist against his chest like an ape. "You want to see what a real man can do? You just come on and find out."

Luke grabbed a handful of Bobby Ray's shirt and threw him to the side, then stepped up close to Malachi. "I'm tellin' you now, get back in the truck," he said through clenched teeth. "You're startin' a fight we can't finish."

The cocky smile slipped from Malachi's face for the first time. "Who's *we*? I didn't say you had to be involved in this. This ain't your fight."

"Don't be stupid. I ain't likely to stand by and watch you get the stuffin' beat out of you, now am I?" He nodded toward the street. "You go on and take your brother home. It ain't right for him to be watchin' this."

Malachi took a look behind him at Noah, giving Bobby Ray the perfect opportunity to lay a punch square in his middle. The blow took the air out of Malachi and bent him at the waist, but it took him only a few seconds to recover enough to come up and land his fist under Bobby Ray's chin.

Dolly screamed in my ear and ran for the telephone. "I'm callin' the sheriff."

"Yeah, I'm sure he'll be a big help savin' a colored man."

"Colored man or not, the sheriff's bound by duty to

protect this post office, so he'll do it or I'll let my daddy know, and my daddy's good friends with the mayor."

The way I figured it, Malachi Jarvis had walked himself into the licking he was getting on purpose, and Bobby Ray Custis didn't have enough brains in his head for anyone to notice if he got them beaten out of him. But the second I saw someone's fist take a shot at Luke's jaw, I was fit for battle. Without even waiting to see Luke's reaction, I settled my finger on the trigger of his pistol and threw the front door open. I sounded one shot into the air and then leveled the gun in the direction of Bobby Ray's head.

He flinched, either at the sight of the gun or at the pain in his jaw—I wasn't sure which—and put a hand out as if to steady me. "Now, Jessie, there ain't no need for guns. We're just having a fair fight here."

"I was in school with you, Bobby Ray, so I know for a fact you at least know how to count to ten. The way I see it, it's six against two, and in my book that ain't no fair fight." I cocked my head to the side. "Now y'all get on."

Bobby Ray reached up to rub his jaw and smiled. Blood ran down from his mouth and he spit it on the post office steps. "You even know how to use that thing?"

I reckon he wouldn't have egged me on if he'd known the hours I'd spent with Luke teaching me how to shoot proper, but it didn't matter to me what he knew and didn't know. Without a single thought to what I was about to do, I squinted one eye, tipped the barrel of the gun to the right, and pulled the trigger. The blast knocked the head off the stone eagle that sat at the entrance to the post office and sent those boys flying for cover. They all swore and looked at me like I'd lost my mind.

"You could have blown my knee off!" Bobby Ray was at the bottom of the steps now, crouched down so he looked half his already-small size.

I tipped the gun back toward him. "Reckon I missed, but I can try again if you want."

He swore at me, but there wasn't much he could do with that gun pointed at him. He spit into the dirt and then glared at Malachi. "We'll be seein' you again. You bet on that."

Like something out of a James Cagney picture, Malachi remarked, "Anytime."

Luke gave him a shove to shut him up, and I kept the pistol on Bobby Ray until they all scattered off down the street.

Once they were out of sight, Luke looked at me and shook his head. "Jessilyn, I swear . . ."

"Don't go gettin' sore at me." I lowered the gun and handed it to Luke. "What'd you want me to do, stand there and watch you two die in front of me?"

He stuck the gun in his waistband without taking his eyes off me. "What was your plan if you really *had* hit Bobby Ray?"

I shrugged. "Didn't have time to think about it." A smile slowly spread its way across my face. "Got lucky hittin' that eagle, though, didn't I? It was a nice touch."

"You got lucky? What were you aimin' at?"

"Anythin' but flesh, I reckon."

Luke shook his head at me with a smile starting to turn up the corner of his mouth. "Do me a favor next time and don't shoot till you know what you're shootin' at."

"Don't get all worked up. It ain't every day I have need for shootin' a gun, anyhow."

Sheriff Clancy came walking up the street so slow, you would've thought he was taking his morning constitutional. "Jessilyn!" he called. "I got other things to do with my day besides keepin' up after you." He stopped at the foot of the steps and surveyed the situation. "You got any ideas about that gunshot I just heard?"

Luke and I looked at each other and shrugged in unison.

"I got me a call somethin' was goin' on down here."

"Nothin' that ain't been handled," Luke said.

In my mind the man was useless, and I made no bones about it in the way I looked at him. "Reckon if you weren't available to take care of what started the trouble in the first place, you ain't got need to take care of what finished it."

"You tellin' me you don't know nothin' about that gunshot?"

"Mostly I'm sayin' there weren't no harm done."

Sheriff Clancy flicked cigarette ash into the breeze and squinted at me. "Well, *mostly* I'm sayin' I don't like people goin' around shootin' up my town." The sheriff leveled his gaze at Luke. "You got anythin' you want to tell me?"

Dolly came out of the door just then with her hands crossed over her heart like it was about to fail on her. "Land's sake, it took you long enough to get here, Sheriff. I thought we'd have a bloodbath on our hands."

"I came soon as you called."

"Then you're the slowest man I ever seen. You know, my daddy ain't goin' to be happy to hear I was in any danger. I reckon he'd expect you to come around good and quick if there's any trouble around here."

"Your daddy ought to know I do my best."

She positioned her hands on her hips and put on her best spoiled-baby face. "Your best! Your best would have been to get here quick. Instead, we were all left here to face them hooligans alone, and if it weren't for Jessie, we'd have all been dead."

Sheriff Clancy looked like he was struggling to keep his composure. "I highly doubt you'd have died."

"How would you know? You weren't here, were you?" She waved a hand at him in dismissal. "Anyways, you may as well leave now since you ain't no use to us. All's well, thanks to Jessilyn." Then she caught sight of the blood on her steps and nearly fainted over dead. "Will you look at that? That might never come off, and I'll be blamed for it. They might take it out of my pay." She pointed angry eyes at Sheriff Clancy. "See what happens when you don't take care of things quick?" She ran inside.

Sheriff Clancy shook his head and sighed. "Y'all quit playin' with guns, you hear?" He walked off as slowly as he'd come, surrounded by a cloud of smoke.

Luke nodded toward the post office and whispered, "What d'you think she'll do when she notices that headless eagle?"

I smiled at him, but our lighthearted moment was interrupted by Noah walking up to stand at the bottom of the steps and glare at his brother. "How long's this goin' to go on?" he asked. "You goin' to keep this up till Momma's got to bury you? Is that what you want? You tryin' to get yourself killed?"

"Noah, I ain't doin' nothin' but standin' up for what's right."

"This ain't standin' up for what's right. It's pickin' fights."

Malachi took the three steps in one leap to land in front of his brother. "I ain't got to be scolded by my little brother. It's my life, and I got the right to do with it as I please."

Noah's whole body shook as he stood there in front of his brother. "Fine, then. You go ahead and ruin all our lives, because that's what'll happen when you end up hangin' from the end of a rope one day."

Disgust ran across Malachi's face, and he turned away to walk off alone. "You tell Momma I won't be home for supper."

"What's new?" Noah called after him. "You just make sure there don't come a day when I have to tell her you won't be home *ever*."

Luke slipped his arm through mine and led me down the steps to where Noah stood. He dropped his other arm around Noah's shoulders. "Don't feel bad. Ain't nobody can get through to him right now."

"I don't feel bad for nothin' except Momma. It'll kill her if somethin' happens to him."

Dolly came back out muttering about "stupid men bleedin' all over her steps," so we wished her the best in cleaning it up and said we'd get on our way.

"Oh," I called to Dolly as Luke darted past her into

the post office, "tell Mr. Bates I'll pay for the eagle's head to be fixed."

Dolly narrowed her eyes quizzically until she caught sight of the beheaded bird. "What in tarnation?"

Luke came back down those stairs as fast as he could without dropping Miss Cleta's bags. "Let's get on out of here before she starts screechin' again." He gave Noah's shoulder a nudge. "Come on, I'll ride you home. You need to let things cool off around here."

We found Mr. Stokes where I left him and sent him on his way, then piled into Luke's truck for the trip home. It had all been fine and good to make jokes about my shooting, but as we sat there next to Noah, his worries spilled out onto us, and it was uncomfortable the whole way. We let him off in front of his house and watched him walk up the steps with the weight of the world on his shoulders.

And there was nothing we could do to help.

Chapter 6

Luke's furniture business had come about all by accident, as he liked to say. It was born of him doing bits and pieces for local folks who told people about his good work, and it just so happened that one of them told the richest man in town. After Luke made him a set of chairs and such for his big house, all his rich friends wanted some too. That was when I found out how rich people often liked to have what the other one had, only bigger. And by the time Luke was done filling orders for the local fancy folk, he had a business going whether he'd wanted one or not. Orders came from all over Virginia until eventually people were asking him to go miles away to craft something special for them.

I was as proud of him as any woman could be, but I envied those blocks of wood because they got to spend more time with him than I did. He still had most suppers with us, and if he hadn't, I doubted I'd get to see his face most weekdays. As it was, he worked some Saturdays, too, but those were the days I'd head over to his place, determined if he wouldn't come to me, I'd go to him.

When I rounded the corner to his house, he was bent over a dressing table with his sandpaper, and I walked quietly so as to keep from distracting him from his work. But when I saw the open book beside him, I stopped in my tracks.

His eyes darted back and forth from the worn Bible my daddy had given him a few years back, his lips moving as he whispered to himself what he read there. My cheeks flushed at the sight of it, and I looked away, feeling I'd interrupted something sacred.

It had been some time since the day we'd lost our friend Mr. Poe, and though I still missed him dearly, the effects of that day had been lessened by time. Mr. Poe had lived a life full of confidence in a God I didn't know or understand, and it ate away at my insides. But no matter how hard I tried, I couldn't find my way to the faith that had possessed his very soul.

It wasn't that way for Luke. The sight of Mr. Poe giving up his life so willingly was stamped on his consciousness like he'd been branded, and it changed him for good. It was like a switch had been flicked, and that light I'd seen in my family and in Miss Cleta suddenly started to glow inside of him. It was a change that brought him closer to the God that had always been a dividing line between me and those dearest to me, and it didn't settle well in my heart.

"It's the best thing possible for Luke," my momma had told me a short time after. "And any woman who loves her man wants what's best for him no matter how it makes her feel."

But I was a selfish girl, I knew well, and I didn't want there to be any kind of separation between the two of us for any reason. It only served to rough up my heart like that sandpaper Luke had in his hands. I said as much to Momma once, and she told me sandpaper eventually smooths things out, so my heart should be good and ready soon. But I wasn't keen on being roughed up, and when Luke stood and stretched, I pushed all thoughts of God and Bibles aside and called out a hello.

"Hey there, Jessie." He turned his body toward me, but I saw him reach out quickly to close the Bible that had once graced the table beside my daddy's favorite chair. He knew as well as I did that it was a sore spot between us. "I was plannin' to come over after I'm done here."

"Looks like you've got some solid work goin' on there, and I know you well enough to know you won't put those tools down until you've got it finished. Reckon we wouldn't be seein' you till church tomorrow at this rate."

He used the back of his hand to brush the sweat from his forehead. "Lady who wants this dressin' table wants it all decorated up with curlicues and whatnot. I swear, you should see her house. There's fancy knickknacks all over the place, like you're afraid to take a step so's you don't knock somethin' over. I ain't never seen nothin' like it."

"She dress fancy too?"

"Taffeta and hats. You'd think she was the queen of England."

I ran my finger along the wood and traced one of the curlicues. "Wonder what it'd be like to wear taffeta."

He set narrowed eyes to the tabletop and grabbed the sandpaper again to smooth a piece of it out. Then he shook his head. "Taffeta don't suit you."

"You sayin' I can't pull off a fancy dress?"

He set the sandpaper down and leaned against the table, arms crossed. "No, I'm sayin' you don't need fancy things to make you pretty."

I looked down to hide my nerves and pulled my skirt sides out on display. "Can't say it would hurt me to have somethin' finer than this old thing."

"You never worried before about what you wore."

"A woman changes her mind a lot, you know."

"Well, a man don't." He reached out to finger my

sleeve. "And I still say you're as pretty in this dress as you'd ever be in a mountain of taffeta." His hand slid from the fabric to trace a lazy river down my arm, leaving a trail of goose bumps behind, and I caught a breath. But before I could even think about running out of air, he pulled his hand away and shoved them both into his trouser pockets like a boy ordered to the woodshed.

I didn't know whether to cry or holler at him, but I'd had enough of his going back and forth to last me two lifetimes. What he'd said about men not changing their minds was nothing but drivel. "You think you can fool me, Luke Talley, but you can't. You know you can't keep your mind off me no matter how hard you try."

He looked over my head, his jaw tensing, but I stood on my toes to look into his eyes.

"You just stay here workin' all day 'cause you're afraid of my daddy's rifle, but I can see it all over your face: you think about me all the time."

I reached out to tug playfully at his shirt, but he caught my wrist in his strong grasp and pushed me backward a few steps until I ended up against the trunk of a willow tree. I gasped and looked up at him, wide-eyed. Our faces were inches apart, my arm pinned between the two of us.

"It ain't funny no more, Jessilyn," he said through clenched teeth. And then as suddenly as he'd taken hold of me, he let me go, turned on his heel, and walked away, leaving me to stare after him in awe.

I couldn't help but be wobbly in the knees as I backed away, watching his house like it would tell me all that went on inside that head of his. I took twelve paces backward before finally spinning around to make my way through the fields toward home, but even then I took the long way.

By the time I got home, the sun was good and high, catching the humidity in the air in just the right way to make my hair curl up all around my face. It was so heavy, I gave up on keeping it in place and pulled the hairpins out.

Gemma was propped up against the oak tree with a book perched on her knees, but she looked up when I came near. "Too hot for a body to be traipsin' about, Jessie." She studied my face a bit and then patted the ground next to her. "Sit down here and get some shade."

I was in no mood to sit, but I was also in no mood to argue, so I plopped down beside her with a long sigh.

"You see Luke?"

"'Course I saw Luke. Why else d'you think I'm down in the mouth?"

"Well, what happened?"

"Same as always happens. He looks good and ready

to say how he feels about me and then he stops and pulls away like he ain't never seen me before."

She hugged the book to her chest and smiled. "He's just confused, is all."

"Well, that's just great, him bein' confused while I ain't a bit confused!" I bent over to trace a heart in the dirt of a bare patch beside me only to promptly swipe it away. "I'm tellin' you, Gemma, I can't wait much longer for him to come to his senses without losin' my mind."

"Jessie, you done lost your mind the day that boy pulled you gaspin' from that swimmin' hole six years ago. Seems to me you ain't waitin' around for him to come to his senses. You're waitin' for him to lose them."

I looked at her for a long moment, then dropped my head to my knees with a groan.

She laughed and pulled me to her like a momma consoling a child with a skinned knee, and I let her, like always. So long as she mothered me with her hugs and not her words, it was fine with me.

I helped fix supper that night with my ears at the ready for Luke's whistle, hoping and praying he'd come despite what happened earlier that day, but I never heard it. So it was a weight lifted from my heavy heart when the slamming of the screen door announced his entrance as we took our seats at the table.

Luke walked in and snatched his hat off his head

awkwardly. "Sorry to be late, Mrs. Lassiter. I lost track of time."

Momma pushed his usual chair out as a sign of welcome and smiled. "Ain't never a worry about that. You set on down here. We were just gettin' started, anyhow."

He thanked her and sat, but he was nothing but a bundle of nerves, and he wouldn't even hint at looking in my direction.

Daddy sat back in his chair and stared at him, but he didn't say a thing. He just shoveled a helping of peas into his mouth and shook his head like he knew an embarrassing secret about Luke.

Then again, maybe it wasn't so secret.

Despite the fact that conversation was barely existent at the table that night, Momma couldn't keep from letting little smiles break across her face at intervals. And every now and then she'd look from me to Luke and then back at me. By the time I'd finished my slice of ham, the silence had become deafening to me. Gemma noticed and nudged me in the knee to get my attention so I'd see the reassuring smile she was sending my way.

There was as little talk for the rest of the evening as there was at supper. I'd never in all my born days known the Lassiter house to be so silent. It was like each of us was afraid to break the spell for one reason or another, and we went about our separate ways like mimes.

By the time I was done with the dishes, a lightning storm had begun to put on a show outside, and I walked onto the porch to watch alone. Not a drop of rain fell to ease the heat, but the jagged streaks lit up the night like fireworks.

I heard Luke's boots on the den floor as he stood, and I tensed at the thought that he was headed out to join me, but my heart sank when I heard him announce that he was leaving.

"Better get on my way. It's gettin' late."

"But it's stormin'," Momma argued. "Why don't you just wait it out?"

"I best get to sleep early. Had a long day."

I turned in my chair so I could peer into the window just in time to see Gemma jump up from the sofa. "You can't go out in the lightnin'!"

"It ain't too bad. Probably just some heat lightnin'."

"I don't care where it came from, Luke Talley; it's lightnin' all the same. You best stay inside, you hear?"

Gemma's face was painted with fear, and her expression didn't leave Luke much room for refusal. He dropped his head and ran a hand through his hair. "All right, Gemma. I'll wait it out."

"Better yet, why don't you stay the night?" Momma tossed her knitting into her basket and stretched. "We could all use an early-to-bed, and I can just fix up the couch for you."

"No, ma'am. I'll just wait it out. You don't need to go to any trouble over me."

"Ain't no trouble and you know it."

Daddy blew a ring of pipe smoke and then used the pipe to point at Luke. "Come to think of it, it'd help me out if you did stay. The truck's actin' up, and you could save us all a walk to church in the mornin'."

That seemed to settle it, and Luke put his hands out to his sides in a gesture of resignation. "If y'all are sure you don't mind . . ."

Momma was already taking the throw pillows from the couch. "'Course we don't mind. Gemma, honey, go grab me the extra sheet, will you?"

I walked inside and looked at them like I hadn't heard a thing.

"Luke's stayin' the night to keep out of the storm," Momma told me. Then she snapped her fingers. "Shoot! I forgot that old spare pillow lost its stuffin' and I ain't patched it yet." She turned to me and waved toward the stairs. "Jessie, fetch him your pillow and you can use the throw pillow tonight."

"No, ma'am." Luke picked up one of the small pillows from the floor and held it in both arms. "Jessie ain't got to give up her pillow for me. I'm fine with this one."

"I don't mind," I murmured. "I don't really even need a pillow. I'll get you mine."

But Gemma was halfway down the steps and tossed me the extra sheet she'd fetched. "I'll get your pillow."

Momma made sure Luke's makeshift bed was fixed up as nice as home, kissed me good night, and headed off to bed with Daddy in tow. Luke and I had one short moment of awkward silence before Gemma came downstairs and plopped the pillow down with a smile. "Sweet dreams, Luke." Then she tucked my arm into hers and led me up the stairs, only she stopped short at the top.

"What are you doin'?" I whispered.

She only nodded downstairs and leaned around to watch Luke. Momma had left the hall lamp on so Luke wouldn't bump into anything, and in the faint light we could see Luke at his perch on the couch, suspenders at his sides. He kicked his shoes off onto the floor beside him, then gave my pillow a sidelong glance. He laid his head down and closed his eyes, but he sat up again in thirty seconds, flipped the pillow over, then lay back down. But it was no good. Twice more he sat up, flipped the pillow, and tried again until eventually he yanked the pillow out from under his head and tossed it across the room.

Gemma pulled me back to our bedroom with a smile across her face.

"What was that all about?" I asked. "You put a brick in that pillow?"

"Not a brick." She grabbed my lavender perfume from the dressing table and held it up in front of her. "Just your scent."

"He threw the pillow across the room! That mean he ain't liked my scent all these years?"

She rolled her eyes at me and fell back onto her bed in dramatic fashion. "Jessilyn, there ain't no brick in that pillow, but there's one in your head." She sat up and pulled me down beside her, waving the perfume bottle under my nose. "How's a man supposed to sleep when all he can think of is a girl? He tossed that pillow away because it smelled like you and he couldn't think straight."

I blinked five times before giving my head a slow, accusing shake. "And Momma talks about my feminine wiles. Gemma Teague, you're a tease!" Then I grabbed her face in my hands and smiled. "But I sure am glad I got you on my side."

I didn't know if Luke got much sleep that night, but I sure didn't. I woke before the sun and decided there was no point in staying in bed. I washed and dressed quickly, then headed downstairs, careful to avoid the squeaky steps. Luke was asleep on the couch, his long legs hanging over the edge, one arm flung across his face. His sheet was balled up on the floor beside him, and I could see his chest rise and fall with each breath. I stood in the dim morning light and watched him for a minute, but he stirred and flipped onto his side, and I rushed to the kitchen to avoid being caught staring.

I set about making pancakes as quietly as I could, but by the time I poured the first ones onto the griddle, Luke came shuffling in.

"You always fuss around in the kitchen before sunup?" His hair was sticking out at odds and ends, his eyes squinty.

"Couldn't help it. Too many thoughts in my head. And anyways, you know there's almost always someone in the kitchen before sunup. That's farm life."

"Not on Sundays there ain't." He wandered up beside me and leaned against the counter.

There were a couple minutes of awkward silence before I decided I'd had enough of the distance between us. I flicked a hunk of hair that was lying across his forehead. "You sleep on your head or somethin'?"

"Why?"

"Your hair's all cockeyed."

He reached up to smooth it down and then ran his

thumb across my cheek. "Well, you're wearin' flour. I ain't the only messy one."

I self-consciously brushed a hand across my face to clear away anything he might have missed and then flipped the pancakes. "I'm a sloppy cook."

"You look good in flour."

"It's a good thing since I wear it so often." I peeked underneath one of the pancakes. "Almost ready. Fetch the plates?"

It felt like something meant to be, Luke and I puttering about the kitchen on an early morning. He insisted on waiting to eat until I was ready, and after fixing him a good stack, I settled across from him at the table with my two.

I ate absentmindedly, watching him plow through his stack in no time flat. "You ever learn how to chew when you were growin' up?"

"I get hungry in the mornin's. You know that."

"Well, you must be extra hungry this particular mornin'. Them poor pancakes never had a chance."

He ran a napkin across his mouth and leaned back in the chair, hands behind his head, legs stretched out. "Maybe they was extra good this mornin'."

I focused my eyes on my plate and pushed a bite of pancake around in the syrup. "You're just bein' a charmer, is all."

"I know good pancakes when I taste 'em."

I pushed a stray lock of hair behind my ear and got up to clear the plates.

Luke beat me to it and put them in the sink. "I'll get the washin' done."

"Don't be silly. I'll get them."

"Ain't no reason I can't wash the dishes."

"There is if you don't know how to do it."

"'Course I know how to do it. I eat some meals at my house. What do you think I do, throw the dishes away after I use 'em?"

"Go on ahead if you want to." I tested the griddle to see if it was hot enough and poured out a pancake. "I'm gonna cook up the rest of this batter, anyways."

Luke grabbed an apron from the hook on the wall and held it up in front of him. "How do you put this thing on?" He pulled the top straps around his waist so the apron hung around his knees. "This don't look right."

"Luke Talley," I giggled. "You look a sight."

"Well, I ain't got any idea how you women wear these fussy things." He held it at arm's length and flipped it one way and then another. Finally feigning triumph, he tied the top straps around his neck. "Knew I'd figure it out."

He was ridiculous standing there in the kitchen, his suspenders hanging at his sides, a frilly apron covering his front, and I shook my head at him and laughed.

"What're these things for?" he asked, holding the bottom straps out in front of him. "They go into a bow in front?"

"You're crazy!" I grabbed them from him and reached around his waist to tie them up behind him, but the minute I had my arms around him, the playing stopped.

There was a woodpecker outside the window making short work of our aspen tree, a clock chiming the hour, and a pancake burning on the griddle, but all I was aware of was me standing there with my arms around a man in an apron. For all I cared, that chiming clock could have stopped dead and let me live in that moment for eternity.

Luke stared at me and lifted a hand to brush the hair out of my eyes, whispering just once, "Jessilyn."

I don't know how long a girl can go without breathing, but I was going for the record when my daddy came into the kitchen and let out a long, heavy sigh.

"For cryin' out loud, boy, if you're goin' to keep this up, why don't you just ask to court the girl?"

We both jumped at the sound of his voice, but we didn't move apart. We just stood there in disbelief, wondering if we'd heard Daddy right.

Luke pointed wide eyes in Daddy's direction. "Sir?"

"I said, why don't you just ask to court the girl? You're

makin' a dang fool of yourself pretendin' you don't want to."

Momma came up behind Daddy and stood on tiptoe to peer over his shoulder. Even with half her face hidden, I could tell she was smiling like our pastor with a full offering plate.

I looked at Luke and he looked at me for a few seconds before he turned back to Daddy. "You sure I . . ."

"Luke, I've known you long enough to know you're a fine man, and you ain't never done nothin' but good for my girls. Jessilyn's a woman now. You want to walk out with her here and there, that's up to her. Go on and ask her." He gave Luke the once-over and let out another long sigh. "You might want to take that apron off first, son."

I slid my arms away and backed away awkwardly, lifting the back of one hand to test the temperature of my cheeks, but the heat in them only made me flush even more.

Luke slipped the apron over his head, then ran a hand through his hair to smooth it down. I was covered with a dusting of flour and he still sported creases on his face from sleep. But none of that mattered. Flour, messy hair, and prying eyes couldn't do a single thing to dull the sheer bliss that had started to fill me from the second my daddy had called me a woman and opened the door to my future.

Luke let his hand drop to his side and then reached out to gently grasp my fingertips, looking all the while like a schoolboy trying to get up the courage to ask a crush to the dance. But then he pried his eyes from the floor and looked at me without lifting his head, a squinty sort of stare that reminded me good and quick that he was no boy.

"Would you like to step out with me, Jessilyn?"

That was it. That was all he said. *"Would you like to step out with me, Jessilyn?"*

And it was paradise.

From the corner of my eye I spotted Gemma's head peeking over my momma's shoulder, and I smiled. She'd blessed my life with her presence from the day she first showed up on our property. It was only fitting she'd be there the day my best dreams came true.

Luke saw my smile and let his own face spread out in a grin. "That a yes?"

I shook my head at him and feigned an angry look. "Luke Talley, you don't know me one bit if you think it ain't."

His smile widened, and the pink that had colored his cheeks spread to his ears. Then he lifted my hand to his lips. It was only for a brief moment, but it was enough to send my heart thumping so fast, I thought I'd pass out.

I glanced at Daddy in fear of disapproval, but he only

sniffed the air and grimaced. "Sakes alive, Sadie, what's burnin'?"

Momma caught sight of the smoldering pancake sitting on the griddle and rushed to the stove to pull it off. The pancake was black as coal, fogging the kitchen in a cloud of smoke.

But my world had just turned upside down. The house itself could have burned down around me and I wouldn't have noticed a thing.

Chapter 7

"Your brother been stayin' out of trouble, Noah?" Gemma asked, her face buried in her work. "I ain't inclined to see him show up at Doc Pritchett's anytime soon."

One afternoon a week Gemma and I would sit together with Noah's sister, Lissa, out in front of the Jarvises' tiny, worn house, sewing drawstrings into tobacco bags. It was a much-needed source of income for Lissa. Gemma did it mostly for the conversation, and though I hated sewing, I always joined in to work on a few so I could sit and gab with them too.

Noah sat near us under a shade tree, a book in his lap. "Who knows? We barely see him these days."

I tilted my head to see better as the sunlight dimmed behind the clouds, though my mind wasn't so much on needlework as it was on Luke. "I reckon he's busy tryin' to find work."

"Work!" Lissa huffed. "He ain't doin' nothin' of the sort. Boy don't do nothin' but laze about and stir up trouble. Some days he comes home three o'clock in the mornin' drunk as a skunk."

Gemma and I lifted our heads in unison, but it was Gemma who spoke first, as usual. "That boy's a mess these days." She shook her head fiercely. "Don't you go followin' in his footsteps, Noah Jarvis. You got too much goin' for you."

"I ain't likely to, Miss Gemma. I got me better things to think about."

I finished my last stitch and laid my work down. "What're you learnin' about today, Noah?"

His eyes came up, but he kept his head tilted toward the book. "Just studyin' history."

"You get into college, what d'you plan on doin' with that extra education? You got somethin' in mind?"

"Boy wants to be a doctor now," Lissa piped up. "Think of that. Dr. Jarvis!"

"So you're pretty serious about that, huh?" I got up and bent down next to Noah to peer at his book. "Tal Pritchett thinks you'd be a fine hand at it."

"It ain't a sure thing. Not even close. I figure I best not go gettin' nobody's expectations up. It ain't likely I'd get into college in the first place."

"Tal thinks you'd get in, no questions asked, and I think

so too," Gemma said. "You keep studyin' hard like that, Noah. I want you takin' care of my children someday."

"Unless you end up marryin' a doctor yourself," I said. "In which case, you already got a ready-made doctor for your children."

"Don't you start, Jessilyn!"

I gave Noah a nudge. "She gets so touchy sometimes."

"I ain't sayin' a word." Noah opened his book and hid his face behind it. "Don't go gettin' Gemma riled at me."

Gemma jabbed her needle into the air in my direction. "I ain't got need of you braggin' about me steppin' out when I ain't, Jessilyn."

"You will be."

"Don't go spreadin' talk!"

"I'm only speakin' truth. Leastways I ought to be. No man could do better."

I could see that she squelched a smile, but she looked away to keep from letting on. "You're just talkin' foolishness."

"I'm only sayin'." I reached up and grabbed a flower from the magnolia tree Noah sat under. "If the man's got any sense, he'll snatch you up, and he'll do it on the quick, too. Not like Luke takin' years of my life away while he got his nerve up."

"Jessie, he weren't doin' nothin' but waitin' till things were good and proper. And I don't need you gettin' worked up over my marital status. It'll happen if and when it's meant to, so don't let it keep you awake nights."

I elbowed Noah. "If I keep this needlin' up, she's bound to box my ears. You know how she can get."

"She'll likely still be doin' it in a few years. Maybe by then I'll know how to mend you up."

"Listen to you makin' jokes, Noah Jarvis," Gemma said. "You're a bad influence on him, Jessie."

"Ain't nothin' wrong with a boy havin' a well-developed sense of humor." I went back to where I'd been sitting and stuffed my things into my sack. "Anyways, least the boy tells the truth."

Gemma jabbed her needle into the tobacco bag and narrowed her eyes. "I ain't never laid a hand on you, and you know it." She stood and filled her own sack. "But heaven knows there was a time or two I thought of it."

"There's a time or two I've thought of givin' Malachi a shot to the head," Lissa murmured. "Yes, ma'am, he could do with a lickin' or ten."

"Well, don't tell me your momma don't give him some," I said, "'cause I've seen it myself."

"Oh, she hands it out good, but it don't make no difference. Don't ask me why it worked with me and Noah but not with Malachi."

"He's stubborn as a mule, that's why." Gemma stretched her arms high, arched her back, and groaned.

"My back's stiff as a board." She walked over to Lissa and patted her cheek. "Don't you worry none, girl. Ain't goin' to do nothin' but give you headaches."

"Ain't possible not to worry when someone you love's in trouble, Gemma Teague. You ought to know that." Lissa finished off by tipping her head in my direction.

I wrinkled my nose up. "Listen to you, makin' it out like I've given Gemma all kinds of worry."

She grinned and tucked her head down closer to her work. "I didn't say a thing."

"Uh-huh! Gemma Teague, you must've told some tall tales about me."

"Only what's true."

"Well, I ain't a girl no more, so you can stop pickin' on me now."

"But it's so much fun."

"Oh, hush!" I slipped my arm through hers and led her off toward the road. "I let her stay any longer and she'll be talkin' nonsense about me all evenin'."

"Nothin' I ain't already heard," Lissa called as we walked away.

Momma was on the porch shucking corn as we came up the walk, and she waved a corn silk–covered hand at us. "You girls get some good work done today?"

"Much as we could with all the silliness goin' on," Gemma muttered.

Momma stood and let the stray pieces of husk slip off her lap. "Oh, what's work without a little silliness to make it better?"

I gave Momma a wink. "Gemma got all bothered because I brought up Tal Pritchett, is all."

"Tal Pritchett's a fine man, Gemma," Momma said. "Seems he means to do some good things here in Calloway."

"He means to snap up my Gemma is what he means to do."

Gemma propped the door open with her foot. "Jessilyn, you're just eggin' me on!"

"Ain't nothin' new about that."

I followed her inside to the kitchen, where Gemma washed up. I could tell by her sharp movements she didn't plan on entertaining any more of my jokes about her and Tal Pritchett. As it was, Luke arrived shortly after, so I didn't feel like talking about any other man, anyway. It had been a few days since we'd talked courting, and I figured he had to come around to asking me to go someplace soon or else he'd look a fool.

So after I put in my fair share of picking up after supper, I walked outside to join him on the porch, where he stood against the rail staring at the moon.

"It'll be full tomorrow night," I noted. "You know what my daddy says about a full moon."

Luke folded his arms and smiled at me. "No, what's your daddy say about a full moon?"

He knew full well since he'd heard my daddy say it every full moon for the past six years. But Luke had me tell him the same stories over all the time just because he liked to hear me tell them.

I smiled wryly at him and then pointed my gaze toward the sky. "My daddy says that the moon fills up a little more every day until it just gets too full and starts to spill out. Then those moondrops fall to earth until the moon disappears altogether and has to fill up all over again. And if you're lucky enough, you'll catch one of those moondrops, because moondrops can make you see the whole world brighter."

Just like always, he asked, "You ever catch one of them moondrops, Jessilyn?"

"Not yet." I turned my eyes to him. "But I got me a feelin' I will soon."

"Well then, we best go out moondrop huntin' tomorrow evenin', you and me. Seems to me we might spot some good ones. We could do a little night fishin' while we wait. Fish are hoppin' at Barter's Lake, so I hear."

After all those years of waiting and wishing for this moment, none of my imagined scenarios did anything to still the nervous flutter of my heart. I hid my shaky hands behind my back and murmured, "That so?"

"So I hear. You reckon you might like that?"

Now for some girls, night fishing to start out courting would have been about as welcome as a snakebite, but not for me. I wasn't much of a goin'-into-town girl, and from my way of thinking, there wasn't a much more fitting way for us to get things started. I did everything I could to make my voice sound nonchalant. "I think I'd like that."

But I knew it would never work. My daddy might have given Luke his blessing, but he wouldn't ever let me walk out alone with Luke at night.

He was way ahead of me. "Gemma already said she could chaperone."

"Gemma likes goin' out on the boat."

"Sure enough."

"I don't reckon Daddy'll mind, then."

"Can't see as he would." He reached out to catch a firefly and held his hand open so it could crawl across it. "In fact, I reckon he don't, seein' as how I already asked him."

I betrayed my attempt at nonchalance and stood on my toes in excitement. "He already said we could?"

Luke nodded. "Gotta be back by midnight, though."

I didn't care. So long as I got to say I'd stepped out with Luke Talley, I didn't much care if we left at seven and had to be home by seven fifteen. I settled back onto flat feet and watched the firefly light up and fly away, a faint ache forming in my cheeks from my wide smile.

I was starting to think maybe I'd caught one of those moondrops after all.

Chapter 8

The day of my date with Luke was a blur. While I straightened Miss Cleta's knickknacks or dusted her furniture, she'd watch me from the corners of her eyes and then start chuckling.

Every time she did, I'd ask, "What's so funny?"

And every time she'd answer, "You're a sight."

The fourth time she said it, I dropped onto the sofa with a loud sigh. "I can't think straight."

"Oh, you can think straight, all right, only you can't think of more than one thing . . . and he's a whole lot nicer to look at than that dust rag." She tipped my chin up with one arthritic finger. "You've waited a long time for this day, Jessilyn. Enjoy it."

"I plan to . . . if I could only get these jitters to go away."

She waved me off. "Jitters are part of the fun. Don't worry so much."

But I worried, and there was no settling down for me that afternoon or evening. After washing up, I sat on my bed, my mind running through all the stupid things I could wind up saying or doing that night.

Momma came in and found me there so distracted, it took her two repetitions of my name before I noticed. Once I spotted her, she gave me that smile only Momma could give and sat down beside me. "You gettin' cold feet?"

"Momma, I swear, after six years, you'd think I'd be ready as anythin' for this."

"But you ain't."

"No, I ain't!"

She put an arm around me and pulled me close. "Baby, first time out with a man is always scary no matter how prepared you think you are. That's just part of life. But let me tell you one important thing: Luke Talley came to care for who you are, plain and simple. Not for somethin' he thinks you might be. Don't go tryin' to be anythin' but you and you'll be good and fine tonight."

"But, Momma, you know me. I'm bound to say somethin' wrong. I always do."

She pulled away and looked at me with a wry smile. "That ever stop him from fallin' for you?"

I didn't know if that was a compliment or a criticism, but I couldn't help but smile at Momma's expression. "S'pose not."

"Well then, you go on and have a fun time tonight and don't go worryin' about nothin'. You just be yourself. And if you start to feel like you ain't sure how to be yourself, you just look to Gemma. There ain't nobody better at puttin' you in your place."

I laughed and leaned into her. "I love you, Momma."

"Oh, baby, I love you too." She kissed my hair and then patted my legs. "You'd best get on up and finish gettin' ready. He'll be here any minute."

I popped up and ran the brush through my hair, stopping to examine myself in the mirror. "Well, that ain't much to look at. This is how I look every other day of my life."

"Don't talk crazy." Momma came up behind me and smiled at my reflection. "You got love all over your face. Ain't no better accessory than that." She tilted her head sideways. "It's missin' one thing, though." I watched her retrieve something from my dressing table. "This'll go just right," she said, holding up the necklace Luke had given me.

I lifted my hair so she could fasten the clasp and then went off to find Gemma so she could do my hair. But not until I'd stopped off in the bathroom to peer at that necklace in the mirror again. I didn't know if it was the necklace or thoughts of Luke, but my eyes sparkled like diamonds. I pinched my cheeks for color and smiled at my reflection.

"If you like what you see so much, I guess Luke'll like it even better."

I turned sharply to find Gemma staring at me from the doorway. "Ain't nothin' you can tease me about that'll make me upset tonight." I picked up the dish of hairpins off the windowsill and handed them to her. "Here. Make me pretty. But don't make it fancy. I don't want to look like Greta Garbo with a fishin' pole."

She set the dish down and stuck two pins in her mouth. "You're already pretty," she murmured around them, pulling the ends of my hair up behind my head. "Ain't no hairpins goin' to improve on that."

"Same thing can be said for you, and you know it." I leaned against her and watched her in the mirror. "I'm glad you're comin' with me."

"Me too. Somebody's got to keep you out of trouble."

A knock sounded at the front door, and I heard Luke open it and yell inside, "It's just me!"

"*Just* him," I whispered. "There ain't no *just* about it. And here I am with my hair in tatters."

"Your momma will keep him occupied till you're ready. That's what mommas do."

She was right. Ten minutes later we found them in the kitchen shelling beans to be soaked overnight.

"There they are," Momma declared when we walked in. "You girls ready?"

"Yes'm." The first glance I gave Luke was a tentative one, all full of bashfulness, a trait I'd never once in my life been accused of. But the way he looked back at me lit me up from the inside out. I made my best effort at being me, just like Momma said.

"She got you workin' already?" I asked. "She ought to know you're slow as molasses at bean shellin'."

Momma patted his shoulder in mock sincerity. "I reckon she's right at that, Luke. I guess you'd best leave the job to me and head on out. You takin' your truck?"

Luke looked at me and Gemma. "Depends on what the ladies want."

The way I figured it, a truck drive was much too fast, and I wanted all the time I could get with him. "It's a fine night to walk." I spoke quickly and then decided I'd better give a reason for my hasty response. "Anyways, we go ridin' up to Barter's Lake with that squeaky truck and we'll scare the fish away."

Gemma and Momma both gave me a look that said they knew exactly why I'd made my choice, but neither of them said a thing.

Daddy was on the porch with his pipe when we came out, and he stood up like a castle guard, arms crossed in front of his chest. "You 'bout ready, then?" He took the pipe out and pointed it at Luke. "You take care of my girls, son. And make sure you're home on time, you hear?"

Luke tipped his hat solemnly. "Yes'r. I'll do that."

Daddy tucked the pipe back into the side of his mouth. "See that you do," he said around it.

I cast one last glance at Momma, but she just winked and waved. "You have fun now."

The three of us wandered off in silence and stayed that way for the first ten minutes of our walk, breaking it only with comments about the weather and such, things we'd never mention under normal circumstances. But these weren't normal circumstances. This was the realization of everything I'd hoped for all these years, and there was a fear coursing through me that it could never measure up to my daydreams.

Gemma hummed a church hymn, a soft melody that blended into the chorus of frogs and crickets. She trailed behind us, never one to hurry about unless necessary, but I figured she was holding back even more tonight so Luke and I could have our space.

He looked at me and waited for me to meet his gaze, then smiled. "Nice night for fishin'."

I smiled back and then closed my eyes to savor the

breeze. "Nice night for anythin'. Gonna make it hard to get used to the real summer heat when it comes in."

"The way it's started out, could be a mild summer."

"Or it could be baitin' us, makin' us think things'll be nice, and then whack us upside the head in a week or two."

"More likely than not, I guess. But I reckon I can stand the heat so long as I spend the summer here with you."

I didn't look at him because I knew I was likely to be wearing the stupidest grin a girl could wear. I just stared straight ahead and hoped he couldn't make out my expression in the moonlight. He tucked his free arm through mine, and though we walked the rest of the way in silence, our journey was charmed from the first step to the last so that I almost regretted it when we reached Barter's Lake.

Luke kept a skiff there, and he helped the two of us in before shoving us away from shore. I waited for Luke to bait my line, and then, as the breeze picked the water up into small peaks, setting the boat to dancing subtly to and fro, I steadied myself carefully and cast off.

I settled back with a contented sigh and glanced at Gemma. She never had been as fond of fishing as me, but she loved the water, and she was already curled up at the far end of the boat, eyes closed, a peaceful smile on her face.

Luke and I sat close as seemed proper, and I nudged him lightly with my elbow. "Gemma's already out. Sure hope we don't tip in this breeze. She'll sink like a lead weight."

"She sure can doze off quick."

I watched the full moon put on a show of shadows about the weedy banks. Each peak of the water shimmered with its light.

Luke dipped his hand into the water and held a small pool of it out to me. "Your moondrops."

I smiled at him, then dipped my fingers into the water and flicked it at him. He blinked away the drops and grinned at me, dropping the rest of the water into the boat before running one wet finger down the bridge of my nose. "Now whenever your daddy talks about moondrops, you can say you already caught yours."

"Right on my nose."

"Best place to catch 'em."

We sat so that our shoulders and knees touched, and I decided then that I could sit like this for the rest of my life and be happy. I figured Luke must have felt the same since anybody within a mile could see he'd hooked a fish, but he just sat still without even a thought of checking the line until that fish wriggled its way off the hook.

Sure enough, we weren't here for the fishing.

True to our whole life together, we once again became as comfortable with each other in silence as we were in conversation, and we floated along across the lake, content just to be together. Every now and again a sleepy grunt would let us know Gemma was still out like a light. Poor Daddy would die from anxiety if he knew what kind of chaperone Gemma made.

I closed my eyes and leaned my head back, breathing deeply of the warm night air. I caught a hint of burning wood on the breeze and figured old Bubba Watkins was out at his fire pit, roasting some animal he'd managed to kill for himself. Bubba had a house near the lake, but I never understood why he had any roof over his head at all, seeing as he pretty much lived outdoors.

But Bubba Watkins could do whatever he dandy well pleased, as far as I was concerned. It had nothing to do with me and Luke floating down the lake to the tune of the wind, the frogs, and the cicadas.

I opened my eyes sleepily to find Luke looking at me, watching me as I drank in the moment so I could write it in my memory for good. For a change, though, he didn't look away when I caught him staring. This time he kept his eyes on my face, studying it hard, like he was making a memory of his own.

Sometimes between people there's a moment that spells out everything you're thinking without having to say a word. I know something about moments like those. I've had a lot of them with Gemma over the years, and in some small way, to that point I'd had them with Luke. But at this very moment at this very place, the moment that passed between Luke and me said more than any other time ever had.

We'd waited a long time for this, he and I. Through all my growing-up years, through all that time waiting for Daddy to come around, through all that time Luke saw me as little Jessilyn instead of the woman I was. We'd waited. And now, out in the middle of the water, with a sleeping Gemma and the night creatures as the only witnesses, Luke and I stepped over that imaginary line that had kept us apart all these years.

In one swift movement, Luke laid his fishing pole on the bottom of the boat and reached to cup one side of my face in his hand, his thumb tracing a path from the corner of my eye to my chin and back again.

There's never a quiet moment in a Virginia summer, not from morning till night. No amount of heat or humidity ever takes the starch out of those noisemaking little critters that dot the outdoors, and if there ever was a moment when a winter stillness crept over a Southern summer day, a body would think the world was coming to an end.

But for that moment, in that night, the noise stopped just for me. It was so quiet I could hear each breath Luke took—short, soft breaths that spoke of a man readying his courage. I could feel those breaths on my cheek as he leaned his head closer, and right before his lips were to meet mine, my eyelashes fluttered closed without me even telling them to, like the moment was too precious for human eyes to see.

Just like we'd waited all those years, I waited for his lips to meet mine.

But they never came.

Luke's breathing stopped altogether, and I knew without seeing a thing that something was wrong.

My eyes shot open and found his face still inches from my own, only he wasn't looking at me. He was looking off into the distance toward the bank of the lake, where all sorts of brush and reeds sheltered the noisy frogs.

"What is it?"

He gently covered my lips with two fingers, then leaned forward, squinting into the darkness.

The water was still lit by the moonlight, shimmering like crystal, but for the first time I noticed more than the white light that came from it. This time I noticed the orange mixed in, the erratic flickering that could never come from the moon that hung so still above us.

I knew that flicker. I'd seen it some six years ago, the night the Klan came and planted that burning cross on our front lawn.

My heart began to beat an unpredictable pattern, making me feel light-headed. Luke's hand dropped from my mouth to my knees, lightly pushing me to the side so he could move in front of me. He kept himself low, creeping stealthily forward. I grabbed his arm from behind and leaned my chin on his shoulder, peering into the dark woods beside the lake.

We could see them clearly now, their white robes dotting the open spaces between the trees, their torches held high. They were circled around a tall cross that burned in the clearing past the trees, surrounded by popping sparks like demons in the depths of hell. I gripped Luke's arm tighter and took a hasty glance at Gemma. Still asleep.

I was grateful for it.

The boat moved quickly with the wind. Luke reached for the oars, but before we even knew it, we were floating precariously close to the woods where a narrow inlet would lead us to the other side of the lake and out of sight. Turning about would be noisy and useless, and I knew as well as he that our best chance of getting out of sight would be to move through the inlet into the other side of the lake, where thickening woods hid the water from the clearing.

I'd grown quite fond of the wind since Miss Cleta had taught me the secrets of it. "It's the breath of God,

Jessilyn," she'd say, lifting her face to greet it. "Just listen to it talkin' to your soul."

I wasn't so sure about it being the breath of God, but I knew I liked the feel of it all the same. When the wind came, it covered up all the rest of the world's noises, pushing trouble away, whispering about sweet memories and voices from the past.

But it betrayed me this night.

As we headed toward the inlet, that wind died down so still, so quiet, we floated to a near halt, drifting like sitting ducks just outside the Klan meeting. For the first time, the voice of one of the men carried through the tranquil air, a ghostly holler that bounced off the water and surrounded us with words we couldn't understand but could feel the meaning of.

I glanced at Gemma to see if she'd wake at the sound, but she only stirred. It didn't matter, though, because her stirring was enough to set the boat to rocking, dipping once so sharply that the water beneath us plopped against the skiff.

The two men closest to our edge of the woods turned their heads swiftly so that the dark slits in their hoods pointed right at us. Luke and I caught our breath in unison, and I felt his hand come down and grasp my ankle hard to warn me against moving a muscle.

They just stood there, frozen in place, staring right

at us, the orange glow of the torches casting shadows around them. Then they leaned their heads together to confer and the closest one trudged toward us.

Luke turned his head to me and hissed, "Get down. Low!"

I nodded frantically and curled up between the two benches, my ear against the floorboard so that all I could hear from one side were the muffled sounds of water against wood. Luke crouched next to me and tossed his hat down. I gripped it tight with one hand like a security blanket and used my other hand to keep a fistful of his shirt.

We floated ever so slowly toward the inlet, tracing a deadly path in the water, and with each inch my fear increased. Not being able to see made it all the more frightening. I could tell that Luke was straining his neck to peer over the side without giving himself away.

I wanted more than anything to know what he saw, but I couldn't dare to speak in even the lowest whisper. So I did the next best thing. I lifted my own head, peering up just till I could see a sliver of land.

I was shocked to see how close we were now, right beneath the banks that rose about two feet above us, sheltered from the water by masses of vegetation. And I was just as shocked to see how close we were to the

Klansman who'd come to scout us out. He strode from the tree line just as we reached the inlet, his torch in one hand, shotgun in the other.

By luck, fate, or the hand of God, I didn't know, but right when he reached the shoreline, the full moon that had promised me moondrops scurried off behind a cloud, shrouding us all in a sudden dimness. The Klansman raised his arm, throwing torchlight out around him. He was so close, I could hear his labored breathing, and I figured a big moonshine gut underneath that flowing white robe had made his trip from the clearing more difficult than it should have been.

At the same time, I saw Luke's hand shoot out of the boat and grab a prickly bush along the shoreline to keep us from moving. Our only chance was to hope the brush that separated us from the shore, along with the darkness, would keep us hidden from view.

Above those reeds and whatnot, I could see the man in white only from the waist up, those black slit eyes scanning the horizon first with sharp, birdlike movements and then more slowly, methodically. Just in time to make life even more difficult, the breeze picked up a bit, and I could see Luke's arm shaking, his hand turning white against the prickly bush, as he strained to keep us still. I wanted more than anything to help, but there was no reaching outside the boat for me. So I closed my eyes to say one of Momma's prayers, the only way I knew to try and help.

The ground beneath the Klansman crackled as he made a move to turn about, seemingly giving up on his search, and I felt Luke's muscles relax a bit at the thought of it. But the man only made it halfway before pausing, standing still to listen hard. Then he turned toward us again, lifted his torch high, and flung it sideways, first to the right, then to the left. The flame whooshed, showering sparks around us like fireworks. We ducked our heads and waited, listening to that torch travel through the air, and it was all I could do not to jump with each move it made.

I tilted my head back again to see Gemma and caught sight of two bright flashes of ash drifting through the air above her, hovering over her bare leg. My heart leaped up into my throat, and I moved my arm as quickly as I dared toward her mouth, reaching it just as her eyes shot open with the sting of the ash.

The pressure of my hand kept her from uttering a sound, but she threw her hand up to mine in panic, giving the boat another soft rock. Her eyes met mine, and I squinted at her, warning her off. I felt awful for her not knowing, waking up to something so frightening as this, but she held her own, nodding at me in unspoken agreement despite being ignorant of our predicament.

The whoosh of the torch bit into the air again. Gemma followed the sound with her eyes, and I winced to see the terror in them once she caught sight of the man who stood so close to us.

We all lay there in that boat, motionless and wordless, expecting discovery at any moment, until we heard the ground crackle beneath him again, this time sounding his retreat. Luke and I watched until he was out of our line of sight and then lifted up carefully to watch his withdrawal.

He sauntered loudly through the woods, had one more conference with the other Klansman, and then both rejoined the group.

Luke let go of the prickly bush and let out a breath so long I would have sworn he'd been holding it in the whole time he'd held us there.

I leaned up on one arm and watched the flames of that cross lick the night sky until we drifted out of view.

Luke reached back to touch my arm. "You okay?" he whispered.

I ran my hand over his and lifted it to my face. Blood covered my fingers.

"Jessilyn?" He whispered my name sternly. "I said, you okay?"

I leaned close to his ear. "Yes, but you ain't." I reached up to Gemma's pocket, where I knew she always kept a fresh hankie, and pulled the folded cloth out. As soon as our boat floated into the open, the clouds parted for the moon like theater curtains, and I sat up and grabbed Luke's hand for a better look. "Dang Klan ain't got nothin' better to do than go around makin' fools of themselves! I swear, I don't know why God don't just strike them all dead."

"The hand's okay, Jessie. Don't let it rile you." He pulled away from me and grabbed an oar, feeling around for the other one. "We need to get out of here."

He could tell me all day not to get riled up, but it wouldn't do any good. I was sick and tired of bad people pushing good people around, and Luke's bloodied hand only made me angrier. "You can't row like that. Your hand's all ripped up."

"Long as I got a hand, I can row, Jessilyn."

"We're out of sight, Luke. Let me at least wrap your hand first. Please."

He took a deep breath, looked around us, and then held his hand out to me. "All right. Just be quick."

The sight of his hand, scraped up beyond recognition, made my stomach turn somersaults, but I used my blouse to wipe some of the blood off, staining it from hem to bottom button. Then I wrapped Gemma's handkerchief around it, knowing full well it wouldn't do much good. But it made me feel better to do it.

As soon as I'd tied the knot, he grabbed the second oar and made his way to the bench, dipping the oars in and out with quick, smooth movements, disturbing the water as little as possible.

Gemma had her knees tucked up under her chin, still shaken by her rude awakening. I watched Luke row until we reached the shoreline well across from the Klan. He jumped into the water, dragged the boat up, and helped each of us out.

Gemma was silent and paced the wooded shoreline, rubbing her arms against a chill that didn't exist in the air. But I couldn't walk on legs that felt rubbery like mine, so I eagerly sat on a fallen tree.

Luke looked around us, now on guard against any possibility, before finally settling down next to me. "You sure you're all right?"

"Guess so." I nodded toward Gemma, who was watching the woods like a hawk. "But she ain't."

"She's got more reason to be afraid than we do."

I kept my eyes on Gemma as I said, "I ain't afraid so much as angry."

He didn't say much, only stared out at the water. Then he took his hat off and ran his good hand through his hair. "We won't be able to go home the regular way, you know. Can't risk goin' through there again. We'll have to walk from here." He sighed loud and long. "We're gonna be late gettin' home. First time out with you, and your daddy's goin' to kill me."

"He ain't goin' to kill you, Luke Talley. He'll understand. You're doin' what you have to do to watch out for me and Gemma, after all." I looked at the boat Luke had made with his own two hands. "What about the boat?"

"I'll come back for it tomorrow." He pushed an arm into my side. "Reckon we should've just gone to a movie."

I shook my head vehemently. "This is just what I wanted to do. Wouldn't have it any other way."

"No other way?"

"Well, maybe no Klan."

He smiled, then stood up, grabbed my hands, and pulled me to my feet. "Well, next time I'll leave the Klan off the schedule." His left hand stayed in my right, and we wandered off to fetch Gemma and start the long walk home.

She shook her head at us when we came up behind her. "Don't go sneakin' up on me. I ain't got my nerves settled yet."

"We weren't sneakin' up."

"You could've at least called after me."

"And call the Klan, too?" I slipped my left arm through hers and bumped her hip with my own. "You just need a little Jessilyn; that's what you need. I'll talk to you all the way home and you'll forget all your troubles."

I didn't look at her face, but I knew by the way she sighed, she'd be rolling her eyes. "It's Jessilyn talk that usually gets my nerves in a bundle in the first place."

"Bundled-up nerves ain't no problem so long as they're bundled in the right way. Seems to me the Klan's way ain't no picnic in the park."

"Well, neither is yours!"

"A picnic in the park!" Luke piped up. "That would've been a better idea than night fishin'. What in blazes was I thinkin'?"

"You were thinkin' of Jessie; that's what," Gemma said. "You know she likes night fishin'. Don't go worryin' about how things ended up when the startin' out was good."

I pulled them both close and took a long, deep inhale of clean night air. There are moments in life when you stop and realize how blessed you really are, and this moment was one of those for me.

And no Klan in white demon robes could ever take that away.

Luke walked us through the woods, picking out the best path he could. I was content just to be hand in hand with him, but poor Gemma seemed as skittish as a new calf. Every noise startled her; every crack in the brush or stray animal crossing our path made her yelp.

So when we heard the voices, she nearly dropped dead at my feet.

Luke's hand jumped up to his waistband, where I knew his gun would be tucked away. He dropped my arm and held his own out to block us from moving forward. I put my arm around Gemma, and the two of us crouched beside a tree, waiting. Luke crept forward between the trees and stuck his head through an evergreen, peering for a few seconds before he sighed loud enough for me to hear. Without turning toward us, he waved us over to his side and then walked on through the brush.

Gemma and I came up behind him to find a group of young colored men sitting beside a fire, carrying on like children. Empty liquor bottles lay here and there, and the group of them sat on old wooden cartons playing cards. We caught the tail end of a dirty joke, and Gemma uttered a noise of disgust. At the sound of her voice, all six of their heads turned toward us in surprise.

Including Malachi Jarvis's.

"Gemma Teague!" Malachi stood up quickly, wobbling, and wildly waved a hand in her direction. "You missin' me so much you came all the way out here to find me?"

Gemma marched over to him with the authority of a drill sergeant and ripped the beer bottle from his hand. "I ain't got no time for no drunk!" She spilled the contents out at his feet and threw the bottle into the woods, where it smashed against a tree.

The other men all looked at each other with smirks on their faces and spluttered before bursting into obnoxious laughter.

"Your old lady's here to take you home, Jarvis," one of them quipped.

Gemma ripped his bottle from his hands as well. "You got somethin' you want to say, Toby Gowans? Hmm?" She turned to the others and repeated herself to each of them. "No? You ain't got somethin' to say?" She threw aside the bottle she held and stabbed her thumb over her shoulder. "You get on home with us, Malachi."

I stood beside Luke in amusement, pleased to see Gemma mothering someone other than me for a change.

But Malachi wasn't amused, and he told her so in no uncertain terms. "You ain't my momma! And even if you was, I ain't got to answer to no momma, anyhow. I'm a grown man."

"You grown enough your momma won't box your ears for findin' you out here spendin' your wages on drink and gamblin'?"

"My momma ain't got authority over me like that no more."

"Fine then." She slowly started to walk off in the direction of home. "I'll just tell her and let her decide what she'll do."

Malachi's momma must have put the fear of God in

him quite a few times in his life for Gemma's threat to make his eyes pop out so far. He threw his cards down and hurried to her side. "Now, don't go tellin' Momma about the card playin'. I didn't mean what I said."

"I figure your momma ought to know. She'll already know you been drinkin', anyhow, the second she sees you. You smell like a distillery!"

"Come on, Gemma. Don't tell her. She hates gamblin'. She'll whack me with her purse every day till I give up cards altogether."

"Sounds like just what you need, too. Hope she's got plenty of heavy stuff in that purse."

"Gemma, wait!" Malachi stumbled after her. "I'll go with you."

Luke and I couldn't help but smile at the whole display, but we both joined them, Luke putting an arm around Malachi to steady his drunken walk. We could hear the snickers and jeers of the other men as we walked away, but it didn't change Malachi's mind any. He had a healthy enough fear of his momma's purse to keep him from doing that. As it was, I figured he'd get at least a few whacks with whatever she had handy when she saw him.

We rounded the corner from the clearing just in time for Malachi to lean over and vomit.

Luke jumped away. "Dang it, Malachi! I ain't goin'

around takin' care of you no more. You're a lousy drunk."

Malachi ran the back of his arm across his mouth and rolled his eyes. "Don't act like no saint. You ain't no temperance woman."

"I ain't had a drink in two years. And don't go usin' me to make yourself feel better. If you're a lousy drunk, you may as well admit you're a lousy drunk."

"That's right; I forgot." Malachi folded his hands in front of his face like he was ready to say prayers. "You came to Jesus, so maybe you *are* a saint."

Luke grabbed Malachi's shirt with both hands. "You can talk all you want about me, but don't you make fun about what I believe in. You hear? It's the same as what your momma believes, too, and it'd kill her dead to hear you talk like that."

Luke's face was so stern, Malachi squirmed under his stare. "My momma knows I don't see things the same way as her."

"Don't mean it don't hurt her none." Luke pushed Malachi back so that he stumbled and landed on the ground. "Just like it's gonna hurt her to see you like this."

"I reckon she's used to it," Gemma muttered. "Ain't no woman should have to get used to a son that does nothin' but waste his God-given life away."

Drunk or sober, Malachi never could beat Gemma,

and he didn't even try to now. He just groaned and slowly got back to his feet, and the four of us took off again for the uncomfortable walk to Malachi's house.

Lissa was pacing on the porch and ran down the steps when we got there. Her shoulders drooped when she caught sight of Malachi. "He been at the bottle?"

"More than one," Gemma told her.

Luke dragged Malachi up to the house, where they were met by his momma. She looked wrung out, her eyes bloodshot and creased with worry.

"Ain't any momma should have to have so much worry as she does." Lissa swiped at a tear that slipped from her eye. "He'll be the death of her yet."

Gemma put an arm around Lissa and pulled her close. "By the looks of her, she can take care of herself."

Malachi's mother gave Luke a kind nod and a word of thanks, but the second she finished, she turned on Malachi, grabbing the back of his neck like she would a puppy. Malachi howled, but that didn't keep her from yanking him inside like that, and I didn't figure I'd want to be around to see what happened next.

We were silent as we walked home that night. There was too much to think about. It hadn't been the night I'd always hoped for. Klan and drunken men weren't exactly parts of what I'd dreamed my first time out with Luke would be like.

But he was here next to me, and that was something. I turned to look at him, and even though he didn't turn his eyes from the road, I could see a smile creep up on his face. His bandaged right hand took my left and lifted it to his lips long enough to remind me that amid all the troubles in life, some good things still outdid the bad.

Chapter 9

The morning of my nineteenth birthday, I woke up in a panic, sweat dripping down my temples. I shot up so fast, I rammed my head on the sloping ceiling. Moaning in pain, I dropped back onto my pillow and threw an arm across my forehead to block out the sun that spilled in through the window behind me. I tipped my head to the side and peered at Gemma's bed, but I'd slept in late, and her bed was empty and made up neatly.

That was best, I figured, since she'd be bound to ask me what my trouble was, and I was no good at lying to Gemma. It was my birthday morning, and I didn't want to even *think* about those nightmares I'd had of Klan and burning houses and bad things happening to Gemma. I definitely didn't want to talk about them.

I got up and padded to my mirror, running the brush

through my hair ten times to divert my attention from the horrors of that dream. It didn't help much. I could still see those images every time I blinked. Dreams were like that for me. They always stayed with me even after I woke, haunting my reality with figments of imagination.

I heard the clamor of Momma in the kitchen and knew she'd be working on my birthday cake. I shook my head in hopes of shaking out the bad feelings that had lodged there and leaned forward onto my elbows, staring in the mirror at my freckles, counting each one with my finger like they could tell me the story of every year I'd lived.

My mind drifted back to my thirteenth birthday, the day I met Luke when he dragged me sputtering and half-drowned from the swimming hole. I recalled his face as he knelt over me, his golden hair wet and tousled, blue eyes shimmering in the sunlight.

If ever a girl could fall in love lickety-split, I'd done it. There was never a day from that point onward that the mention of his name didn't make my toes tingle. But there was more than toe tingling to be had now. What I felt for him had settled into something deeper, something that couldn't be touched by time or tragedy . . . or freckles. What I felt for Luke Talley made me feel like I could do anything, like nothing and no one could steal away my life and meaning so long as Luke was by my side.

The very thought of all he meant to me sank into my skin, and my reflection looked back at me and smiled. What I saw in that mirror was no longer a girl but a woman whose mind knew all it needed to know about life and love.

And I was bound and determined that the love I had so firmly entrenched in Luke would get us through anything. I gave my reflection a firm nod. "It'll be fine, Jessilyn," I murmured determinedly. "You wait and see."

I heard the screen door slam, heard Daddy call, "Sadie! What's this here package on the porch?"

I ran downstairs. "What package?"

Daddy held up a small, carved wooden box wrapped in a ribbon. "I imagine it's for you, Jessilyn. Though I don't know where it came from. Figure maybe your momma wrapped it on the porch and left it there."

I took it from him, examined it, and knew right off the bat where that wooden box came from. "Momma didn't wrap this, Daddy. This here ain't no Momma-tied bow."

"Well then, who . . . ?" He stopped and looked at me, then took his hat off and wiped his forehead with his arm like a man nearing surrender. "Open the box, Jessilyn. That boy's obviously got somethin' up his sleeve."

My fingers shook when I untied that cockeyed bow that could only have been tied by Luke Talley's calloused carpenter's hands. The box was so beautiful in detail, I handled it like glass, afraid to spoil any bit of Luke's handiwork. Daddy watched me without a word, but that didn't keep him from puffing out two long sighs before I managed to get the lid off.

All I found inside was a purple wildflower. I picked it up between two fingers and held it in front of my face.

Daddy narrowed his eyes at the flower and grunted. "Boy sure goes to a lot of trouble to give a girl a weed!"

I twirled it in front of my face twice before realization dawned on me. "It's from the patch beside the gazebo."

"What's that got to do with anythin'?"

"It's got everythin' to do with everythin'!" I reached up to land a kiss on Daddy's cheek. "I'll be back soon. I promise!"

I ran outside and down the steps in a fashion that would have made Momma's hair stand on end, but I slowed up once I realized I'd make myself hot and sweaty, and I didn't want Luke to see me any way but ladylike today.

I tried to calm my excitement, but by the time I reached the gazebo, my heart was pounding out of my chest. I climbed the two steps inside and spotted another box lying alone on the bench seat my daddy had built twenty years ago for my momma. Picking the box up gently, I sat and untied yet another awkward ribbon.

Inside the box was one slightly ripe strawberry. I smiled and lit out again for the strawberry patch where I'd spent more than a few summer mornings with Gemma. I walked down the rows of strawberry plants before I finally spotted the box nestled on the ground.

This one held a single leaf, big and proud, and I knew without a second thought it was from the sprawling oak in Luke's backyard. I took a moment to compose myself, tucked a few stray hairs into place, and then set off for my journey across the creek to Luke's house.

When I arrived, he was nowhere in sight. I stood there at the outskirts of his property drinking in the sight of the house he'd built with his own two hands over the past few years. Little by little, he'd constructed a home that put his old cabin to shame. The shack he'd once called home now sat off to the side, serving as a shed, making the memory of his living there seem absurd.

The house was beautifully simple. Painted white with black shutters, a long porch trailing from front to back, it was the picture of peace. A porch swing rocked by itself in the breeze. Gemma and I had planted flowers around the house and filled the window boxes he'd made. Every time I looked at that house, I swelled with pride.

But now wasn't about the house. Now was about the

huge oak off to the side of it that had been one of my favorite things for as long as I could remember. That tree was regal somehow, like the king of nature, spreading its branches out to cover its kingdom. I watched the leaves flicker in the breeze, creating that rustling that sounds like music on a beautiful summer day.

I walked to the trunk and started circling it, letting my fingertips run across the rough bark, my eyes on the ground below me in search of another box. I didn't notice Luke walk out onto the porch.

"You're lookin' in the wrong direction!"

My head snapped up at the sound of his voice, and I looked at him questioningly.

"Look in front of you, not down."

I stepped away from the tree trunk and looked around me, wondering what could possibly be within this tree that would be from Luke to me.

If he'd made me a birdhouse, I was going to be sore.

But it was no birdhouse. It was no box, either. There, hanging from the most majestic branch of all, was my old wooden swing, the wind tilting it this way and that. He had prettied it up with a nice glossy stain and a scrolled design that bordered the edges. The ropes were new and sturdy. It was a sight that tugged at my heart so soundly, there was no hiding the tears that pricked my eyes, but I didn't so much care just then.

Luke took the porch steps in one leap and hurried toward me in an uneven lope. I turned and moved to the swing, running my hand down the rope and across the seat. I reached beneath to feel the bottom.

"It's still there." Luke was only a few feet behind me now, his hands in his pockets, watching. "Turn it over."

I used both hands to flip the seat. One of my tears slipped off my eyelashes and plopped down right in the center of my initials. I ran my thumb across to wipe it away and then flipped it back over.

When I twirled to look at him, I found his expression somber, his eyes glistening with something that wasn't tears but spoke of a sincerity I'd not seen from many people outside my family.

"Luke . . ."

He fidgeted a bit under my gaze. "Thought you might like to have it back up, is all. . . ."

"It's perfect." My words came out quickly, cutting off any other nervous thing he might have tried to say. "Perfect."

He blinked three times fast, like it would ward off his nerves, then pulled his hands from his pockets and strode toward me. "Here," he said, taking hold of the swing to steady it, "try it out."

I stared at him from the other side of the swing and took the ropes in my hands. We watched each other for several seconds before I stood on my toes to kiss his cheek in a way I'd never dared to before.

I lingered there for a moment, our faces so close, and watched him like he was the most beautiful sight I'd ever seen. I loved everything about this man. The way he moved, the way he smiled, the smell of his clean shirt, the rhythm of his breathing—which was quickening by the moment. Everything.

Before it happened, before my whole world got flipped upside down, I heard him whisper my name once. And then I felt his lips on my forehead, lightly, so that I instinctively tipped my head up in search of more. I felt his hand move up my back and circle lightly around my neck, his thumb tracing a path up my throat before his face drifted down to mine and our lips met.

His kiss went beyond anything I'd ever dreamed. Even the most overactive imaginations can't come up with anything to match what happened between us that day. No words can explain it, either. That moment was something only the two people sharing it can ever understand. The way he held me and kissed me was pure innocence, but it left no doubt about his feelings whatsoever. Each second his lips remained against mine popped my doubts like balloons until I was left with nothing but absolute certainty that Luke Talley wanted no one but me.

When he pulled away, my knees buckled. I gripped his shirt for support, but I didn't need to. His arms tightened around me, and I leaned against him, desperately wishing I could stay this way forever. Eventually, I lowered down off my toes and turned to slide into the swing, leaning back against his chest. He held the swing there for a short time and then gave me a gentle push.

I tipped my head back into the breeze and closed my eyes, filled with the peace of knowing everything would be all right. Luke Talley had brought part of my home to his, and that only made reality of what I'd always dreamed. Someday, maybe soon, his home would be mine.

We stayed there together for some time before he slowed me down and lowered his head to my ear. "It's gettin' toward noon. Best be gettin' home."

He came around to face me and put his hands at my waist to help me down. Again we lingered longer than we had to, but for once I was in no rush. He pulled away reluctantly and held his hand out to lead me to the truck, but I nestled my hand between his arm and his side instead. "Let's walk."

He tipped his hat at me and smiled. "Whatever the lady wishes."

I returned his smile. "She wishes to walk."

"Then we'll walk."

There were no words on that walk. Not one thing. We were comfortable in that silence, surrounded by the songs of creation, and I reveled in it all the way home.

When we turned the corner into the front yard, we saw Gemma standing next to Tal, who was sitting on the ground, cajoling our dog, Duke, to fetch a stick. He looked up when he heard us crunching across the gravel drive. "This here dog of yours won't do nothin'. May as well keel over dead for all the good he is."

"He's old as the hills, that's why." I picked up a bone that was lying on the ground and tossed it his way. "Try this."

He grabbed the bone and ran it in front of the dog's face. "C'mon! Fetch. Move. Breathe!"

Duke did nothing but let his droopy eyes trail up to Tal's face and then back down to the ground.

Tal poked the animal gently in the nose, but he didn't budge. "I think he's dead."

"His eyes are movin'."

"Maybe that's some sort of nerve reaction. Like the way a snake wiggles after you chop it in half."

"Well, don't go choppin' him in half to find out." Luke took a deep breath of the sweet-scented air. "It'd ruin my appetite for Mrs. Lassiter's barbecue sauce."

I gave him a nudge with my elbow and left them behind to go in and freshen up. As I walked, I turned slightly to cast Luke one last glance and caught his eye. I smiled, then turned back just in time to avoid tripping over the steps.

"Ain't you goin' to marry that girl yet?" Gemma whispered her words, but that whisper was akin to another person's normal volume, and as much as I wanted to hear Luke's answer, I wanted even more to smack Gemma across the head.

"Gemma!" I called. "I reckon Momma could use our help in the kitchen." My voice was pointedly light-hearted, but my face told her she'd best get inside unless she wanted to be sleeping in the shed tonight. She gave me a smile that told me she considered her job well done and sauntered up to the house with her famously lazy walk.

"What on earth are you thinkin'?" I hissed.

"Just lightin' a fire where one needed to be lit."

I raised an eyebrow at her. "Well, I don't need you to go lightin' no fires, thank you very much. If you're intent on lightin' a fire somewhere, why don't you light one under Tal Pritchett?"

Gemma didn't say a word to that, and I figured I'd given her a good taste of her own medicine. I sauntered past her in triumph only to catch the toe of my shoe on the threshold and sail into the kitchen.

"Jessilyn!" Momma looked at me, planting flour-covered fists on her apron-covered hips. "You been at the bottle?"

My eyes widened at my momma, the temperance woman of temperance women, making a joke about alcohol. "Momma!"

She smiled at my shocked expression and nodded toward the kitchen table. "Gemma, honey, dredge those tomato slices for me, will you? And, Jessilyn, you could put on an apron and get them fryin'." She looked at my dress and cringed. "Oh no, you'll get your dress all splashed with oil. Here." She grabbed my arm and switched places with me, then tossed an apron over my head and tied it tight. "Roll out this cobbler dough for me. You look like you could use some calmin' down."

I picked up the rolling pin and tried to focus on getting the thickness just right, but I wasn't having much success. Neither was Momma, because after she'd filled the frying pan with the first few tomato slices, she said, "Oh, it ain't no use" and grabbed my arm with one of her messy hands. "I can't concentrate on a single thing, Jessilyn, until you tell me what went on with Luke this mornin'."

Gemma dropped a tomato into her bowl and jumped up to huddle next to me and Momma. "I can't neither!"

I didn't need any urging to tell all about it, and I did

so in detail, with Momma holding a hand up every so often to make me stop so she could check on the tomatoes. Only I left out the part about the kiss. For some reason, I had a sacred feeling about that kiss, so sacred I couldn't even think of telling anyone about it. It was something for me and Luke to share between the two of us only. But it didn't matter a bit. They were both pie-eyed when I finished anyway, and I leaned back and sighed at the memory of the look on Luke's face that morning.

Momma stared off at nothing for a few seconds and then dreamily scooped the tomatoes from the pan and onto a plate. "That's a man to keep, Jessilyn," she murmured. "No doubt."

"I aim to, only I ain't certain sure I've caught him yet. Leastways there ain't no weddin' talk."

"Oh, he's caught, all right." Gemma dunked another tomato, but she wasn't paying much attention to it. "Just 'cause you ain't got no ring on your finger don't mean nothin'. He's as caught as a man can get."

"What man?" Daddy walked into the room and looked at each of us expectantly.

"Oh, nothin', honey." Momma picked up a tomato and distracted Daddy with food like she'd done many a time. "Taste this for me, will you?"

Daddy obliged and gave her a loud "Mmmm-hm!"

in return. "Sadie Lassiter, that's good eatin' right there. Yes'r!"

He reached for another, but Momma shooed him away. "Get on out there and check the barbecue. That pig's been smokin' an age now. Anyways, you stay in this kitchen, you'll end up dippin' your fingers in everythin'."

Daddy peered out the kitchen window. "I see the boy's here." He nodded at me. "You find out what he was doin' with that crazy boxed-up weed?"

"Yes'r." I blushed at the very thought of what my daddy would think if he knew about that kiss. I turned my face away to hide my burning cheeks.

He waited for me to expound but got impatient when I didn't. "Well?"

"It was a game of sorts, Daddy; that's all. Like hide-and-seek."

"Hide-and-seek for what? Weeds?"

Momma sighed and plopped another tomato on the plate. "Harley, don't be so ornery."

"Well, I'm just wonderin' what the girl's talkin' about."

"No, you're bein' ornery. And she ain't no girl; she's a lady, so you may as well take to the idea good and quick. Luke gave her nice little clues to get her to where his gift was, and his gift was that old tree swing she loved all prettied up and hangin' on the big oak tree by his house." She plopped a few more slices into the pan so forcefully, they splashed oil all over. "Now, don't go makin' a fuss over somethin' sweet and nice."

"I ain't makin' no fuss." Daddy could see he'd gotten her goat, and he never much liked doing so if he could help it. He rubbed the back of his neck and made sure to lower his voice when he spoke again, but his words weren't much calmer. "Just seems to me he could've found a different place to hang the thing. This here's her home, after all."

Momma eyed Daddy so fiercely, she could have near about had the same effect by tossing the frying oil in his face. "Maybe you best start gettin' used to the idea it won't always be."

Gemma and I locked eyes nervously. I gave the dough two more swipes with the rolling pin and yanked my apron off. Gemma did the same after she finished up her last slices, then followed me from the kitchen.

Most days Momma and Daddy got on fine as could be, but every now and again they had a disagreement that got heated, and we knew to leave them to it. We headed upstairs to fix ourselves up, knowing they'd be over and done with the spat by the time we got back downstairs. That was the way with Momma and Daddy's quarrels. They'd start out all smoldering and then catch on fire for a few minutes before they came to some sort of compromise that put the flames out for good. Gemma and I knew from experience how it all worked.

Only we didn't much care to be around when the fire started.

After we ate more than our stomachs should have been able to hold, Momma expelled me from the kitchen since it was my special day and sent me and Luke off for a walk to Miss Cleta's. "I told her since she didn't feel up to comin' to your birthday dinner, we'd send her down some leftovers. The fresh air will do you good, anyways."

There was more than the fresh air to do me good. Walking alongside Luke couldn't help but put a spring in my step, and as we headed down the road toward her house, I held on to his arm like my life depended on it.

After all, sometimes it seemed like it did.

Chapter 10

Young love is a step apart from reality. It paints over the crudities of the world with pretty colors and strokes until everything's just a watercolor. Only problem is, when you cover something up, you don't really get rid of what's beneath.

I guess I knew all about that better than most. I'd seen the ugliest sides of life in my nineteen years. But when a woman wants to see life through the lenses of love, she has a way of doing just that, never mind what's really going on around her.

So I went through those first days of knowing how Luke cared for me without a worry, figuring all would turn to rights—*had* to turn to rights—in a world where a love such as ours could exist.

That is, until the evening of June 15.

I'd forgotten all about the meeting at Cole Mundy's barn the minute Luke Talley made me burn that pancake. The time since had been filled with so much catching up for the time we'd lost, talking and laughing and looking into each other's eyes like people I'd laughed at before I knew what it felt like, that I'd been able to mostly forget about white-robed men and burning crosses. These were days I cherished for the time we had together as much as I did for the knowledge that they couldn't last. Soon enough, he'd be hard at work filling orders and then setting out to deliver them.

But for this Wednesday evening, I wasn't thinking about work orders or meetings in Cole Mundy's barn. I was thinking only about Luke Talley and the wisps of blond hair that were tickling his forehead with the breeze.

He studied the chessboard. "You been practicin' while I was away."

I gave him a wry half smile. "Got to have somethin' to do with my time while you're away."

"Uh-huh. Ain't got nothin' to do with wantin' to whup me at chess."

"I'm not as competitive as you think I am."

"Jessie, if you ain't competitive, then a pig ain't got a snout."

I kept that half smile on my face and tipped my head at the board. "You gonna talk or play?"

He sighed and moved a piece.

"You gave me the game with that move!"

"Weren't nothin' else for me to do. I ain't like to sit here for hours waitin' for my doom."

I studied his pieces for a minute or two and then tented my fingers in front of my mouth. "Huh!"

"Huh! That's right. You got me fair and square."

"Reckon I got better'n I thought." I tapped his shoe with my own and leaned toward him across the table, knocking over a few pawns as I did so. "Reckon I'm more trouble than you bargained for."

He leaned over the board and brought his face six inches away from mine. "Reckon that's a risk I'm willin' to take."

Now, normally, Gemma was my right hand in times like these, giving me and Luke the space my daddy so rarely gave us. She'd ask my daddy questions to distract him or start humming so Daddy couldn't eavesdrop on us. But on this evening Momma and Daddy had gone off for a visit, and here Gemma was, bursting through the screen door at the worst possible moment. My poison look told her so.

She didn't catch it, though. I could tell by the look in her eyes she was lost in her thoughts, and most times I couldn't find her too easily in times like those. I turned my attention back to Luke, but he'd slipped back into his seat, stealing the moment away with him.

I sighed and pushed my chair back. "Gemma, somethin' wrong?"

She didn't answer, just stood there hanging on to the porch rail, looking off into the sky, her lips forming words her voice didn't. Prayers.

I gave Luke a sideways glance and nodded in her direction. "Won't hear a thing when she's like this." My voice was flippant, but my insides didn't match. Gemma usually got this way when she was sad or worried, and I didn't much like thinking about her feeling either way. I got up and put my hand on her shoulder. "You okay, Gemma?"

She just shook her head. "Somethin's wrong."

"Where?"

"Don't know." She wrapped one arm around her middle, tight. "I just know somethin's wrong. I can feel it."

I knew what she meant. Impending trouble always settled in my stomach before it went anywhere. But for this night, it was Gemma alone who carried the weight, and I didn't ask her why. I knew what she'd say. She'd say the Lord told her, and she was meant to pray about it. That's what she always said. Sometimes, right smack in the middle of the night, I'd hear her slide off her bed onto her knees and pray right there in whispers.

I didn't much believe in God talking to people unless it had to do with Moses or Balaam. To me, those were ancient stories, and I could figure enough about a God that would talk in times like those.

But speeches from God or not, I believed Gemma had a sixth sense about certain things. I trusted her more than I trusted myself, and I figured if she said trouble was coming, then trouble was coming.

Luke, he was different. He watched her like he figured any second an angel would appear beside her. Over time, I'd watched Luke think more and more about the things Scripture said, and I knew now as he stood there watching Gemma that he believed she'd heard the voice of God.

I wasn't sure how to feel about that, so I just pushed those thoughts aside and cleared the pieces from the chessboard one by one to pass the time. I'd only gotten halfway through when I heard Gemma speak.

"The colored church." With that announcement, the dread that she'd already had written across her face turned a shade darker, and her next words came out in a sort of moan. "Tal's there."

That was all she said, but it was all she needed to say. Her finger pointed off into the distance. I followed its direction until I saw what she did—three wisps of smoke, like gray fingers pointing to the heavens.

Luke disappeared inside, and I knew he'd be calling for help. But all I could do was stand and stare. Some six years back, the sight of such a thing sent us all into the worst time we'd ever known. The plumes of smoke that day were signs of a fire that left Gemma an orphan, and if I never saw such a thing again in all my life, I knew I'd be the better for it.

But Gemma, she'd been there. She'd seen the bolt of lightning that lit up her house like kindling. She'd heard her parents' cries and been forced to leave them behind, knowing they'd gone on without her and there was nothing she could do to change that.

I remembered the look on her face when I found her curled up in a cart while her house burned in the distance, and I saw that very same look now.

She pointed her eyes at me. They were glassy with fear, and when she spoke, her words came out in agonizing gasps. "There was a meetin' there tonight. We've got to go."

I knew all about that meeting. It was a meeting to talk about how to peacefully stand up against prejudice in our community. I knew about it because Gemma had complained about it to me just this morning.

"Ain't no reason to go stirrin' up trouble," she'd said. "Best to leave well enough alone."

"Only it ain't well enough," I'd replied.

She only shook her head at me. She didn't want to argue.

And there was no arguing with her now. Her whole body shook with the certainty that she could lose another loved one to flame and smoke, and I ached at the very thought of her having to go through that again.

"Gemma, you stay here." I used my hands on her shoulders to turn her full around to face me. "You know you can't go out there and see that. It'll rip you up."

"I have to."

"No, you don't. You can stay here and wait for Momma and Daddy, tell them where we've gone."

"A note'll do the same. I'm goin'."

"Don't be a stubborn mule!"

"I'll be whatever I need to be, Jessilyn, and don't you go sayin' different. If I've got to go, I've got to go. Don't matter none if you think it wise or not."

I knew I'd get nowhere, so I shut my mouth and watched her head off to take a determined seat in Luke's truck, her arms crossed as tightly as they could be, quivering as they were.

Luke came out and grabbed my arm. "Called the sheriff, and ain't it a surprise, he's not in! Got one of them dim-witted deputies of his, says he'll let it be known there's trouble at the colored church." He lowered his voice even though Gemma couldn't hear a word from where she was. "You ask me, there won't be a single soul there to help . . . least not one that's white." He steered me down the steps to the truck and helped me in before hopping up beside me.

Gemma's church, the only colored church in our parts, sat a good half mile away from town, an old, rickety building all alone in a field of goldenrod and ticks. Despite being painted up a shiny white and kept clean as a whistle, most of the time it looked like it was going to come down on somebody's head. I'd told Gemma many a time I was worried she'd be buried alive there.

She always dismissed me with the same words. "If I go to Jesus praisin' Him, I reckon there ain't no better way."

Gemma's feet tapped the floorboard in a nervous dance, but I didn't put my hand on her knee to urge her to stop. I knew all sorts of things had to be stirring in her soul, and she needed to get by somehow. The trip wouldn't take long in minutes, but it would seem like an eternity in thoughts.

The acrid smell of burning wood floated into the truck through open windows, making our eyes burn and water. Gemma's lips moved in whispered prayers. I gripped Luke's sleeve, readying for what figured to be a trying time.

The sky was orange over the treetops when we rounded the bend to the church, throwing me right back to that day at Gemma's house like I'd been transported in time. The air was heavy with smoke, making it hard to breathe. Gemma pulled a handkerchief from her pocket and held it over her nose and mouth. The second the truck skidded to a stop well away from the burning church, Luke tied his own handkerchief around my face and then jumped out of the truck. "Stay back!" he ordered.

That old building had gone up in flame so quick, it was almost a pile of ash already. The roaring of the fire, popping and cracking with a life of its own, was deafening, but not enough to cover the agonized screams and wails of the soot-covered mass of bystanders.

Gemma started to fuss with the door handle, but her hand was too shaky to grasp it.

"Don't, Gemma." I held her arm. "Don't go out there."

She coughed hard, and there were tears streaming down her face, but she kept jiggling the handle. "I need to know, Jessie," she murmured when she could breathe again.

"Then let *me* go. Why don't you stay here and wait for help while I go look?"

She turned to face me, and with that handkerchief over her mouth and nose, all I could see were her bloodshot eyes, but they told me all I needed to know. "They already done their helpin'!"

I knew what she meant. The way she saw it, the only white hands that would have anything to do with this scene before us had struck the matches and poured the gasoline.

And that was the way I saw it too.

Gemma still fumbled with the door like a child, and I watched her sadly for a few seconds before hopping out and running to her door to let her out. I took both her arms in my hands to help her down and let her steady her legs before letting go and following behind her.

About a dozen colored people huddled together in the tall grasses a good distance from the fiery remains, most of them with blackened and torn clothes, ministering to each other in between sobs. About a dozen more were futilely trying to squelch the fire with buckets of water from a nearby well.

I held on to Gemma as we wove in and out between them searching for Tal. I called out his name, but Gemma couldn't.

Funny how our voices sometimes don't work when we need them most.

As we walked by a large woman who cradled two weeping children in her arms, the woman reached out and tugged on Gemma's skirt.

"Just like that, Gemma Teague," she murmured. "It went up just like that. I saw them walk by the window, but I didn't know what they was up to." She covered one ear on each child and lowered her voice. "They looked like demons from the depths of hell, and they got to be if they's the kind that can set a church full of people on fire like that."

Gemma pulled away, her whole body shaking now. "Tal Pritchett," she managed to stammer.

"What's that, girl?"

"Tal Pritchett," I answered for her. "She wants to know if Tal Pritchett was here."

"Oh, he was here. He was up front speakin' when it happened."

I gripped Gemma harder. "You seen him after the fire started?"

The woman pulled the children closer and rocked back and forth. "Don't know, honey. Just don't know. It happened so fast."

Gemma's legs betrayed her, and she nearly tumbled to the ground before I managed to steady her. Afraid for her well-being, I searched the area for Luke, but he was several yards away from the church, coaxing a couple of anxious horses across the rough ground. Someone had hooked them up to a plow in an attempt at creating a sort of firebreak around the church property, but

I didn't have much hope that would stop the spread of the fire.

I turned Gemma to face me. "Won't you please wait at the truck? It'll be safer there, and I can go look for Tal."

She only shook her head and tugged me onward. I slipped my arm around her waist and desperately searched the darkness, terribly afraid that this night would be yet one more scar on Gemma's memory. As we walked on, the gasping breaths she took told me she feared the same.

We had scanned the faces of the group who milled about up front and were making our way around back when I heard Gemma cry out and felt her weight slump against me. I froze and looked ahead with a searing dread.

I didn't want to see what Gemma's eyes had seen.

But when I spotted Tal Pritchett, covered in soot and ash, stumbling toward us, I never wanted to stop looking. His face was creased with strain and streaked with sweat and tears, but his eyes were lit up from the sight of Gemma. He swept her into his arms, and once her weight was transferred to him, my legs gave out and I slid to my knees. As I knelt there, crying silently, watching my best friend weep out her terror, my bones turned brittle at the very thought of what could have been done to the man she so clearly loved with all her heart.

And at the thought of the men who had almost made it happen.

I leaned back on my heels and watched the flames lick at the starlit sky, and I thought of what those people must have felt like when it all happened. I could picture them sitting in the pews, alive and well, listening to folks talk about how to live a better life in a white man's world. And then I could see that fire erupt in the church like they'd been dropped into the pit of hell. I could see them struggle to escape amid the smoke and heat, screams of anguish ringing in their ears. In my head, I could see it all.

But these people had seen it all with their own eyes. Over the years, they'd seen a great deal with their eyes, all because they'd been born with dark skin. And as I watched Gemma and Tal, as I looked around at the horrified faces surrounding them, I was filled with rage. I stood up with fists so tight, my fingernails dug into my palms.

I pictured those hooded men, unmasked by now, no doubt sharing moonshine and laughs in Cole Mundy's barn, and my heart burned with the kind of hate my momma had told me was an abomination before God.

But I didn't care. I looked around and saw there was nothing I could do here but watch the world fall apart for a congregation of colored people. I turned without a word, marched to Luke's truck, and pulled away.

There were no thoughts in my mind then. That's the funny thing about hate. It makes the brain fuzzy and mixes things up. It covers up all the good things you've learned over the years and lowers your inhibitions like alcohol. I'd never taken a drink of liquor in all my life, but I'd seen the effects of it many a time, and I figured this was as close to getting drunk as I'd ever be.

The truck rattled over the uneven dirt roads so that my ribs ached, but I didn't slow down one bit. By the time I pulled up at Cole Mundy's house, I was possessed by a kind of senseless rage I'd never known. I didn't think twice about what I was about to do, didn't worry that I was unarmed and would be outweighed by every man inside. Their raucous voices drifted out to me, and I got out of that truck, slammed the door, and barged into that barn like I owned it.

The air was so thick with smoke, it would have choked me had I not been forced to inhale it from the time I got within a mile of the colored church. There were a good twenty men there, and I recognized every cigar-smoking, liquored-up one of them.

Including Sheriff Clancy.

The chatter stopped the second they set eyes on me, except for the few muttered curses that were aimed in my direction.

Delmar Custis was the first to speak. He slid his filthy boots off the table they were propped on and let them hit the floor with a thud. "I think you got the wrong place."

"No, I ain't. I was invited, don't you remember? Got me a nice little notice tacked up to my front porch."

"That weren't no invitation. That was an announcement, is all."

"You mean it was a threat." I looked around the room. "Looks like you got yourselves a nice turnout, anyways. Not so many as you'd like, though. Bet if you'd have put 'We'll be torchin' a colored church' on your invitations, you'd have gotten more of a crowd."

Several of the men sat up real straight when I said that, but Delmar waved them off with his cigarette. "Girl, you ought to know better'n any other in this here town, you don't go makin' accusations to certain people unless you want trouble comin' your way. We don't know nothin' about no colored church bein' torched. Shame if it's true, though." He took a puff of the cigarette. "Heck, you got yourself a nigger, ain't you? Sure hope she ain't got singed or nothin'."

To this day I think maybe I could have kept myself together but for one thing. He laughed. Right there in front of me with the sin of attempted murder on his hands that very night, he looked at me and laughed at the thought of my Gemma being caught in that burnt-up church.

I marched to him in three quick strides, yanked the cigarette from his mouth, and put it out on his arm. He screamed and lunged for me, but even when he had me pinned between his sweaty body and the wall, his gasping breaths tainting the air, I didn't care. It was as though some part of me had begun to leave, the part of me that had always believed good would eventually win out over evil. It wasn't gone completely, not yet. But it was starting to fade away, chipped at like peeling paint.

Delmar had my hair in one hand, yanking my head back so I had to look up at him. Past him I could see the other men closing ranks to watch the show. "You gonna kill me now?"

"I ain't killed nobody, girl, but if I aim to start, I can't say I'd be too sorry to start with you."

"But you'll kill someday." I made an effort to swallow even though it was hard with my neck stretched backward. "Men like you, they don't go through life without killin' someone."

His grip loosened a bit, but he still pinned me with his chest. I took the opportunity to tip my chin down some, and when I did, I caught Sheriff Clancy's eye. "What sort of law they hire you to uphold these days, Sheriff? Or don't you hold to the law none at all?"

"Ain't no lawbreakin' goin' on in here, Jessilyn. Least not until you showed up. I could arrest you for assault."

"I didn't say nothin' about lawbreakin' goin' on in here. I'm talkin' about over at the colored church."

He watched me for a second and then took a long swig of his beer.

"That stuff give you courage, Sheriff? Or does it just make you a better liar?"

Sheriff Clancy spit and shifted his wad of chewing tobacco. "You got a big mouth on you, girl!" But despite his vehemence, he clamped a meaty hand on Delmar's shoulder. "Let her go."

"Don't feel like it."

"I didn't ask if you felt like it. In fact, I didn't ask you nothin'. I told you to let her go."

Delmar didn't even flinch until the sound of a pistol being cocked caught his attention. I looked down and saw Sheriff Clancy holding his pistol by his right thigh.

"Like I said, Delmar . . . let her go."

Delmar gritted his teeth so hard, I could hear them scraping together, but he let me go. Not without giving me one last shot, though, and his sharp release sent my head back into the wall. I bit my tongue with the force of it, blood immediately awakening my taste buds. I ran the back of my hand across my mouth where some had trickled from the corner of it. As I walked toward the door, I looked into the face of every man in that room, then made a mental note of their shoes. If a man was bound to hide his identity under a white hood, you could always figure him out by his shoes.

The sheriff kept his hand on his gun, apparently to stave off any trouble, but the look he aimed my way said he'd just as soon put a bullet in my head. I opened the door and hurried outside. It had started to rain, and the feel of it was like a slap to the face. My knees started to shake from the realization of what I'd done, and I ran to the truck awkwardly and peeled out of the gravel drive.

The rain had put a damper on the fire, but it still burned freely and had taken over most of the church property. Luke was standing on the roadside, his clothes wet and sooty, as I drove up.

"Jessilyn!" He waved and I slowed to a stop, turned the engine off, barely able to look at him. "Where you been?" he asked. "You had me worried sick. Gemma and Tal took a few of the ones who were worst off over to the Jessups' barn to look after them, and everyone else headed out when they realized there weren't nothin' to be done. Next thing I know, I'm all alone, and you ain't nowhere to be found."

I hopped out, still unable to look him in the eye. I knew he'd want to wring my neck if he found out where I'd been, but it wasn't likely I'd get by without saying. I put it off for a few more seconds and reached up to smooth back his wet hair.

He pulled my hand away to lay it over his heart. Then he leaned forward. "Jessie, what's goin' on? Don't shut me out. Ain't nothin' worse than that."

I felt so guilty. While Luke had stayed to help good people, I'd gone off to cause more trouble with the bad ones. I slipped my hand away from his and held it over my own heart, where a pain was starting to make it hard to breathe.

Luke looked at the back of my hand and then leveled a sharp glance at me. "Why's there blood on your hand?" He pulled me to him and gave me a once-over. "You get hurt somehow?"

I shook my head and started to cry.

Luke took my face in his hands. "Jessilyn, you tell me what happened. Now! You hear?"

"I left." My voice shook, and I had trouble working in my words around the gasps as I cried.

"I know that. Where'd you go?"

"To Cole's."

"Cole Mundy?" He dropped his hands and studied my eyes. "What in blazes would you do somethin' stupid like that for?"

"I don't know." I knew my words were as stupid as my actions, but it was the truth. I didn't know. I had no idea what had come over me from the very start of it all, and I couldn't explain it to the man I loved just now, either.

"You don't know? Jessilyn, they could have killed you out there, you know that?" He turned and walked off about ten feet. I knew he was likely thinking he could kill me right about now too, so I left him alone to work out his anger before he turned his attention back to me.

He turned around then and pointed at me. "Where'd the blood come from?"

"I bit my tongue."

"You bit your tongue!"

"It's the truth, Luke!"

"How?"

I stood there silently, afraid he'd retaliate after hearing Delmar had been rough with me, and I didn't want Luke getting hurt because I'd been a fool.

But Luke wasn't taking my quiet for an answer, and he took three quick steps toward me. "Jessilyn, how?"

"He just gave me a little shove, is all. It was my own fault. I just bit my tongue because I got surprised by him."

"Who's 'him'?"

"Delmar Custis."

"Delmar Custis put his hands on you?"

He had no idea how much, and I wasn't about to let

him know. I only shrugged. "He shoved me a little, like I said."

He walked past me and opened the truck door, but I caught him by the arm. "Luke, wait! It wasn't nothin'. It was my own fault. I lost my temper, and I went over and accused them. It ain't like he didn't have reason for it."

Luke didn't look at me. "Get in the truck, Jessilyn."

"Where are we goin'?"

He didn't say anything, but the set of his jaw told me enough. I slid my way between him and the truck door. "Luke, don't do nothin', please. It was my fault. Me! If you get into trouble because of my stupid ways, I'll be sick, you hear?" I was frantic by now, all sorts of images flashing through my head, and not one of them ended without Luke being hurt. Or worse. I took his face in both of my hands and made him look at me. "If you care about me at all, don't go over there. Just let it go."

His blue eyes locked with mine. "Jessilyn, you know how I feel about you."

"Then don't go."

He watched me for a good solid minute, every muscle in his face tense. I held my breath the entire time I waited. Finally he leaned his forehead down against mine and sighed. "You wear me out, Jessilyn. You know that, don't you?"

Relief swept over me and I fell against him, no longer

feeling able to hold my own weight. But I didn't have to worry. He held it for me. And as we stood there in the rain, the smell of fear and hate mixed with the smoky air around us, I clung to him out of desperation, desperation about what life would bring us.

About the thought of who it might take away.

Chapter 11

I could see it start to happen right from the minute Gemma had met Tal on our front porch. Even with Malachi bleeding on the floorboards, she'd shone from top to toe, a flush dusted across those high cheekbones of hers like I hadn't ever seen before.

Just like she was shining now, strolling up the walkway beside him.

I leaned the broom against the house, stood at the top of the porch steps, and waved. "All done for the day?"

"For all I can tell." Tal held up a chicken by its scrawny legs. "Gemma's prize for her services today. She's a soldier to do what she does for some fried chicken."

I wrinkled my nose at the sight of it. Ours was mostly a planting farm, and any slaughtering that was ever done was done by a field hand or my daddy. "I hate the sight of those things unless they're already ready to be dredged and fried."

Gemma smiled at my discomfort. "That mean you ain't gonna pluck it and whack it up for me?"

"I will soon as hell freezes over." I retrieved the broom and nodded toward the house. "Momma's asked you to stay for supper, Tal." Then I looked at him long and hard and said, "Long as your friend don't come with you. Daddy's in the shed. You can leave that critter off with him."

"That's mighty good of your momma. Tell her I thank her kindly." He tipped his hat at me, then at Gemma, and went off to dispose of Gemma's wages.

Gemma took the broom from me and swept the pile I'd made into the bushes. "That man put in more work today than most do in a week. He's got six folks hurt from that fire, and he ain't got nowhere to take them since the hospital won't accept coloreds. You should see him tryin' his best to care for folks in that empty old barn." She stopped sweeping and tossed the broom against the wall so hard, it slid sideways and clattered to the floor. I didn't say anything. I just watched as she took a deep breath to calm her nerves and then bent over to pick up the broom and settle it upright. "I swear, Jessilyn, sometimes it all just feels like too much. I ain't sure how much more I can take."

I took her face in my hands and stood almost nose to nose with her. "Gemma Teague, most days it's me get-tin' a reminder from you, but today it's my turn. All the stuff goin' on—it's a bunch of nonsense, ain't no doubt in that. Men like the Klan shouldn't be allowed to run around destroyin' people's lives. But I've had you tell me time and again to look at the good, and I'll tell you what's good this here day. It's that you got Tal Pritchett here to care for them sick folk at all. He could've been lost yesterday. You remember that."

Her eyes moistened up right off the bat, and she leaned her forehead against mine. "I know." Her breath caught, and she took her time before repeating, "I know it, Jessilyn."

I used my thumbs to swipe at her tears, then wiped away my own. "Now, more importantly, you two seem to be gettin' on right nice." I lowered my voice and put my mouth close to her ear. "Reckon he's got some thoughts about you that don't have to do with workin'."

"Shh!" She gave me a playful whack with the back of her hand. "Don't you go startin' somethin'."

"Oh, please! Everybody in these here parts knows what's goin' on between you two. It's clear as day you're in love with him."

Gemma's cheeks turned pink as Momma's roses. "Be quiet, I said. I don't need the whole world knowin' my business." But no matter her stern words, a grin played at the corners of her mouth. "He is a fine man, though, ain't he?"

"And fine-lookin', too, you ask me."

I waited for her to scold me for such talk, like usual, but she just took a glance in Tal's direction and said, "Mmm-hmmm. He sure is."

I stepped back and put my hands on my hips. "Gemma Teague! If that ain't the first time I ever heard you talk saucy."

She tilted her chin up and gave me the look of a woman who knows what she knows but ain't interested in the rest of the world knowing. "I'm just sayin', he's a fine man who's fine-lookin', and that's all I'm gonna say about it."

"Uh-huh. I hear you. And I'm just sayin' I got me a sure bet to lay down that there ain't a soul in Calloway who don't know what's what with you two."

Gemma still had her eyes on Tal, who was talking to Daddy outside the shed. "Ain't your momma taught you better than to lay bets?" She sashayed past me and paused at the door. "I'll be upstairs freshenin' up." Then she dashed inside with a hop in her step.

With a smile gracing my face, I glanced at Tal again, studying him while he stood there in conversation with my daddy. Sure enough, I figured he'd fit in right nice with us even if the people of Calloway did fuss and fight over another colored person joining the Lassiter family. Adding Tal to our family, though, meant losing part of Gemma, and as much as I teased her, I wasn't ready for that yet. I wasn't sure I ever would be.

But there were plenty of things in life that weren't up to me. I'd found that out many times, and I knew tonight was no exception the minute we sat down to supper.

Luke had stayed home to work this evening, and from the second I took my seat, I'd felt like the odd man out. From the faces at the table, I could see there was something stewing that only I wasn't part of, and it stung at my pride like an angry bee. Daddy kept looking Tal over with that intuitive eye of his, and Momma kept jerking a little, so I knew she was giving him little kicks under the table to make him stop. Gemma sat all uptight and quiet, and Tal was having so much trouble swallowing his food that he ate his peas in singles.

I pushed my mashed potatoes around my plate, making peaks and valleys out of them, and wondered what had suddenly gotten under everyone's skin. Finally I leaned back in my chair and announced, "Miss Cleta got a new carpet for her livin' room."

It wasn't exactly groundbreaking news, but it was something to fill the unbearable silence. I looked at Momma. "She says you're welcome to her old one if you want it. Miss Cleta thinks it's awful threadbare, but it looks just fine to me. Might help take the chill out of the den in winter."

Momma smiled but didn't reply. I tapped my foot quietly beneath the table for about thirty seconds before deciding I couldn't take any more. I let my fork slip out of my hand and clatter to the table beside my plate.

"All right, now this is too much. What on earth is goin' on around here?"

"Jessilyn," Momma breathed, "what's gotten into you?"

"Only whatever's not bein' said at this table. I'd like to know what's got everybody so out of sorts."

Daddy's right eyebrow shot up, but he didn't take his eyes off Tal, and Tal shrank under his watchful glare.

I gave Gemma a nudge under the table, and she looked at me nervously. "You want to tell me what's goin' on, Gemma?"

She gave me one of those long stares with wide eyes that said I should keep quiet, but I wasn't interested. I just returned her stare and said, "Well? Say somethin'."

Tal cleared his throat and forced himself to look at me. "She can't."

I looked at Tal expectantly. "Why not?"

"'Cause she don't know what's goin' on."

"Well, do you?"

"Yes'm."

"Oh, don't 'yes'm' me, Tal Pritchett. I ain't your momma. I just want to know what's got this family all atwitter."

"Jessilyn, it ain't for us to say." Momma saw Daddy's mouth open and gave him another swift kick. "Tal will say what he needs to say when he's good and ready."

"So he does have somethin' to say, then." I turned to Tal and tipped my chin up. "Well, if you got somethin' to say that's makin' this table so uncomfortable, I reckon you best up and say it."

The second those words came out of my mouth, I regretted them. The nervous way Tal's hands shook when he plopped his napkin onto his plate, the way his jelly legs barely held him up while he stood—it all fell into place in my head like pieces of a puzzle, and suddenly I didn't want to hear it anymore. But it was too late.

His words spilled out so clumsily, they sounded like gibberish to my ringing ears. I heard him like he was twenty miles away, and when I saw Gemma's tearful, smiling nod, I closed my eyes against the sight of it. Daddy grudgingly rose from his chair to clap him on the back, Momma grabbed them both in a bear hug, but I . . . I just sat there, numb from head to toe, faced with the fact that all my teasing about Tal had more to it than I'd taken the time to recognize. This was the first time

I'd stopped to accept the fact that soon I would have to say good-bye to my best friend.

I forced myself to stand and say all the niceties that people say to couples who were promised to wed. But behind my phony smile sat a heart weighed down by emptiness.

"I thought I'd burst with waitin'," I heard Momma say when my ears started to pick up sound again. "He asked Harley for permission this mornin', and I've been a nervous wreck since, scared I'd drop somethin' and spoil it all." She gave them a soft push toward the door. "You two go on out for a walk or somethin' and have a little time to yourselves. You don't need us gawkin' at you at a time like this."

Tal took Gemma's arm and walked them out of the kitchen, and Daddy followed them to the door. Then he plopped down in his green chair and lit his pipe.

I left Momma humming at the sink and ambled off to sit on the arm of Daddy's chair.

He sighed loud and long and put an arm around my waist. "Now, what do you think about all of this, Jessie girl?"

I leaned my head back against the chair and stared at the ceiling, where a group of gnats sat in a circle. "Reckon I saw it comin'."

"But it don't seem real till it comes, that right?"

"Yes'r."

"Well, I didn't see any reason to say no to the boy. He's a fine man with a fine occupation."

"Didn't make you feel any better about givin' Gemma to him, did it?"

He took his pipe out and sighed again. "Jessilyn, ain't no time I feel good about losin' either one of my girls." He took a puff and leaned his head back like me. "Guess I'm just selfish, is all."

I let my head tip over so I could look at him. "Guess I get it from you, then, 'cause I don't want her to go neither."

He reached to cup his hand around my chin. "We got one thing to remember, you and me. No matter who marries who or who goes where, we're always family till the day we leave this earth. You hear? Ain't no weddin' bells gonna change that."

I nodded slowly and swallowed the lump that was stuck in my throat. "Yes'r."

Daddy stuck his pipe in his mouth, and we sat there without a word, Momma's humming filling the background. I looked around at the old den furniture—the ragged gold sofa with the afghan lying across the back, the pictures of stone-faced family members that hung on the wall, Momma's rocker with her knitting basket beside it. Nothing had changed from the day I'd been able to form memories. And as much as I spouted about wanting change, there was a part of me that loved the sheer sameness of this room.

But I knew life was not like den furniture. It changed. And most often it changed when you least expected it and in ways you didn't much want it to. There wasn't much I could do about that, though. One thing I could do at this moment, pregnant with change as it was, was treasure what I had while I had it. I settled back in my daddy's grasp, on the arm of my daddy's old green chair, with my daddy's pipe smoke tickling my nose, and I closed my eyes.

Some things never change.

Chapter 12

First thing the next morning, I made my way through the fields, colored pink by the light of dawn, on my way to Luke's house. I hadn't slept a wink the night before, tied up as I was by thoughts of Gemma's leaving. It had been discussed the night before that Gemma and Tal wanted a wedding with little fanfare, and it was to happen in just a couple weeks. I wondered what all the hurry was, but I knew there wasn't any good reason for them not to. If any two people had been cut out of matching cloth by God, it was those two. They were the same in thinking and believing, and I'd known from the second they'd met, there wasn't much question they'd make each other happy till the day they died.

But that didn't mean *I* was happy about it, and the

dark circles under my eyes made my feelings good and clear to anyone. Luke was already hard at work, but the second he saw me, he let his chisel drop with a clatter and came to meet me.

He didn't greet me, only took my face in his hands and stared into my eyes. "Somethin's wrong."

I shrugged. "Depends on who you're talkin' to."

"I'm talkin' to you."

I slid from his grasp and wandered over to the bureau he was working on, tugging the door open to look inside. "It's beautiful."

"Jessie, you're avoidin' the subject."

I ran my hand down the smooth edge of the door, then closed it gently and turned toward him with a sigh. "Gemma's gettin' married."

He stuck his hands in his pockets and leaned against the tree where my swing sat motionless in the still, wet heat. "I figured that'd happen soon enough."

"Well, so did I, but . . ."

"That don't make it easier to swallow."

The sudden lump in my throat took away my ability to talk, and I replied with a shake of my head.

He walked over to me and slid a hand under my chin. "She'll still be here for you, Jessie. You know that."

I couldn't look at him. I nodded my head halfway and then buried my face in his shoulder. His arms slid around me, and I rested there as I had so many other times in my life. And just like so many other times in my life, he whispered in my ear that everything would be okay.

He let me rest against him for a few minutes and then gave my hair a playful tug. "Reckon you'll be a maid of honor, huh? All dolled up in some nutty dress with ruffles all over it."

I dried my tearstained cheek against his shirt and tipped my head up in defiance. "I'll do no such thing. She even tries, I'll pin her ears back."

"Oh, there'll be some pinnin', all right. They'll be pinnin' flowers on you, pinnin' baby's breath in your hair—"

"Stop it."

"Before you know it, you'll look like Dolly Gooch."

I shoved my knuckles into his ribs. "Don't you start with me, Luke Talley."

"I'm only sayin'."

"I ain't wearin' no fluff and nonsense. Besides, Gemma wants a quiet weddin' at our house. I'll end up helpin' Momma make me somethin' simple I can wear to church after the weddin'."

He leaned down, picked a violet, and stood up to tuck it behind my ear. "Don't matter if you've got ruffles or flowers, Jessilyn. You'll be beautiful all the same."

He leaned in for a kiss that was nothing more than

a flutter against my lips, but it was enough. Just as I'd hoped, my weary walk across the fields had made everything seem better.

Luke threw his tools into his toolbox and tucked an arm through mine. "I'll walk you home."

"You don't have to do that."

"I want to."

"So you can be with me, or so you can have some of Momma's hotcakes?"

Luke cocked his head sideways. "Well . . . maybe a little bit of both."

I gave him a shove with my hip but couldn't help smiling. Then again, even the very mention of his name did that to me.

Luke and I were a sight at the breakfast table that morning, making eyes at each other like two fools. Tal had come by to eat before he and Gemma started out their day, and all four of us making like lovestruck idiots was driving my poor daddy to distraction. But the way I figured it, Luke and I had a full six years of feelings all cooped up inside, and so long as all we were doing was making eyes at each other, it was to be understood.

The crunching of gravel signaled a visitor pulling into the driveway, dragging our attention away from each other.

Daddy got up and looked out the window. "It's Nate Colby."

"Nate?" I got up to see for myself. "What's he doin' here this time of day?"

Daddy pushed the curtain aside and called out, "Hey, Nate! What can we do for you?"

"Miss Cleta's sick. Don't know what to do for her since she's so stubborn and all, but she don't seem right to me. Figured one of y'all could talk some sense into her."

"Sick?" I leaned in closer to Daddy. "She's not bad, is she, Nate?"

"I don't know. She says she won't see no doc but the colored one, but I done told her that just wouldn't do."

I think we all cringed at that comment. Everyone but Tal, that is. He just slid his chair back and sauntered up to the window behind us all. "I'd be happy to see her, so long as you can take me back."

Poor Nate looked near about ready to melt into his shoes when he saw Tal's face at that window. His shoulders drooped and his chin pointed to the ground. "Reckon so" was all he said. He didn't put up a fight about social viewpoints or any such thing, just turned back to his truck and hopped inside.

Momma was already packing some soup she'd cooked up from the chicken bones the night before, doing what she did whenever she got nervous—fixing food. She threw in some herbal tea she'd put together herself. "You make sure she gets some food in her. Don't let her be a stubborn mule about it, you hear?"

I took the basket she'd packed. "Yes'm. I'll be sure."

Daddy told us to call from Nate's if we needed something. Luke piled into the back of Nate's truck with Tal, Gemma, and me for the bumpy ride down the road.

Nate's two-year-old daughter, Grace, was sitting in the truck bed with their dog, and I plucked her up and pulled her onto my lap. "Hey, baby. You're out early." I kissed her mussed-up hair. It smelled like honeysuckle.

She reached a finger up to touch my eyelashes. "Miss Cleta's sick."

"So I hear. I'm sure she'll be fine. We'll see to her."

But as we bumped along the road, I thought how easy it was to say such things to children. Much easier than believing it as an adult. That short ride down the road seemed a lifetime to me just then. By the time we got there, I'd run through a whole slew of ideas of how we might find her, and not one of them was in the least bit pleasant. I scurried out of the truck the second we pulled up and handed Grace to Nate.

"She'll be inside." I pointed the way for Tal, like he'd have a hard time figuring out where she lived or something.

But Gemma took hold of his arm before he could budge. "You wait here till I talk to her first."

"Gemma!" I looked at her like she'd lost her mind. "Miss Cleta needs lookin' after."

"Not till I talk to her first." She lowered her voice. "This here ain't no small thing, Jessilyn. Miss Cleta bein' seen by a colored doctor? That'll get around this town like wildfire, and she won't never live it down."

"Miss Cleta asked for him."

"I want to make sure before she goes through with this. I don't think she realizes what she's doin'."

Tal stood by and listened, but I could see he was none too happy to do it. Then he put a hand on Gemma's to get her attention. "I see what you're sayin', Gemma, but that don't mean I can sit by and not help someone who's sufferin'."

"You're like to see her suffer more if you do help."

Luke spoke up then. "I say we quit bickerin' and let Miss Cleta have her say. She's got a strong mind of her own, no doubt, and she wouldn't take kindly to us tryin' to run her life for her."

"You already know how I feel about it," Nate grunted. "No offense, Doc." He tipped his hat at us and shifted Grace's weight from one arm to the other. "Got to get the little one home for breakfast. I'll stop in later to see how Miss Cleta is."

"Thanks for comin' to get us, Nate." I watched them leave and then took Luke's arm. "Luke's right. Let's get on inside and let her figure this out before she up and dies of old age."

We found Miss Cleta resting uncomfortably in a rocker in her front room, softly humming a tune.

I knelt beside her. "Miss Cleta, I hear you're sick."

"Stuff and nonsense! I'm just havin' a touch of the rheumatism."

"You're lookin' mighty pale for the rheumatism." Up close, I could see that her face was gaunt and pained. Her right hand was clutching at her chest, and I put my hand over it. "You got chest pains, Miss Cleta?"

"Girl, you come up with some funny ideas."

"Ain't funny the way you're holdin' your chest. Now, stop bein' so stubborn and tell me what hurts."

She scrunched her nose up at me. "You're gettin' bolder with age, Miss Jessilyn."

"I ain't been nothin' but bold all my life, and you know it. Ain't nothin' different except I'm worried for you. It ain't kind for you to be stubborn when people are tryin' to care for you, so you best up and tell me what's wrong." Her hand had begun to shake beneath mine, and I was afraid she was getting worse right there in front of me. "Looks to me you need to see a doctor, and I don't want no arguin' about it, you hear?"

Miss Cleta shook her head weakly. "You do beat all."

"You wouldn't like me so much if I didn't."

She smiled and put her other hand on my face. "I don't want to see that doc in town."

"Then we'll take you in to the hospital," Gemma chimed in on her way to the kitchen.

"That's too far away. Don't want to make that trip, especially when they'll just tell me I'm fine except for gettin' old."

Gemma came back with a glass of water for Miss Cleta. "But we ain't got no other choices. It's the hospital or the doc."

"That ain't so." I glared at Gemma over my shoulder. "We got Tal Pritchett with us, Miss Cleta. He was havin' breakfast with us when Nate came."

Miss Cleta took the water in her shaky hand and sipped twice before saying, "Well, that sounds right fine. Isn't that just the way the good Lord works? I hear tell Doc Pritchett fixed Peeboe the milkman's bursitis up in two weeks flat."

"He's a colored doctor," Gemma argued like Tal wasn't even in the room.

"So?"

"So, last I looked your skin was white as paper."

"Gemma Teague, I ain't got need of you to tell me what color I am."

"But, Miss Cleta, you can't have a colored doctor work on you. It just ain't done."

Miss Cleta struggled to sit up straight, but she managed. And she managed to shoot Gemma some daggers while she was at it. "Seems to me there was a day a body could've said it weren't done for a white family to take in a brown girl, but that happened, now didn't it?"

I grabbed Miss Cleta's hand tighter, so grateful at times for her hardheaded determination. "If that's what you want, that's what you'll get." I waved Tal over from his post by the door. "This here's Tal Pritchett, Miss Cleta."

He knelt beside Miss Cleta and smiled at her. "You sure you're fine with me treatin' you, Miss Cleta?"

"So long as you ain't no witch doctor, I got me no complaints."

He laughed and patted her hand. "No, ma'am. I ain't no witch doctor. Ain't got me no spells or potions or nothin'."

"Well then, get on with it." Miss Cleta closed her eyes, her white face creased in discomfort though she persisted in playing at wellness. "But you'll find there's nothin' wrong with me at all. Just a bunch of fuss over nothin'. Y'all are gonna be stuck here till all hours over some silly worryin'."

"Don't matter to me none how late I'm here," I said. "It's my day to work here, anyhow, remember?"

"You got to sleep tonight, ain't you?"

I narrowed my eyes at her and played tough. "Now, Miss Cleta, I ain't goin' nowhere today or tonight, or tomorrow for that matter, so long as you ain't well. You may just as well get that through your stubborn head. Way I see it, we got two choices. We can make the best of it, or you can be bullheaded and make us all miserable while we're here."

One of her eyes opened, giving me a vicious glare all on its own, but I knew she was having to try hard to keep her lips from curling up. She liked my stubbornness, and no matter her stony face, I knew her thoughts were softer.

She closed her eye again, settling her head more deeply into the cushion attached to the wooden rocker. "You're a mulish sort, Jessilyn Lassiter."

"Yes'm. In that way, I think I take more after you than I do my own momma."

That smile of hers crept out of its hiding place, and she rubbed my arm with a worn hand. "Anyways, ain't nothin' wrong here that can't be cured with an aspirin and a good night's sleep."

I noticed that magazines sat on the floor next to Miss Cleta's chair, an empty teacup on the table behind her. If you ever had tea with Miss Cleta, you knew you'd best hang on to that cup until you'd finished every last drop or else she'd swipe it and have it cleaned before you could blink. That was her way, neat as a pin and quick on the draw.

That dirty teacup told me more than words could.

"Well, if that's all you need, I imagine the doc'll give it to you. Meantime, there ain't no harm in gettin' looked at."

Tal put his hand on my shoulder. "Reckon you best leave me to it, then."

"I'll wait just outside. You tell me if you need anythin'." I started for the front door, but then I looked back at Miss Cleta. "And you do as he says, hear? Don't you go givin' the doc a hard time so he don't never want to come back here again." I glanced at Gemma. "In fact, he and Gemma are fixin' to be married, so you best be extra good to him 'cause he's family now."

Gemma's eyes teared up at that, but there wasn't time to say a word before Miss Cleta hooted louder than any sick old woman should ever do. "Land's sake, if that ain't news! Don't nobody tell me nothin' no more?"

I dug my fists into my hips. "Don't go hollerin' at me, Miss Cleta. I told you more'n once I figured Gemma liked the new doc."

"You didn't tell me she liked him enough to marry him."

"Well, I didn't know that until just yesterday."

Miss Cleta pursed her lips. "Next time you keep me in the loop, you hear?"

"Yes'm." I sighed. "But I still say I told you all I knew to tell."

She waved me off and then grabbed Gemma's arm to tug her close. "Come here and give me a squeeze, child. Ain't nothin' to brighten an old woman's day like news of a weddin' for two fine people." She embraced Gemma and gave her a kiss that left a lipstick mark on her cheek. Then she looked at Tal. "I may not know you yet, but I figure any man who wins this girl's heart must be a fine one at that." She looked around at us with a sigh. "Well, you see there, now I feel good as new. All I needed was some good news, and here I have it. You may as well head on out."

"Oh no you don't." I threw out my arm to block the doorway. "He ain't goin' nowhere. You're lettin' the doc look at you, and that's all there is to it. I'll be on the porch with Luke."

Miss Cleta opened her mouth to argue, but she didn't have a chance to utter a word before Gemma stuck a thermometer in her mouth.

Luke and I waited outside, and I folded my arms against a chill that suddenly bit into me even though it was hot as hades. "I'm worried about Miss Cleta."

"She's a tough lady."

"But she ain't no spring chicken. She don't look right, and she ain't baked or cleaned up like usual lately, neither." I sat in one of the rockers made by Miss Cleta's late husband, smoothing my hands over the wooden arms. "Sully knew how to make a comfortable chair," I murmured. "Miss Cleta's right." I'd heard her rave about his woodworking skills so often, I felt that I'd known him, and her words ringing in my head made tears prick at my eyes.

Luke crouched in front of me and took my hands in his. "She's gonna' be fine, Jessilyn. That doctor will fix her up better'n ever. You watch."

He'd comforted me a million times since I first laid eyes on him, but I loved how his way of comforting had changed since then. His words were much the same, but his ways weren't, and I had to bite my lip to keep the tears at bay now that his eyes spoke volumes of sympathy.

"Aw, Jessie, don't cry." He reached up to wipe away the tear I'd let slip out. "Miss Cleta wouldn't like it, anyhow. You know what she always says. It takes more time to cry over a problem than it does—"

"To fix it. I know. But there ain't nothin' I can do to fix this problem."

He leaned down to kiss the top of my right hand, and then his voice came out so light, I could barely hear him. "We could pray over it."

I looked down at him even though his eyes weren't visible to me, but I didn't know what to say. I suppose it should have warmed my heart to hear him say such things. After all, the best people in my life had a faith in God unlike anything I'd ever known. But then, that was why it bothered me to hear it from Luke, because for those early years together, we had shared the same apprehension about the faith that my momma and daddy, Gemma, and Miss Cleta had in common. We had been in it together, him and me.

He knew good and well it made my nerves ache to hear such things from him. The air between us became too thick for comfort, no matter that it was true Miss Cleta needed prayer. His hands slipped away from mine, and he stood up slowly and leaned against the porch railing. We stayed there in the quiet for quite some time, neither of us willing to break the heavy silence.

Eventually I stood and peered through the screen. "He's listenin' to her heart, and she ain't raisin' a bit of a fuss."

He came to stand beside me. "That ain't good." We watched side by side while Tal listened, then jumped out of sight when Miss Cleta glanced our way.

We sat back down and rocked on that porch, the tension building as time passed with no word. Then Luke got up and stretched. "Can't sit no more."

"You nervous?"

He ran a hand through his hair before turning to me. I could see he was trying to keep me from getting scared again, but he couldn't lie, either, so he just avoided the question altogether. "She's in good hands."

"I know that well enough, Luke Talley. That don't mean there ain't cause for worry."

He shrugged and leaned out over the porch rail. I got up and put one hand on his shoulder, leaning my weight against him. "It's times like these you realize how much a body means to you. I swear, she's like my own kin."

He moved his arm around my waist and pulled me tight. "Things'll be fine. You'll see."

The squeak of the door opening caught our attention, and we turned to see Gemma peering through the doorway. "Look at you cuddlin' on the porch while Miss Cleta's in there sick and lowly."

"Ain't nobody sick and lowly in here, Gemma Teague," Miss Cleta said from behind her. "And there ain't never a day I want people to stop livin' their lives on my account."

All three of us jumped to attention at the sound of her voice, and Gemma gave her a submissive "Yes'm."

"Miss Cleta, what're you doin' up?" I hurried to the door and looked inside. "Where's the doctor? You didn't knock him out or anythin', did you?"

"Don't be ridiculous! He's in the kitchen, mixin' up some sort of tonic or somethin'. Says it'll help me feel right nice. Don't know why I got to take a tonic, though. He already made me take a pill. Maybe he *is* a witch doctor."

Tal came back in with a short glass. "Just some herbs to settle your stomach, Miss Cleta. My momma's recipe. I've used it for years."

She took the glass with a wrinkled-up expression. "Y'all best come on in." She waved her hand inside and then shuffled back to her chair. "If I collapse and die from drinkin' this potion, least I'll have some company."

Gemma went to straighten the cushion behind her head, but Miss Cleta shooed her away.

We all stood by watching as she took a drink of that tonic, like we were waiting to see if she'd double over in a seizure from it or something. She finished one good, long swig and gasped for air. "This tastes like manure." Then she pinched her nose and finished the thing in two long gulps before setting the glass down with a clatter. "Tal Pritchett, you tell your momma she needs to work on flavorin' that conconction. The taste alone could put a body six feet under." She nodded at me. "Doc says he's comin' back this evenin', but I think it's bullheaded nonsense. Nonetheless, he says it's either that or the hospital so they can poke and prod."

Tal shook his head at her. "Miss Cleta, I figure you're just fine and well. I ain't got no worries about you. All's I'm sayin' is I ain't God, and just 'cause I think you're fine don't mean I shouldn't keep an eye on you. You'll have Jessie with you here today like always, and I can come back later and see how you're doin'. I won't be at peace if I don't." He nodded toward Gemma. "I spoke with Gemma, too, and we'd both feel best if she stayed the night with you tonight."

Miss Cleta waved a hand in front of her face like she was swatting a pesky fly. "Nonsense! I'll be good as new by then, I told you."

Gemma crossed her arms, ready for battle. "It ain't like I can't sleep on your sofa just as well as I can in my bed. That way, I'll be nearby if you need somethin', and I can keep some supplies here so we can keep an eye on your blood pressure and whatnot."

Miss Cleta sighed, but she gave in without a fight, a testimony to the fact that she wasn't quite convinced she was okay.

Her resignation worried me, and I knelt in front of her to take her hand. "It'd make me feel better too, Miss Cleta."

"Well, least I got me a doctor who can admit he ain't God," she remarked. "If you're determined to, you may as well, Gemma. I'd be right grateful if you'd stay on tonight. But you won't be sleepin' on no sofa. I got me a spare room with a fine bed in it that Sully made with his own two hands. You'll sleep a good many winks in there, and there won't be no reason for you to be tendin' to me in the middle of the night, I can tell you that. I'll give you the same pay I give Jessilyn."

Gemma got into battle stance again. "Oh no, ma'am, you won't. I won't take pay."

"Gemma Teague, are you in the medical profession or not?"

"I'm only an assistant."

"There ain't no *only* about it. You're an assistant to the doc, and you're stayin' here to help me; that means you get paid sure and simple. There's no fightin' about it."

Gemma's face turned two shades of pink, and Miss Cleta put up a hand to stop her. "Don't argue with an ornery old woman who just drank the potion of hell, child. It won't profit you none." She stared Gemma down for a second to make sure she didn't try a rebuttal and then snapped her feeble fingers to get Luke's attention. "As for you, Luke Talley, you can come on back here at five o'clock and walk Jessilyn home. I don't like her walkin' off by herself, and I ain't got it in me to worry today."

"Miss Cleta, you ain't got no cause to worry about me walkin' home in broad daylight."

"Don't go tellin' me what I can and cannot worry about, Jessilyn."

"Yes'm."

"Well then . . ." She looked around at everyone like she'd suddenly tired of her audience. "Get on with you, all of you. I'm sure you've got better things to do than watch an aged woman deal with a case of indigestion."

"We'll be goin' then, Miss Cleta." Luke leaned down and planted a kiss on her cheek. "You get some rest, and I'll be back for Jessie later."

"Land's sake, boy. Don't go givin' me palpitations!" She laughed out loud, a sound that brought a little more peace to my heart.

They all left us, and I sat and stared at Miss Cleta so hard, she reached over after a few minutes and whacked my leg.

"I ain't got to be watched like an egg 'bout to hatch, for heaven's sake. Get up and find somethin' to do, else you'll freeze up in that position like some statue." She picked up the stack of magazines and plopped them in my lap. "Here, find some place for these infernal things. Don't know why I even buy them, all full of silly stories and girdle advertisements and foolishness like that."

I did what she asked, but it didn't keep me from eyeing her every chance I got. Whether it was taking a glance while she wasn't looking or studying her reflection in the curio glass, I couldn't stop thinking about her well-being for two seconds together.

"I can see you starin' at me, Jessilyn!" she finally said in a huff. "I got eyes, you know."

"Miss Cleta, I'm worried about you, is all." I sat next to her and took her hands in mine. "You're family to me; you know that."

She pulled one hand away to cup my cheek in it and looked me sternly in the eyes. "Honey, you're like the granddaughter I never had, that's true enough, but I don't want you concernin' yourself over all this. The rate I'm goin, I'm likely to live till a hundred."

Her words came out with conviction, but I spent the rest of the day mostly hovering over her, even though she scolded me for it every five minutes. By the time Luke came whistling up the sidewalk, I was a bundle of nerves.

He came inside, took one look at my face, and said, "Everythin' okay here?"

"Everythin's fine. I ain't had even an itch all day, but this girl of yours hasn't been able to keep her eyes off me. I couldn't so much as breathe without her rushin' to my side."

"Oh, that ain't true." I touched her forehead to check for a fever, but she was cool as a cucumber. "I only did my job."

She gave my hand a push. "I ain't got no fever. I ain't had a fever in thirty years. All you do is fuss over me." I pulled my hand away, but she grabbed it in her frail hand and held it to her face, suddenly meek. "And I love you for it, dear girl. Don't you ever doubt it."

Luke put a hand on Miss Cleta's shoulder. "We don't plan on knockin' off that fussin', neither, Miss Cleta, so you best get used to it."

Tal and Gemma came in and looked at our little huddle.

"Everyone all right here?" Tal asked.

Miss Cleta waved them in. "We're fine and dandy. Ain't doin' nothin' but gettin' sentimental. Come on in and make yourselves at ease."

Gemma set a basket by the door. "Jessie's momma sent some supper with us, so we'll be eatin' fine."

"Sure enough." Miss Cleta sniffed the air. "That momma of yours does magic in the kitchen, Jessilyn. You tell her so when you get home."

"Yes'm." I kissed her cheek. "You get some good sleep tonight, you hear? I'll be by bright and early to check on you."

"You ain't got to check on me bright and early. Either I'll be fine or I'll be dead, and there ain't no excitement in neither. You just get your sleep and take your time gettin' over here, Jessilyn."

Luke gave me his arm as we walked down Miss Cleta's steps. Clouds had gathered in the sky and the sun only peeked out for quick glimpses.

We were quiet as the grave for the first half of our walk until I got tired of the silence and decided to get our minds on something else. "You see the way Gemma and Tal looked at each other?" I asked, even though I knew full well he had. "You'd think there weren't no sick person in the room at all, for mercy's sake."

"They got eyes for each other, no doubt. Leastways they won't get tired of lookin' at each other after they get married."

"Well, I hope Tal keeps his eyes on Miss Cleta, too. She is the patient, after all."

"Doc says she's fine, and I think so too. Her color was comin' back when we left, and I ain't never seen a body feisty like that in the face of death."

"You can't judge Miss Cleta's health by her feistiness. I wouldn't be surprised if she reached out of her coffin and gave me one last scoldin'."

He laughed and pulled my arm closer, but we walked on in silence after that. Beautiful silence. The cicadas sang sonnets, and the clouds that had rolled in were carried along by a soft breeze. I closed my eyes and drank it all in, my footsteps guided by Luke's arm, and I didn't open them up until I felt him slip his arm away from mine. My heart sank when he pulled away, but it skipped the moment I felt him grab my hand with his own. His grasp was gentle and tight all at once, and the way his touch made my heart turn somersaults, you would have thought he'd declared his undying love for me right there in the middle of the dusty road. Neither of us said a thing.

There weren't really words that would work, anyway.

The next morning I got to Miss Cleta's by six thirty and found Gemma cuddled up next to Tal on the porch. I held my hand up to shield my eyes from the sun and smiled at them. "Lookin' right energetic this mornin'," I said in a voice laced with more than a little suggestion. "Guess things are fine here, then?"

Tal stood up like a gentleman and returned my smile. "The patient's doin' fine, Jessilyn. Probably just a bad case of indigestion. The way I see it, she'll live to be a hundred. Maybe more."

"I have no doubt she will. She's got too much to live for, bossin' me about and all."

"Then get on in here, Jessilyn Lassiter, and let me start today's bossin'!" Her voice made me jump, the strength of it confirming the doctor's clean bill of health.

I rolled my eyes and opened the door. "Yes, Miss Cleta."

Tal and Gemma followed me in, and he took Miss Cleta's pulse one last time. "Good and steady. Miss Cleta, I wish all my patients were as good off as you."

"Don't you go takin' too good care of me, now. I ain't too keen on bein' long on this earth."

Tal looked at me sideways.

"She figures she's better off in heaven," I said. "But I wouldn't worry about her jumpin' off any bridges or anythin', if that's what you're thinkin'."

"Land's sake. I ain't goin' to do myself in, boy. 'Course, drinkin' that potion you gave me yesterday was near about kin to it." Miss Cleta waved a hand at him. "You can get on your way now Jessilyn's here. See to it Gemma gets home safe. And don't forget your fee. It's on the table."

It was clear Tal had known enough cranky patients in his day, and he took her instructions in stride, tipping his hat in a gesture of compliance. "Yes'm. You let me know if there's anythin' more you need, you hear?"

Once they'd left, I settled Miss Cleta in with a nice, fresh cup of tea. She took a few sips and then tapped her toe like she did when she was thinking about something particular. "Seems we have a weddin' comin' up, then."

I busied myself straightening things that didn't really

need straightened so my feelings wouldn't show when I answered. "Yes'm. Right soon, too, I reckon."

"Mm-hmm." She set her teacup on the side table. "And just how're you feelin' about that?"

I only shrugged. "Just fine."

"Just fine!" She made a little hissing noise between her teeth like something a cat would say. "If you're fine about it, then I'm Eleanor Roosevelt."

"Well then, we'd best get you back to the White House."

She wagged a finger at me. "Don't you go gettin' fresh with me, Jessilyn Lassiter. You know good and well what I'm talkin' about. You ain't never been fond of the idea of lettin' go of Gemma, and I figure rightly you're feelin' none too good about it just now."

I gave the framed picture of Sully on the piano one last push to get it where I wanted it and then turned to face Miss Cleta with a bit of sass all my own. "Well, what's a girl supposed to feel when she's losin' her best friend? You tell me."

"Lots of things."

"Like what?"

"Like sadness, frustration, happiness."

"They don't much go together."

"Sure they do. When you love people, there's always a mix like that. You think lovin's easy? It ain't. It's hard work. Awful hard work. But if you find good folks to love, it's worth all the feelin's you get from it." She patted the chair next to hers, and I slid into it reluctantly. "Now listen here, ain't nothin' wrong with you feelin' sad about Gemma leavin' your house. Nothin' at all. Ain't nothin' wrong with you wantin' things not to change, neither. But fact is, they do." She gave my chin a little flick. "Anyhow, what d'you figure on doin' once Luke gets up his nerve to ask for your hand? You plannin' on stayin' with your momma and daddy? or with Gemma?"

I tipped my head sideways to acknowledge what she was gettin' at. "No, ma'am, you know I ain't."

"Well then, you need to find that part of you that can accept the changes as necessary. And you got to find that part of you that's happy for Gemma 'cause she's happy. I know that part's in you somewhere because you ain't a selfish girl."

A surge of guilt at how I'd felt of late filled me up when she said that. I laced my hands in front of me, staring at them. "I wouldn't say that, Miss Cleta. I think I'm likely to be good and selfish."

"No, you ain't. Not like I'm meanin' it. If you were really selfish, you wouldn't want what's best for those you love. But I believe you do, else you wouldn't fuss and bother over me like you do. Nor would you fight so hard for people who have a hard time of it, like you do for Gemma, or how you did with Mr. Poe, rest his soul." She lifted her cup to her lips again, pursing her lips as she swallowed. "No, ma'am. You ain't a selfish girl, leastways no more'n most of us are. Ain't a body on this earth that don't feel a little possessive about ones they love when push comes to shove. But once you get over the shock of it, you'll feel right fine for Gemma. You like Tal, don't you?"

"Ain't many better, Miss Cleta. If I'm goin' to think thataways, I can't pick a better match for her."

"I reckon I'd agree with that from what I've seen."

"He's a good man, and Gemma will make him a good wife. I'm sure they'll be happy together." I leaned back in the chair and stared at the ceiling. "I reckon I just wish she could do both—marry Tal and still live with me like my sister. But that's child's talk."

Miss Cleta let out one of her short, hooting laughs. "Land's sake, honey, once you got a weddin' ring on your finger, you won't want no sister livin' with you!"

I could feel my cheeks blushing, but I just waved her off. "I ain't even got a proposal yet."

"You will. And once you and Gemma are both married, you'll be livin' no more'n a stone's throw away, and I reckon you'll end up sittin' on one another's porches, watchin' the children play together and talkin' about life. Things likely won't be as different as you're thinkin' they'll be, and more likely than not they'll be better."

I laid my hand over hers and gave it a squeeze. "I reckon so, Miss Cleta. You always make more sense than most of Calloway put together."

Chapter 13

There was a table full of girls in the corner of the diner that kept casting hopeful glances in Luke's direction and then giggling. I knew full well that Luke had been pick of the litter since the day he came to Calloway, and his soaring business had only made him more so. I knew that well enough to know the sting of jealousy like an old friend.

Other girls had always had more feminine ways than I did, and they could flirt better than I could ever know how. But I just scooted a little closer to him and ignored all those fluttering eyelashes and ridiculous giggles because today I figured I had one thing they didn't.

Luke Talley.

We'd come to the diner after church with our old friends Buddy Pernell and Dolly Gooch, but they were so lost in each other, it was like having the table to ourselves. Those two wouldn't have noticed a tornado two feet away. They certainly didn't notice a table full of gawking girls.

I could tell by Luke's pointed resistance to look their way that he knew full well what was going on, and to his credit he paid no attention to anyone outside of our table. When the girls finally left, they sashayed past our table like a row of beauty contest hopefuls, but Luke kept his eyes on his peach pie.

Luke tossed back the last bite and pushed his plate away. Then he smiled and leaned close to me. "Did I tell you that you look pretty today?"

Heat crept up my neck, but I willed it to stay away from my cheeks. I looked away, feigning hurt. "No. Guess you had your mind on other things."

"Ain't had my mind on nothin' else. Couldn't even tell you a word the pastor said in church."

It was a little piece of magic, the two of us sitting there, sharing a look that nobody else could ever share in a million years.

That is, until a dollop of whipped cream landed square on the tip of my nose.

I rolled my eyes. "Buddy Pernell, you're such a child!"

Luke smiled at me and ran his finger down my nose to clear it away. "Looks good on you."

Buddy laughed a laugh that hadn't changed since the time we were children together, even though the rest of him had. "I owed you, didn't I? Anyways, that ain't near as bad as stuffin' cake up my nose like you did."

"Well, you almost drowned me. I win." I dipped my napkin in my water and scrubbed the sticky residue away. "For a man fixin' to marry, you sure act like a boy. I swear, Dolly, you got your work cut out for you, marryin' him."

"That's what his momma says."

Buddy shook his head and pointed his straw at Luke. "You see how these ladies talk? Just once, I'd like to hear what goes on in one of them sewin' circles they have."

"'Oh, Dolores,'" Luke sang out, "'I do declare that husband of mine will be the death of me! He don't do nothin' but eat and sleep and cause me trouble.'"

I shoved my spoon into my chocolate sundae and eyed Luke up one side and down the other. "What in tarnation is that supposed to be?"

"Woman talk, of course."

"Ain't no woman this side of the Mason-Dixon Line got a voice like that."

"You sayin' you met every woman in the South?"

I rolled my eyes in disgust. "You make us women sound like crazy people."

Buddy and Luke exchanged a glance that said, *Maybe*

they are crazy, but I ain't goin' to be the one to say it. I was just about to protest when Gemma came in, breathless from having hurried over.

"There's trouble brewin' over at the meetin' place," she called out. "And Tal's right mixed up in it." Then she scurried back into the street. All four of us rushed out of the diner, following in Gemma's wake.

The meeting place was a field behind the lumber-yard, a wide meadow dotted with shade trees, perfect for picnics and such. Today it was being used by the colored church for their monthly social, but nobody in particular owned it. It just sat there on the outskirts of town to accommodate anyone who wanted a place to picnic or laze about on a fine afternoon, one of the few places in or near town where there were no *Whites Only* signs or separate entrances. After all, it was nothing but God's country there, and there wasn't anybody who had the right to put such stipulations on that.

Or so I thought.

By the time we got there, the arguing voices were raised in the kind of way that doesn't do anything but make a body nervous, and I knew without even think-ing who one of those voices belonged to.

"Malachi," I groaned in Luke's ear. "He's at it again."

"But he didn't start it." Gemma tugged at my arm to get my attention. "It's Cole Mundy and Delmar Custis.

They come over here all liquored up—on a Sunday no less—and start fussin' at Tal, and then they go tellin' the rest of us we ain't got the right to use this here meadow no more. 'We is too,' Malachi says. 'Ain't no laws against it.' So Delmar, he says it's white people that make the laws, and any self-respectin' white man knows there ain't no excuse for no group of . . . Well, you can guess what he called us. He says ain't no excuse for a group of us to be ruinin' the scenery for law-abidin' folks who want to come into town of a Sunday."

"Delmar Custis!" I narrowed my eyes at the man's back. "He ain't nothin' but a Klansman at heart. Always has been, always will be."

"Well, you can bet Malachi couldn't keep his mouth shut, so now he's over there arguin' with those two, who ain't got half the sense God gave a mule on a good day. When they're liquored up, there's no tellin' the trouble they'll cause." Gemma glanced nervously at Delmar, who was now pointing and yelling like some sort of hellfire-and-brimstone preacher on revival Sunday. "And you know that Cole Mundy's always got his huntin' knife on him. Maybe even a pistol, too. I'm afraid he'll start somethin'."

Luke and Buddy edged forward to intervene, but Dolly grabbed Buddy's arm. "Don't you go gettin' yourself shot, Buddy Pernell, you hear?"

"I ain't aimin' to." He gave her a wink and sauntered off beside Luke.

"I declare, that boy's goin' to up and get himself killed one day the way he dabbles in trouble." Dolly crossed her arms and clucked her tongue like we weren't watching more than a picture on a movie screen. "He'll leave me a widow one day, you watch . . . if we even make it to the altar before he meets his Maker."

Gemma and I looked at her like she'd gone crazy, but we knew she was just being herself. Dolly Gooch had always been a kind soul, but she hadn't ever been much for serious thinking. Her mind had only been on looking pretty and setting up house ever since we were ten years old.

Well, she may have been the type to sit back and watch, but I wasn't. I walked off behind Luke, with Gemma at my heels, stopping only when I got to the edge of the crowd so Luke wouldn't yell at me for getting in his way. Tal stood off to Luke's left, his arms crossed tightly over his chest.

"You get Sheriff Clancy?" I whispered to Gemma.

"He ain't there!" She shook her head hard. "I tell you, that man's about as worthless as pig slop. He's probably off playin' poker somewhere."

Luke whistled to interrupt the arguing, his hand at his waist so he could get a feel for his pistol. "This sure is a lot of noise for a fine Sunday," he said when eyes turned toward him. "Seems a shame to waste such an afternoon on a spat over nothin'."

"You ain't got no business here, Talley." Delmar stared him down and then spit his chaw on Luke's foot. "Why don't you and your friend here clear out and let me take care of these niggers?" He jerked his head in my direction. "And keep your girlfriend there from shootin' willy-nilly. Seems she almost shot up my boy the other day, but I ain't like to let her get away with it same as he did."

Luke casually looked down at his shoe, stared for a few seconds, then flicked his foot to the side to knock the chaw off. "I see you got yourself as much class as ever, Custis," he murmured. "Now, why don't you head on out before this here trouble gets out of hand. The way I hear it, in this town, the meetin' place is open to all folks. Ain't no lawmakin' for a place that belongs to no one particular man."

"Anythin' ain't man-owned is county-owned, the way I see it." Cole Mundy stood a full four inches shorter than Luke, and he nearly stood on his toes to bring himself up to Luke's face, making him look more like a child at a circus than anything else. "Now, like the man said, clear out!"

"You ain't never had no problem with the colored

church meetin' here before, Mundy. What's got you so riled up now?" He leaned toward Cole and sniffed. "Aside from the fact that you've been at the sauce."

Tal was standing just behind Malachi, and he moved forward, raising one hand in the air like he was waiting to be called on by the teacher. "I reckon I'm the one got them riled up. There was a couple white boys playin' over by that fence there." He pointed off in the distance and waited for Luke to nod his understanding before he continued. "Well, one of them, he fell down and hurt himself, so I went on over to check and see if there was somethin' I could do to help. These men here, they saw me talkin' to the boy, and Mr. Custis says it ain't fittin' for a colored doc to touch any white boy."

"He didn't call him a 'colored doc,' neither," Gemma muttered.

"This boy ain't got no call to put his filthy hands on a white boy, nohow. But it was this one got uppity—" Delmar jabbed his finger in the air toward Malachi—"sayin' it ain't my business to go about tellin' a doctor who he can and can't tend to. I ain't a man to stand for one of his kind talkin' to me like dirt. I want some respect from him!"

Malachi shook his head, smirking. "Shoo-wee! This here fella wants me to have respect for him." He gave

Delmar a once-over and laughed. "I'm confused. You want me givin' you respect for your fat gut or for your tobacco-stained teeth?"

Delmar took a leap at Malachi, but Malachi just stepped out of the way and let the heavier, slower man fall to the ground.

On another day, in another situation, I would have struggled not to laugh at the sight. But on this day, with one white man being humiliated by one colored man, in front of a group of colored folk, no less, I knew the minute Delmar Custis kissed the dirt, we were in for trouble the likes of which we'd never seen before.

You could hear a pin drop in that meadow. Every face in the crowd drooped in worry. Even Malachi's. There was no way in this whole world retribution wouldn't come for this, and there wasn't a single soul who didn't know it.

Malachi's poor momma was standing behind him, held in Noah's tight grip, crying like she had a crystal ball that foretold all kinds of pain in their future, all over this one encounter. The pain in my stomach didn't leave me much hope it would be otherwise.

Luke pulled his gun out, shoved Malachi out of the way, and pointed the weapon at Cole, who was reaching in his pocket, no doubt for something to wreak vengeance with. "You just head on out, Mundy, you hear?

You ain't got your right senses about you just now, so you head on out."

Cole lowered his hand the second he stared into the barrel of Luke's pistol, but the look on Delmar Custis's face when he peeled himself up off the ground was like a premonition. It held more violence than I'd seen before, and I'd seen some mighty fierce hate in my day. For a brief moment I thought he might reach out and snap Malachi's neck where he stood. But just now he was in ready range of Luke's pistol, and he didn't have much choice but to back away.

Just before he turned, however, he leaned forward and spit right in Malachi's face. Buddy wrapped his arms around Malachi before he even had a chance to react.

"I said, head on out," Luke repeated through clenched teeth, now pointing his pistol toward Delmar's chest.

Delmar aimed eyes at Malachi that carried the kind of hate you'd expect to find only in the depths of hell and pointed one finger in his direction. "You're dead, boy. You hear that? Stone-cold dead." He took one last hard look at Malachi and then backed away several steps before turning to saunter off from the group.

Silence reigned as those men backed away from us, staring us down like wild animals eyeing their prey. The sight of them made my skin crawl, and for those few moments, while time seemed to stand still, the thought ran through my mind that I wouldn't care one bit if Luke's gun went off and shot Delmar Custis square between his beady eyes, that Delmar Custis could drop dead in front of me this very moment and I'd smile. But it took only two seconds for me to realize what kind of evil my thoughts were made up of, and I rubbed my arms against the unusual chill that descended on me. I'd had many an idea run through my mind in my life, but this was the first one that had me thinking kindly about seeing a man meet his Maker right in front of my eyes. I swallowed hard and tried to look at Delmar Custis without hate in my heart.

I had more trouble doing it than I was comfortable with.

When Delmar and Cole disappeared around the corner, a collective sigh spread over the meadow, but it wasn't a sigh that spoke of confidence that peace was coming to Calloway County anytime soon.

It was one that told of coming horrors instead.

Chapter 14

Monday evening, Luke's truck picked up gravel and flung it every which way when he tore into our driveway. I was taking clothes off the line, two clothespins propped between my teeth, but I dropped the trousers I held the minute I saw him drive up like that. There was no other reason for him to do it except that there was trouble brewing somewhere.

I ran to meet him. "What's happened?"

He slammed the door. "You seen Noah?"

"No, why?"

"His momma ain't seen him since this mornin'. She said he headed into town and ain't been seen since. Malachi was supposed to meet him in town and walk him home, but he ain't to be found neither."

"I reckon we can all guess where he is."

Luke stood there for a second, his head down, and then he reared back and kicked one of his tires hard. "Doggone it! What's he thinkin'? Goin' off half-cocked like this, throwin' his life and money away. And on what?"

Gemma came out onto the porch. "There trouble?"

"Can't find Noah," I said. "You seen him?"

She shook her head, her hands gripping her apron, twisting it into a thin line. "You goin' to look?"

Luke nodded.

"I'm comin' too."

I untied my apron and tossed it on a nearby tree branch. "Leave a note for Momma and Daddy. They can help look when they get back from Mrs. Tinker's."

Gemma ran inside, and I let Luke help me into the truck.

No one spoke as we drove, but I knew where we were going. We'd been there once before, that night we'd seen the Klan on the banks of Barter's Lake. If we wanted to find Noah, the best place to start was with Malachi, and we knew exactly where he'd be.

The din of raucous, drunken men filtered through the open windows as we approached, and Gemma jumped out before we'd even pulled to a stop.

Malachi saw her and ducked behind his hand of cards. "Don't let her see me. She'll beat me with somethin'."

"I see you fine, Malachi Jarvis. I ain't blind." She stared him down, hands on her hips. "You put them cards down and get on in the truck."

"I can't go yet." He talked around a cigarette that hung from the side of his lips, all droopy and ashy. "I'm workin' a straight flush." He turned the cards around to show her. "See?"

The rest of the group muttered and threw their cards onto the crate that served as their table.

Gemma marched over to him and looked around angrily in search of something. Then she grabbed the hat off the man next to her, knocked the cigarette out of Malachi's mouth with the back of her free hand and proceeded to whack him over the head with the hat.

"Hey! Hey! Are you crazy, woman?" He jumped up to escape and tottered toward the woods, but she followed him and whacked him over and over until Luke came and dragged him to the truck.

"You look like a fool," Luke muttered. "No, I take that back. You *are* a fool." He shoved him into the truck bed so hard, Malachi slid forward and smacked his head on the side.

Malachi rolled over and glared at Luke. "What's your problem?"

"What's my problem?" He gave Malachi's chest a shove. "My problem is your little brother's missin' and you ain't been no help to your momma or sister because the only one you can think about is yourself."

Malachi froze. "What d'you mean he's missin'?"

"I mean ain't no one seen him since this mornin'. If you hadn't been so busy gettin' sauced and gamblin' your money away, maybe you'd have noticed."

"We have to find him." His glassy eyes were tinted with fear. "He could be hurt somewhere."

"No kiddin'!" Luke gave him another shove, then secured the back of the truck bed with an angry slam and hopped in next to me.

A hush fell over us as we scanned the roadside, except for Malachi, who called Noah's name with every exhale. I turned to look out the back window and saw him leaning over the side of the truck, peering into the growing darkness. His voice was anguished, slurred by the alcohol that no doubt blurred his vision as well. What help he would be, I didn't know.

I turned back in my seat. "He's bound to fall out if he leans any farther."

Luke grunted. "Would serve him right."

The ride was the quietest I'd ever had in Luke's truck. I spent the entire time scanning the roadside with trepidation, fearful of what sort of things I might see. I'd lived less than two decades, but I'd had enough time on earth to see plenty of the violence life can bring. With prejudice rearing its ugly head in Calloway again, all those old memories of violent hate began to trickle back into my mind. Every now and again I would blink hard in hopes of coaxing the images away, but they filled my mind the moment my eyes opened again.

But I couldn't spend the ride with my eyes shut tight.

Gemma reached out to take my hand. She was shaking like a leaf, and when I met her eyes with my own, I was petrified by the look I found there. We both knew, deep down inside, something was wrong.

Desperately wrong.

We were only a quarter mile from the Jarvis house when we discovered how wrong.

The moonlight lit up the horror with shapes and shadows that magnified what was already a sight that will haunt me for the rest of my life.

There was a slight breeze in the air, but that body hung so still and limp from the dying oak tree, I had to blink three times to make sure I was seeing what I was seeing. In the cockeyed light, the arms could have been broken branches, the legs withered tangles of the wisteria vine that had choked the life out of the tree.

But the sight before us was no trick of the eye, and I reached out to grab Luke's wrist, my fingernails digging in so deeply, he gasped.

He pulled the truck to a stop. "Jessie . . . ?"

"He's there." My voice didn't work properly, and my words came out in only a whisper. Gemma was focused on the opposite side of the road, but she turned to watch me as I spoke.

"Where?" I could feel Luke's pulse quicken under my palm. "Jessie, what'd you see?"

I couldn't speak after that, but I lifted a hand to point into the moonlit distance. Luke and Gemma followed my finger, squinting.

They didn't see at first, but the wail from the truck bed told the story like I never could.

Malachi Jarvis tumbled out of the truck like an animal. He stumbled past Luke's window, his breathing coming out in broken sobs from a place I didn't know existed in a human being. A chill ran down my spine at the sound of it, freezing me in place. Luke and Gemma shot from the truck, but I remained immobilized. He was several yards away, but I could see from where I sat that Noah Jarvis was gone from us as sure as if God had plucked him right out from our midst and rushed him up to heaven.

There should have been a crowd of mourners here witnessing the loss of life so untimely, it had stolen away the brightest hope our town had. There should have been good men here striving to untie the knot that had stolen the air from his lungs and the life from his body. Where were the decent people who should have had the goodness and the strength to stop the efforts of such wicked men?

Nobody was here. Nobody had tried to stop the bloodshed. Nobody had defended the innocent.

And nobody knelt to pray for forgiveness.

I slipped from the truck and walked on leaden legs toward the place of execution. As I watched, Malachi scampered up the tree, climbing out over the branch until he reached the rope. He was sobbing, searching desperately in his pocket for his knife. "Help me get him down!"

Luke was beneath the body, holding Noah's legs in anticipation of his weight falling onto him once Malachi cut him free. Gemma was sobbing, shaking so violently there couldn't have been any strength in her, but she clung to Noah's calves as though she could help relieve Luke's burden.

I didn't move to help. I couldn't. There was barely enough strength inside me to stay on my feet. All I had in me was rage, a feeling that coursed through my blood so quickly, it became part of who I was. That kind of hate doesn't know how to cry. It barely even lets you breathe.

Malachi's moans were otherworldly and filled the

warm, clear air, drowning out the night sounds. Or maybe the crickets and frogs knew what they were witnessing and had fallen silent out of respect.

Malachi's knife snapped through the rope, and Luke and Gemma fell to the ground with Noah, burdened as much by the weight of what had been done here as by the weight of his body. I dropped to my knees beside Noah, forcing myself to look at him. If he'd suffered alone that night, the least I could do was face what he'd been through.

The men who had choked the life out of Noah Jarvis had first removed his shirt, beating him ruthlessly, as evidenced by the scrapes and bruises that covered his chest. Blood matted his hair and trickled down from the corners of the mouth that had once spoken wisdom far beyond his years. The hands that had once seemed destined to treat the sick bore the wounds of a struggle to fend off blows. His cheeks were bruised and swollen.

I guess hanging him from a tree to die wasn't enough.

Luke was at my side, his breaths coming in loud gasps, and he ripped off his shirt and laid it carefully over Noah's face. With that act of finality, Gemma dropped down on the grass, her sobs ringing through the night.

Malachi slid down the tree and flung himself across

his brother, his cries joining with Gemma's in a dirge. Luke reached out to touch Noah's arm, but Malachi shoved his hand away.

"Don't touch him!" He ripped away the shirt Luke had placed across his brother and cradled Noah's bloodied face in his hands. "I said I'd come," he moaned. "I didn't come." His words were strung out, the saddest song I'd ever heard. "I didn't come. I didn't come."

His words of apology tumbled out with every sob, and as the realization continued to sink in, he looked up at Gemma with horror in his eyes, his voice coming out in high-pitched cries. "It should have been me. They wanted me!"

Gemma put her hand on Malachi's head, but he pulled away as though her touch were a searing reminder of how he'd failed his brother.

Without realizing it, I was rocking back and forth on my knees, my arms wrapped around my waist so tightly, my ribs could barely expand with a breath, and I was gasping for air.

Luke came behind me and pulled me into his arms. "Don't, Jessie."

I struggled against his grasp, but he held me tight until I gave up.

Malachi's sobs kept on until I couldn't hear anymore, couldn't watch anymore. I slipped out of Luke's embrace and leaped to my feet. There was nothing we could do to calm Malachi, just as there was nothing we could do to bring his brother back to life, and I had to move. I couldn't sit there anymore, helplessly watching the living mourn the dead. On legs that felt like rubber, I paced a patch of dried-up grass, gasping for air, squeezing my hands into fists until the blood ran out of them.

Malachi leaned over and tucked his arms beneath his brother's body, struggling to rise to his feet. Luke moved to help, but Malachi called him off with a grunt and hoisted his brother on his own. His knees buckled like a new calf's, but he passed up the truck, seemingly determined to carry his brother home, like Noah was his cross to bear. But I knew that this trip would never be enough. Malachi Jarvis would carry the burden of his brother for the rest of his life.

We stumbled along behind him down the road, a haunting procession mourning all that we'd lost. For me, it was more than a singular loss. From the day I'd come to know what prejudice could do to people's hearts, it had stolen from me. It had stolen innocence, security, loved ones . . . and now it had stolen my hope. What hope could I have in a world that took the promise of a bright future and snuffed it out with such force? As I followed behind Malachi Jarvis, who would forever live with a burden no man should have to bear, I no longer struggled to understand. I didn't want to understand.

I only wanted them to pay for what they had done.

Chapter 15

I couldn't sleep. Every time I closed my eyes, I saw Noah swinging from that oak tree. So I paced the porch into the wee hours of morning, the creak of the floorboards a steady reminder of my pain. Of all our pain.

Gemma had fallen asleep in Momma's arms well after midnight, and Momma had followed suit shortly thereafter. The two of them were still on the couch resting fitfully, but even fitful sleep sounded good to me then. Daddy was asleep in his favorite chair, but every so often he'd wake up and peek out at me.

"You okay, baby?" he'd ask.

I'd just look at him and then back out at nothing.

"You should get some sleep."

"Can't."

And then he'd sigh and head back to the chair.

This exchange happened half a dozen times before the sun started to cast a glow over the dark that had haunted me all night long. The birds chirped songs that seemed out of place in my world just then, a ridiculous chorus of happiness for a day that spoke of nothing but sorrow to me.

Momma opened the screen door and looked at me through swollen eyes. "Baby, Daddy says you've been up all night long. Come on in and get some food in you."

"I can't eat, Momma."

"You'll get sick."

"I already got sick behind the bushes three times last night. Don't need more food to throw up."

My tone was harsh, and I felt sorry for it. But at the same time I wondered why everyone couldn't just leave me alone. Momma had her arms wrapped tightly around her, and though any other time she would have given me a slap for speaking to her like that, she just went back into the house without a word.

I never left that porch all morning. By the time I decided to sit on the porch swing, my legs felt like they weren't attached to my body anymore. Everything in me felt drained and parched, and I couldn't do much more than stare in one direction. All I wanted was to see Luke. I needed to hear him say things would be all right.

Most times that had been Daddy's place, but more and

more I'd been relying on Luke for things I'd once left in Daddy's hands, and now that Luke and I had shared the horrors of Noah's death together, he was, more than ever, the only one I wanted to be comforted by.

But the events of that night had marked him profoundly, and I could see in his face as he'd left our house that he was in a dark place all his own. He needed to be alone, and all I could do was wait for him to be ready.

Daddy headed into town about ten to talk to Sheriff Clancy, but he was back by eleven, looking like a man beaten to the core. I overheard him talking to Momma a little, but I knew enough of Calloway County justice to know what had happened without even hearing the whole story. Sheriff Clancy would put on a show of duty, promising to interview witnesses and look at evidence. But in the end there wouldn't be one soul around who would admit to knowing a thing, and Sheriff Clancy would say there wasn't much any lawman could do to convict people of a crime there wasn't any evidence or testimony to support.

I walked the fields a lot that day, mostly not thinking much of anything. There's a place that terror takes your mind where there aren't any thoughts or feelings. It's an empty place, so empty it seems all the world has come to a stop. That's how I walked that day, wandering mindlessly because thinking hurt too much. It was late afternoon by the time I took my place on the porch swing again. Momma came out at suppertime to try and offer up some more food, but I couldn't even think of eating.

"Gemma won't neither," she said, brushing hair back from my forehead. "She's sick at heart, just like you. Crawled into bed at dawn and won't budge." And then she broke into tears so violently, she ran off into the house, leaving me to stare at nothing like I had for hours.

By the time I saw Luke again, it was getting dark. My body was more weary than I'd ever felt it, but my eyes were wide open like I'd propped them up with toothpicks. At that moment, nothing frightened me more than closing my eyes. I couldn't do much of anything when I saw Luke, as I watched him walk up like a shell of himself, with a day's growth on his face and mussed hair. It seemed to take every ounce of energy he had to climb the porch stairs. Then he looked at my face and cupped his hand under my chin.

When my chin started to shake, he crumpled and dropped to his knees in front of me. We huddled there together, crying like two children, and even though it was the worst way for us to be together, I was glad we were, nonetheless. I clung to him like the next breeze would blow him away from me for good. The tears stopped when we had no more, but words didn't follow. We were out of those, too, and we sat there on the swing until the moon was high.

Luke stayed at our house that night, but he was distant. It was after midnight when I went to bed, but I couldn't sleep, and after an hour of fending off nightmares, I bundled up in a robe and padded downstairs, afraid to bother Luke on the couch.

But he wasn't there, so I crept over to the window to look outside for him.

He was on the porch, sitting on the front steps, slumped over like a man with the weight of the world on his shoulders. I put my hand on the door to go out to him, but something stopped me. I could hear him whispering, prayers like those I'd heard from the lips of my daddy, and I suddenly felt intrusive. I turned slowly and crept back up the stairs.

I finally managed to doze from five thirty to six o'clock, and I was surprised to find Luke gone when I came downstairs. Momma was cleaning up after Daddy's breakfast, humming in a broken voice, as though she had to hum in order to find some peace.

I walked up behind her. "Luke gone already?"

She turned and wrapped an arm around me for a long squeeze. "He had some work to do, baby. Daddy's off already too. These men, they can't sit still for long."

Her words ended, but her hug didn't, and I could see her eyes misting over as she looked at me. "You sleep at all, baby? You look plumb tuckered."

"Can't sleep, Momma. Sometimes I wonder if I'll ever sleep again."

"You will, Jessilyn. One day soon. With every day that passes, things will seem to turn right again."

"Things won't ever seem right again, Momma. Not in this world."

"God's as good this mornin' as He ever was." She took my face in her hands and held on like my head was about to fall off. "Jessilyn," she said with a quiver in her voice, "God had His eye on Noah that night, and He's got His hand on him right now up in paradise. He has a plan for all things, even the ones that seem so terrible. There's hope in everythin' if you remember that."

I watched her in wonder. Only two days ago bigots murdered a child full of hope and promise, nearly murdering his whole family with the sadness of it, and ever since, my momma had cried through her chores. But here she was this morning, praising God through her pain like the world had suddenly turned topsy-turvy and there wasn't such a thing as evil and bitterness.

Bitterness. That word hung on my heart like a lead weight, and as my momma went back to her dishes, humming a church hymn with a shake in her voice,

I felt sick at the idea of her knowing any measure of what my vengeful heart felt. I grabbed a biscuit and ate it standing up, forcing each bite down over the lump that had formed in my throat.

I didn't know how Momma could see hope in a morning that had filled me with such rage, but I didn't ask. Instead, I made my way wearily upstairs to ready myself for the day. I figured I'd be early to Miss Cleta's, but I couldn't stay in the house. I was too anxious this morning, all mixed up inside.

On my way out, Momma gave me a sack of biscuits. "Run these out to your daddy, Jessilyn? It'll save me a trip."

I took the sack without a word and trudged through the fields with a million thoughts running through my head. Only problem was, not one of those thoughts was complete, and together they were just a jumbled mess. I lifted my head into the breeze, hoping it would scatter them from my mind, but it didn't work, and it must have showed on my face when I found Daddy.

"You feelin' sick or somethin', baby?"

I shrugged and lied. "No, sir."

"What's a shrug got to do with a 'No, sir'? That mean you don't know if you're sick or not?"

"No, sir, my body's fine. It's my heart that feels like it's dyin'."

He put his arm around me, and though I'd normally

have sunk into it like it could save me from every bad thing on the earth, today I stiffened at his touch. Not even Daddy could make me feel right again. No doubt he noticed, but he didn't say a word, only kissed my hair and then reached for the sack of biscuits. He gave it a sniff and sighed, but his sigh came out all broken, just like Momma's hum. It seemed we were all trying not to cry today. He ran an arm across his eyes real quick like I wouldn't notice. "Your momma's biscuits can always wake a man up." He tossed the sack onto the seat of his tractor and eyed me with the intuition he'd always had about me. He took my shoulders in his hands. "Everythin' will turn out fine, Jessilyn. Don't you go worryin' yourself over it."

"How, Daddy? How can I not worry over livin' in a world full of such evil? I've barely slept a second since that night. All I can see when I close my eyes is Noah hangin' there." I balled my fists at my sides and felt anger spread from one end of my body to the other until I was bathed in it. "And all I can think when I'm awake is how I'd like to see Delmar Custis or Cole Mundy or Sheriff Clancy himself hangin' up there in his place."

"Jessilyn, don't you go thinkin' like that." His grip on my shoulders tightened as his eyes narrowed. "I'm tellin' you right now, you'll up and kill yourself if you let hate build up inside of you, and it won't bring a bit of justice to them men, you hear? You leave vengeance to God."

"There ain't no vengeance from God, Daddy. I know. I've lived long enough to see wicked men do wicked things without so much as growin' a wart on their nose. God ain't in the business of justice, so I see it."

He whipped his hat off and wiped his forehead with an angry swipe. "It ain't your place to say what God is and ain't. It's God's place, and He already told us in His Word that He's a just God. Don't you go blasphemin' my Lord. You leave this to Him."

His words crawled under my skin like chiggers. "You sayin' we're supposed to just sit around and do nothin'? let them run this town into the ground just 'cause they feel like it?"

I could see Daddy didn't much like my tone, but he readjusted his stance and took a breath. His voice was good and stern all the same. "Jessilyn, I'm only sayin' it's up to us to do the right thing. Sometimes that means battlin' back; sometimes that means settin' still. I don't know what we need to do yet, but all's I'm sayin' now is we ain't goin' to be well off if we walk around heavy-hearted and filled with rage. We got to think sensible in this, and the only way we can do that is by turnin' our fear and things over to God and lettin' Him help us."

I looked past him, trying to gather myself. Being an

adult myself still didn't mean I was accustomed to yelling at my daddy. But even though my words came out in a mostly respectful tone, the words themselves were anything but, considering who I was speaking to. "God didn't do much to help Noah Jarvis, did He?"

All that anger that I'd seen Daddy breathe his way through melted into sadness the minute those words came out of my mouth, and I immediately regretted them. But there was nothing I could do. I'd said them.

And I'd meant them.

Daddy looked at his shoes for a few seconds and then off into the distance. "God does what God does because He knows best and has the right to do with His creation as He pleases." He squinted at me from under the droopy brim of his hat. "Didn't you learn nothin' with Mr. Poe's passin', Jessilyn?"

His words cut into me like a knife, but he didn't apologize for them. He just nodded toward the house. "Ain't you supposed to help Miss Cleta some today?"

"Yes'r."

"Then you best get on."

It was as sharp a dismissal as I'd ever received from my father, and I knew I'd put a wound on his heart that wouldn't soon heal. The further I got away from a God I barely knew, the further I got away from those that I loved . . . because they loved Him.

It was with a mixture of anger, sadness, and fear that I walked to Miss Cleta's. The air was sticky as molasses, and in five minutes, wet spots were starting to dot my blouse.

When I reached her house, I found Miss Cleta fanning herself on the porch. "Land's sake, Jessilyn Lassiter. Ain't felt heat like this in an age. It's like the gates of hell opened up and breathed on the earth."

"By the looks of the people round here, maybe some of them demons escaped while those gates were opened."

She shook her head and blinked back tears. "I heard tell ain't no one seen Malachi Jarvis these past two days. Poor boy blames himself."

"It's the Klan who need blamed."

"Oh, rightly so. But I feel for their momma. Poor woman's lost one son; ain't right she should lose another."

I sat next to her with a sigh. "He'll come back, I imagine, and when he does, I reckon he'll be rarin' for a fight."

She sat back and sighed, fanning herself harder. "That would be the worst thing he could do, and I hope he doesn't. Won't help anybody for him to come back here stirrin' up more violence, least of all his momma."

I sat up straighter. "Don't tell me you think we should just up and forgive those men."

"Certain I do! Don't mean they shouldn't go to jail or hang by a rope themselves, but forgiveness is for *our* benefit, Jessilyn, not theirs. Unforgiveness ruins us; it don't do nothin' to them."

"Forgivin' them is the same as actin' like Noah never existed."

"No, forgivin' them cleans up our hearts. Unforgiveness is a poison, Jessilyn Lassiter. A poison! It'll eat you up inside sure as you're sittin' there. Don't you go throwin' your life away on it. You do, and you're no better'n they are."

I was tired of a lot of things in my life. I was tired of waiting to marry Luke, tired of watching my loved ones hurt, tired of unbearable heat and worrying about money and watching my parents work their lives away with worries chasing them all the while. But most of all, on this particular summer day with death still tainting the air, I was tired of being lectured. And poor Miss Cleta got the brunt of my fatigue. "How can you say that?" I asked her with a temper that my momma likely thought she'd whipped out of me when I was younger. "How could you say I could be like them?"

I should have known better than to ever think of Miss Cleta as *poor* Miss Cleta. She reared back at my tone for about five seconds, and then she met my vehemence with plenty of her own. "Because whatever's in your heart will come out one day, Jessilyn Lassiter. You count on that. And if you've got hate in there like they have in theirs, it'll come out just like theirs spilled out all over Noah Jarvis." She looked me over once and then pointed her fan at my face. "Heck, anybody can look at you and see it's already startin'."

Anger pulsed through my veins at her words, and I stood up sharply, sending my rocker banging against the wall. "Just once, I'd like to see God do some justice on this earth instead of lettin' the no-good parts of His creation wander around destroyin' people's lives. Just once I'd like to see Him do what He said He'd do."

She stopped fanning and laid her hands in her lap. "Well then, Miss Lassiter, let me tell you what I think. I think all men will pay for woundin' people, one way or another. Either they'll come to Jesus and have to deal with the heartache of realizin' they helped nail Him to the cross by their wicked ways, or they'll reject Him and suffer an eternity of hellfire." She tipped her head up to look me in the eye. "You think that's good enough punishment?"

"I don't know if I do."

Miss Cleta sniffed and looked away. "Well, too bad. You ain't God. He is."

"Well, if you ask me, He ain't doin' much of a job of it."

The look on her face was about the same as it would have been if I'd hauled off and slapped her. "That's blasphemy!"

I didn't say a thing in reply. Blasphemy or not, I didn't care one way or another what came out of my mouth at that moment, and I figured I'd just proved it about the best way I could.

Miss Cleta turned sharply away from me, and I watched her as she studied the geranium plant that hung from her porch ceiling before she turned to me again. "Let me tell you somethin', Jessilyn. You've heard about God your whole life. You've been taught time and again about how His Son came to this here earth to suffer a horrifying death just so sinful people like me—and you, might I add—could be forgiven our debt and spend an eternity in paradise with Him. Time and time again, you've wondered if you could believe, and I always told you I believed you would. But time's a-wastin', and if you start thinkin' you know best, and if you start decidin' it's your place to take God's job of handin' out vengeance, that heart of yours will harden up like cement and there won't be any gettin' in for Jesus. You hear me? You keep on burnin' inside with hate, and it'll eat you up from the inside out. You'll lose your sense, you'll lose your goodness, and you'll lose everythin' that's important to you. And that includes me and your momma and daddy. Gemma too." She stood and put her quivering hand beneath my chin for emphasis. "And Luke."

My whole body shook from a combination of my

rage and her dressing-down. She'd taken that knife Daddy had pricked my chest with and plunged it right into my heart, twisting it a full turn for emphasis. I didn't want to look into those eyes of hers, the ones that seemed to see my dirty soul for what it was, but I couldn't look away.

"This ain't no time for talkin' about me and Luke."

She pulled her arm away from me sharply. "Ain't no time for doubtin' God, neither, Jessilyn, but you're doin' a fine job of it." She opened the screen door and looked over her shoulder at me. "I reckon I don't need your help today after all. Maybe you best spend this day takin' good stock of things in your own life."

She walked inside and closed the door behind her, shutting me out.

Bitterness and anger are evil twins that can follow a body around wherever she goes, and they whisper things in her ears that only make bad things worse. Maybe I didn't know much about most things, but I knew there wasn't much good in me that day, and I walked away from Miss Cleta's house stewing in hot juices, just wishing for my chance to give back some of the bad stuff that had come my way. And that's why, when I decided to walk into town, I took the long route instead of the short.

There was a part of me deep down in the middle

of all that anger that knew good and well what I was doing, that the long way around would take me past Cole Mundy's house. But I worked hard to keep my conscious parts from admitting to it. I didn't have a single idea what I was planning to do if I caught sight of him. All the same, I burned inside to have a look at even one of the men I knew must have helped string up Noah Jarvis, and Cole Mundy lived the closest to me.

Back in the day when my grandparents were young, most people would have fallen down dead in shock to see what was going on in Calloway these days. Back then, it was accepted fact that whites and coloreds didn't mix. I remembered my granddaddy telling me that colored folks were just as much God's children as the rest of us and there weren't any reason to hate nobody because of how God chose to paint their skin. In the same breath he also told me there would be peace between white folks and colored folks so far as the colored folks kept their place. "They wasn't created for much more than dirty work, anyhow, Jessilyn."

I guess Granddaddy Mac reckoned God had better feelings for some of His children than He did for others.

My daddy didn't feel the same as his daddy did, and he made a point of telling me more than twice. He made a point of telling Granddaddy Mac, too, which is when Granddaddy Mac would shake his head and walk out of the room no matter if Daddy was finished talking or not. When that happened, Granny Rose would sigh so that a whistle came out of the space where one of her front teeth had been. "That man don't know his Bible," she'd say. Then she'd pat my daddy on the back and wander off to find another chore to keep her mind busy.

For three weeks after Granny Rose's death I listened to my granddaddy rattle on about what a good woman she was, how she was kind and good and selfless and he never deserved her. He held on to her Bible, worn and wrinkled as it was by years of reading, like it would run away if he loosened his grip.

I remember Daddy watching after him when he was lying in bed all sick at heart over Granny's passing, talking to him about what it was that made Granny a better sort than most. "It's that Bible you're clingin' to there, Daddy," he'd said. "It's those words inside that Momma believed in so much that changed her heart and made her so good."

And Granddaddy Mac would nod and cling harder to the Bible. It was like that tattered book kept him alive, and every evening he'd ask my daddy to tell him what was inside. Daddy would get his own Bible, and I'd sit in the next room and listen to him flutter through the thin pages until he landed on the place he wanted to read from. Then his strong, fluid voice would recite the words until Granddaddy fell asleep, and even after if Daddy wanted to hear the words for himself.

This went on every day Granddaddy Mac lived without Granny Rose, all twenty-two of them. That's all he could do without her, just twenty-two days. And on the evening of that twenty-second day, as I watched Granddaddy Mac struggle to pull in air, I listened to my daddy tell his daddy all about Jesus and what He did to save us all from our sin. I watched my granddaddy, all hardened by years and work and pain and loss, well up with tears and nod.

"I believe it now, Son," he'd said at length. "And I know I'll see your momma soon, sittin' at the feet of Jesus."

I barely ever saw my daddy cry, but he cried something good when he heard his daddy say those words. There was such peace in his eyes that night, even in the face of loss. A half hour later Daddy sat at Granddaddy Mac's bedside with his Bible next to his heart, his other hand on his daddy's arm, just waiting for the life to drain out of him, and said the Lord's Prayer.

My granddaddy had never been a spiritual man, but he knew the Lord's Prayer, and his lips moved to recite the prayer along with my daddy. But his breath ran out before he got to the part about trespasses, and he stopped to murmur his very last words in a whisper so soft I could barely make out what he said.

Two seconds later, Granddaddy Mac died with a Bible in his hands and a prayer on his lips. But the very last words he said to my daddy were "Don't let them put me in the colored graveyard."

I thought about him as I walked toward Cole Mundy's house. I wondered why, if God's so good, a body could come to know Him lickety-split like Granddaddy Mac did but still have bitterness left in his heart. What's the point in asking Jesus into your heart if He doesn't clean it up right off when He gets there?

Anger burns the soul like matches, in little flames that singe and sting but mostly don't do much. But those little singed spots smolder, and after a while they can build up into an inferno that no bucket of water can put out. That's the kind of anger I had now. I'd had six years of angry matchsticks striking against my heart, and there wasn't much now that could cool things down.

Walking down that road with enough anger in my heart to weigh a body into the ground, I figured it was too much work to find goodness. Daddy had always told me we need to keep a watch on what we let in our hearts because what we let in there is what eventually comes out, only it comes out stronger than how it went in.

"It's like when Duke goes sniffin' out some critter," he'd told me once, "only he wanders into a skunk's house and comes out without any dinner for himself and with a good ol' stink on him. That's what happens when you let the bad stuff inside you. You think it's gonna get you somethin' good, but all it gets you is a whole lot of rot that don't do nothin' but make you stink."

Well, I'd been sprayed by a skunk before, and the funny thing is that after a while you get used to the smell. It's like your nose just up and changes its mind, and you don't care so much about whether you get cleaned up or not. It's not so much like that for the people around you, though, and I remember my momma and daddy trying everything from tomatoes to vinegar to get me smelling right again. And I fought tooth and nail against every new cure they tried without thinking once about how uncomfortable my smell made them.

As I rounded the corner, thinking about those bygone days, a tiny little doubt started to tickle my brain, one that made me think maybe I shouldn't put my momma and daddy through the stink of me again. After all, here I was walking around with a dirty heart and a vengeful mind with no regard to how unhappy it made life for them. What kind of good was I to them if I brought them nothing but heartache?

Or what about Luke? I well remembered how worried he'd been that night I left him behind to come here and confront Cole Mundy alone. How long could I continue to act as though my desires were the only ones that mattered?

As I came upon Cole Mundy's property, what little good sense I had started to eat away at my anger like ants at a picnic. We had enough trouble around here that I figured maybe I didn't need to go stirring it up myself. I stopped at the front of the house and stared at it, telling myself to walk away for a change, to just let it go.

But sometimes things don't happen the way we plan; in fact, I've learned that *most* things don't happen the way we plan.

As I began to walk away, I heard the sound of something I hadn't heard much in my life. But it was the kind of thing that sticks in your head once you hear it. It was the sound of a man crying like his life was pouring out through those tears. It was a sound much like I'd heard from Malachi Jarvis just a short time ago, and it twisted my already-nervous stomach into a knot so tight, I wasn't sure it would ever give loose.

Creeping slowly so as to avoid making any noise, I approached the side window of the Mundys' barn and peered in, knowing full well I was interrupting a sort of privacy nobody should have to forfeit to another human being. But conscience wasn't my strong suit just then, and I squinted to see past the row of shovel and rake handles that striped my view until I caught sight of Cole Mundy sitting there in a heap on that dirt floor, his head in his hands. The wails that came from him didn't seem to come from his throat but from deep down inside of him in some place most people don't even know exists.

I didn't know what to think. Here I was all set to pour my hatred out on this man, one of the men that had become akin to Satan in my mind. My every thought had been on people like Cole Mundy and Delmar Custis, on how they were evil in suspenders and should all die and burn in hell for eternity. I had all sorts of ideas about who they were deep down inside, but I can tell you with certainty that not one of those ideas ever had anything to do with them sobbing out their troubles on the dirt floor of a dirty old barn.

What little bit of conscience I had left finally tickled my heart and made me look away. I stared off into the sun that now sat half-shrouded by a black cloud and marveled at how it reminded me of myself, a woman with a heart that was meant to shine but was being overshadowed by grief and rage. I stared at it for a few seconds and then turned my back on it and on Cole Mundy's anguish, and I walked away.

Unfortunately, I took my hate with me.

Chapter 16

I didn't go into town that day I saw Cole Mundy on his knees in his barn. Instead, I walked to the pond and sat staring at my reflection in the water for most of the day. It was likely the worst thing I could have done because thinking too much can sometimes be the enemy of good sense, and the more I thought about the things I'd been through in my life, the more sense just slipped on out of me. At nightfall I made my way home and walked up to my room without so much as an exchange of hellos with my momma and daddy.

Fear can haunt you anytime of day, but it's especially fond of the nighttime. During the day, things can seem a little brighter, but once the darkness settles in, all sorts of fear likes to creep on in with it. And that night, evil thoughts swirled around my head like the very demons of hell were walking circles around my bed. In fact, Gemma would say that was exactly what was happening. ➤

Gemma believed in Satan and demons and all that sort of thing. I believed in God and heaven and hell, so I figured there had to be someone in charge of hell, but I didn't quite believe in the kind of Satan Gemma did. The way she saw things, this whole earth was just covered in good spirits and bad spirits, all fighting against each other every day like some sort of perennial battle of good and evil. But Gemma was a hand-raising, Jesus-praising Christian, and I figured her ideas of such things were as dramatic as all her other church ways. I'd told her as much in the past.

Every now and again, though, I'd get a feeling in the middle of the night like someone was choking the air out of me. My whole body would freeze, fear would fall over me like a wet blanket, and I'd shoot up in bed gasping for air. Gemma would wake from the ruckus I made, and as soon as I told her what happened, she'd point at me and say, "You see that? That's them evil spirits I'm talkin' about."

To which I would reply, "You believe in voodoo dolls, too?" Then I'd roll over, pretending I was going right back to sleep.

I never really did, though. Most times I just spent the

rest of the night tossing and turning, trying not to think of evil spirits camping out in my dreams and blaming Gemma for putting those thoughts in my head in the first place.

Fear had a hold on me this night, only it wasn't the kind of fear I'd had before. This fear had its roots in the thought of living my life with murderers going unpunished, and by the time the dawn peeked in through the window, I was bound and determined that in some way, sometime, I'd make those men pay for what they'd done.

I'd been three full nights without sleep. I'd gotten past the weariness that comes at the beginning and gone on to some sort of emergency mode, where I seemed to be running on high speed, fueled by all my imaginings of white-robed men hanging from trees.

I quickly readied myself for the day and made my way out of the house before anyone would spy me. Today was Noah's funeral, and I knew Daddy wouldn't have anyone working in the fields in honor of that. We'd seen plenty of death in Calloway over the years, and Daddy never let a stitch of work be done in the fields on funeral days. "In honor of a day's mournin'," he'd always said.

I set out down the road, compelled by some twisted part of my soul to go back to that old tree by the roadside where I'd watched Noah Jarvis's dead eyes plead for help. The thought had come to me in the middle of the night while I'd wrestled with those evil spirits Gemma talked about, and I was determined to go there as soon as the night drifted away.

I reached the tree just as the sun started to turn its branches to gold, and I was amazed at how innocent it looked, as though no boy had given up his life on it just days ago. That was until I caught sight of the six inches of rope that still hung from the branch where Malachi had sliced through it. It hung there like a shadow over the earth, reminding me of the full force of man's evil. With steps like a child, I slowly walked beneath the tree until I was level with the rope and stared up at it until the muscles in my neck began to burn.

I wondered what went through his head as they beat him with their fists, kicked him, dragged him down the street against his will. What was it like as they tied that rope around his neck and he waited for his life to drain away? Did he hear them laughing, jeering at him as his body twitched and struggled for freedom?

What kind of men look a young boy in the eyes and laugh with the knowledge that by the time they've had their way, he will no longer be part of the earth he was rightfully born to?

I knew the answer. I knew those men, and I'd seen the hate in their eyes for myself. I knew who every one of them was. And I knew that not one of them deserved to live another day.

By the time I pulled myself away from that tree, I was so overcome with emotion, it was as though I was watching myself from outside my body. I don't even remember how I got from there to the colored cemetery. The cemetery sat well behind where the colored church once stood. I knew it would be only a few short hours before they would gather in memoriam on that burnt-out grass and then proceed to lay Noah Jarvis to rest here. The hole had already been dug, and I sat by the empty space in the ground that waited for Noah's body to fill it. Just as that tiny bit of rope hanging from the oak tree had absorbed every part of me, so did this deep, dark hole in the Virginia clay.

Fittingly, the clouds began to overtake the sun, dimming the landscape to fit the somber occasion. If you sit in faint light and stare at one particular spot for long enough, everything surrounding you seems to fade away, like you're entering a dark tunnel. As I sat there staring into the dirt, it seemed as though there was no end to that chasm in front of me, almost as if once they began to lower Noah's body, it would keep going deep into the earth, never finding the bottom.

I don't know how long I sat there. No thoughts went through my mind, no wild imaginings or vengeful schemes. In fact, there was nothing inside me, like everything that had once filled me up had spilled into that yawning tomb in front of me. If anyone had seen me there, my shoulders slumped, eyes staring vacantly into the dry earth, they would have packed me up for the asylum. But no one saw and nothing diverted my attention until murmuring voices announced the arrival of the first few mourners.

They were still out of sight, and I managed to shake a small piece of myself free from the solitary place I had retreated into and stand, brushing the grass and dust from my skirt.

The first person I recognized was Miss Taffy, who had worked with Gemma at the Hadley home some years back. And then there was Poinsettia Watts, wearing one of her bright floral dresses that couldn't do a thing to brighten the sadness on her face. Her daughter, Posy, walked alongside her. There was a smattering of other folks with them, people I mostly knew by sight but not by name.

Miss Taffy caught sight of me crossing the grass and reached both hands toward me even though we were still twenty yards apart. I stared at her vacantly, loath to have any sort of funereal conversation: *How sad to see such a young life cut short* or *His poor momma, she's bound to die of a broken heart.* But Miss Taffy, she didn't say two words to me outside of my name. Then she grabbed me so hard it hurt, and I wondered where on earth this woman had gathered up this newfound sensitivity. Once upon a time, she'd sooner knock me upside the head with her purse than give me anything even close to a hug.

But I suppose death does that to people. It sort of makes us all equal since we have one thing in common—a broken heart. I didn't have the strength or inclination to return the hug, but I slipped into it all the same, grateful to be held up since I couldn't much see fit to hold myself up tall anymore.

Before she let me go, she whispered in my ear, "He was a fine boy, and I hear you was a fine friend to him too."

If I'd had any tears left, I would have shed them right there on her lavender suit, but I was fresh out. She reached up and patted my cheek before making her way to greet the others who were now filing into the meadow.

"There you are."

I glanced back to see Gemma and Tal walking up behind me. She took my arm in her hand and turned me about, but once she caught sight of me, her whole face drained so much of color, you might have thought we actually could be related. "Jessie, you look like . . ."

She caught herself, but I finished for her. "Death?"

"What's wrong with you?"

I looked away from her prying eyes. "I ain't slept much, is all."

She meant to say more, I know, but she didn't get the chance to before we were joined by Momma and Daddy, followed behind by Luke, who was escorting Miss Cleta with expert care. Nobody said much to me. I suppose there really wasn't much for anybody to say to anybody else.

Momma kissed my hair and murmured, "Mornin', baby," but that was all she said. That was all she could say.

What I remember about that funeral comes in bits and pieces, like chapter titles without all the story filled in. I remember how the wind picked up so that the ladies' scarves flapped into their faces and they had to keep a hand on their hats. I remember standing next to Luke with his arm around my shoulders. I remember Gemma on my other side, keeping a clawlike grip on my hand. I remember the preacher talking about how Noah Jarvis would be sitting at the feet of God, worshiping, looking down at us every now and again thinking we were crazy to mourn over him being in paradise.

But most of all I remember the way Noah's momma watched that casket like maybe the top would lift off and her youngest would sit up and come running to her, like the Lazarus of Calloway County. She didn't cry much. I figured she'd run out of tears just like I had. But she sure watched that box like a hawk, so much so that I wondered if she could see something we couldn't.

A roll of thunder rumbled across the sky, and all I could think was *Not now*. I'd loved thunderstorms from the time I was small, and I didn't want them tainted by the memory of this moment, doomed to think of death every time a bolt of lightning lit up the sky.

I supposed that was how it was for Gemma. I think that was the first time I fully felt the depth of her pain and understood how the memory of a horrible time could haunt you for life. At the sound of the thunder, her fingernails dug deeper into my hand, and I peered at her in time to see Tal slip his arm around her waist.

It was good of him to take care of her like that. Maybe he even took care of her in a way I never had.

The preacher told us all to bow our heads to pray, but I kept my eyes open, watching the tops of people's heads, listening to the murmurs of some of the colored folk, who every now and again would repeat the preacher's words in a whisper or say, "Yes, Jesus. Thank You, Jesus."

All I wanted was an explanation for why they would thank Jesus that they were standing at the graveside of a boy who'd been cheated out of life. That prickle of anger started in me again, and it occurred to me that I was thankful to discover I at least had some feelings left in me.

But those feelings weren't any kind of good, and as I stood there while the pastor finished up his prayer, they grew inside me like the rumble of thunder as the storm drew closer. The second he said *amen*, he launched right into the first verse of "Amazing Grace," and even though I knew it, I didn't have voice or heart to sing it.

The voices around me grew louder with the thunder like they were bound and determined to be heard over it. Miss Taffy was the loudest. Her eyes were closed, those thick hands of hers raised to the heavens, and I watched her as she swayed from side to side, praising the God who had taken Noah away.

Without thinking and without a word, I slipped from the grasp of my two best friends in the world and walked away from that place toward the noise of the thunder, almost as if I could escape into the clouds and never come back. The singing continued without me, and every few steps I would increase my pace in hopes of outrunning the melody of those words. *"We've no less days to sing God's praise . . ."* Who could praise when death had wounded the soul?

By the time I reached the woods, all I could hear was the trickle of the brook that ran through the trees.

I slipped my shoes and stockings off and walked in, letting the cool water run across my feet. I didn't flinch when Luke walked up to the water's edge.

"Jessie?" He didn't even bother to take his shoes off, just splashed on in after me. "Jessie, what can I do to help you?"

"What can you do?" I turned to face him, all those hours of lost sleep suddenly clinging to me like the wet summer heat. "What can anyone do? He's gone, Luke. He ain't comin' back."

He dropped his head and stared at his feet, his hands on his hips. When he lifted his head again, his eyes were wet with the tears I wished I could cry. "I know he ain't."

"Then what do you want me to ask you to do? You want me to ask you to say it's all goin' to be okay? Because I already know the answer to that. It ain't!"

"Not for a while, maybe. We've got mournin' to do, sure enough. But someday we'll have to find some way to get back where we were."

"And how're we goin' to do that? Stand by and watch the Klan burn this town and take it all to hell with them? Let Delmar Custis and them boys run roughshod over colored folk in Calloway while Sheriff Clancy does nothin'? Are we supposed to just stand by till every tree hereabouts has a colored boy hangin' from it like decorations on a Christmas tree?"

My words made him cringe, and he took two steps closer to me. A bolt of lightning lit up the sky, and it occurred to me fleetingly that both of us might just get electrocuted in the brook and that would take care of everything in one fell swoop.

"I'm not sayin' we're supposed to not do anything, Jessie. But I can see what it is you want to do, and I can tell you right now that it ain't the answer."

"I didn't say what I think we should do."

"I know you. I know what you're thinkin'. You're the same girl that marched on over to a barnful of Klan that night the colored church burnt down." He took a step toward me so we were face-to-face. "You're the same girl who shot at Klan when you were only thirteen, and you're the same girl that's had hate growin' in her heart toward those men ever since. Don't you tell me no different."

"I ain't about to."

He tipped my chin up so I had to look at him. "Jessie, this ain't the answer. I don't know just yet what is, but what you're doin', what you want to do . . . this ain't it."

I slipped away from his touch and watched a school of tadpoles swim past my feet. "Well, singin' praises to God ain't no answer neither." I figured I knew the look I'd see on Luke's face, so I didn't seek it out. It was bound to be the kind of look that made my heart hurt, and I wasn't inclined to gaze on it just then.

He didn't say anything for a few minutes, and we stood there alone in that brook with a foot separating our bodies but miles separating our hearts. "I don't know," he finally said, his words coming out like he'd just run a marathon. "I don't know about much of anythin' no more, least of all about you. Or about us."

I don't know what I was thinking then. For all I know, maybe I'd lost all ability to think sense at all. But when I opened my mouth next, all that came out was "Well, maybe you got some thinkin' to do."

Standing there in those woods with the heat of anger and sorrow suffocating us, those words came out sounding like the death of all we'd thought we'd be together. My next breath caught in my throat, and as he turned away from me and walked off alone, I wondered if I'd ever see him again.

Once someone becomes a part of your life like Luke had in mine, that person's absence steals part of you, and for the next hour as I made my way home, I felt like more and more of me drained away. Momma, Daddy, and Gemma had gone to the reception at Noah's aunt's house, so no one saw me when I stumbled up the stairs into bed. The lack of sleep took me over the second my head hit the pillow, a sweet relief from the wreck and ruin my life had tumbled into. I slept for sixteen hours straight, but when I woke up, it took me only sixteen seconds to remember the sort of mess I'd left behind. My body felt numb as I dressed, but my mind was anything but, and I wished I could stop the endless stream of horrible memories that ran through my brain.

When I finally managed to steady myself and stumble downstairs, Momma broke into tears at the sight of me. She held out her arms to me like she had so many times when I was a child. "Baby, come here."

I ran to her just as I had back then and clung to her while we wet each other's shoulders with our tears. The sleep had cleared my head in such a way as to make the whole of the past week seem too crystal clear to manage, and I spilled out all my sadness onto her. By the time I stopped bawling in her ear about how I couldn't live with the pain, how I was so angry inside it hurt, and how I'd let it all ruin everything between me and Luke, she was almost smiling at me.

"At least I got my baby back," she murmured. "You can still talk the hind leg off a horse."

"Momma, this ain't no time for jokes."

"No, it ain't." She shoved me down into a kitchen chair and went about getting me a plate of food. "But it also ain't time to give up on life and happiness, either."

She slid the plate full of chicken salad and diced toma-toes in front of me. "This ain't much for gettin'-out-of-bed food, but you need somethin' right away, and this is all I've got ready. You're pale as a ghost and five pounds lighter."

I was hungry enough to eat lard, so I obeyed her without a fight. She sat across from me and watched me so closely I thought at any second she'd pick up my fork and start feeding me. When I was finished, she reached a hand across the table to grab my own. "Baby, you got to tell me what's goin' on with you, you hear? Why's this got you so eaten up inside?"

"That ain't no mystery."

"But we've seen bad things before in our time, and I ain't seen you this bad off. Even after Mr. Poe left us— God rest his soul—you weren't like this."

I lowered my eyes to the table and shook my head slowly. "Nothin's ever been like this. Nothin'." I fingered my skirt nervously with my free hand for a minute, then looked up at her. "There's one thing to lose somebody you love. There's another to see them hangin' dead from a tree, all beaten and bruised. That don't leave you the same."

"Oh, Jessilyn. Baby, think of what you just said."

I narrowed my eyes at her quizzically.

"You're right, there ain't nothin' like seein' a man

hangin' dead from a tree, all beaten and bruised. You're right, that don't leave you the same. That's what I've been tellin' you for all these years. The day I realized that's just what my sin did to Jesus Christ didn't leave me the same, neither."

"Momma . . ."

"Jessie, you think on that. That's all I ask is that you think on what I'm sayin'. Right now you're feelin' like you'll never heal. Right now you're all full of anger and sadness. And right now's when you need to think more and more about what I'm sayin' because there ain't nothin' none of us can do to help you. Not even you can help you. You need help from somewhere that you refuse to turn to." She slid my plate out of the way and leaned toward me as close as she could across the table. "But whenever you're tempted to think of Noah hangin' from that tree, you think of Jesus there. You think of that because He did all that willingly and He did all that for you. Noah Jarvis knew that, and if you want to make his death worth somethin', then you do what I'm tellin' you."

She let go of my hand, sat back in her chair, and changed the subject so fast I got whiplash. "Now, let me ask you one more thing. Do you want to see Luke?"

"I want to see him so bad it hurts, but he won't want to see me."

"Funny, then, that he's pacin' out in the front lawn."

I hopped up and peered out the window, and there he was, wearing a circle in the brown grass.

"But, Momma—"

"Jessie, love ain't so weak as you seem to think it is. He came over lookin' for you last night and asked if I'd call him the minute you woke up. So I did as soon as I heard your floorboards creak."

I could have jumped out the window for all I felt inside. I ran past Momma, out the door, and into his arms.

I wanted to stay there forever.

Chapter 17

I watched Gemma in the mirror as she pinned the last piece of hair in place, and then I helped her fasten the veil on just so. Gemma's dress was simple, one that could be cut down later and worn to church, but that veil was a work of art. Momma had made it with more love and care than anyone else could have, sewing each bead on perfectly. I lifted the gauzy material over her head and let it flutter down across her face, and the second I did, all those pent-up tears started to flood my eyes. I looked away to keep her from seeing, but it was useless trying to hide anything from her.

She flipped the veil from her face and stood quickly, pulling me to her.

"Don't," I said. "I'll cry on your dress."

"Ain't no tears that ever stained anything." She pulled

me in so tight, I could barely breathe. "Besides, I got my own tears on here already."

We were a tangle of brown and white, she and I, bonded together by love if not by blood, and the agony of losing her spilled out of the little box in my mind I'd put it in and dripped down over my heart.

As if she could read my mind, Gemma whispered, "I ain't never really leavin' you, Jessilyn. You know that."

I nodded, but that was all I could do.

"I'll be just down the road, and anytime you need me—and I mean anytime—you just come on over, you hear? Or you call. Tal's havin' a phone put in at the new house. After all, a doctor's got to have some way of hearin' from people."

I smiled over her shoulder. "You're ramblin'."

"So what if I am." She pulled away and swiped at the tears on her cheeks. "A girl's allowed to do whatever she wants on her weddin' day, ain't she?"

Momma came in and characteristically burst into tears the second she saw us standing there together, Gemma all in white, both of us tear-streaked.

"Don't you start too!" Gemma planted her hands on her hips. "I already done told her it ain't like I'm leavin' town or nothin'."

"It ain't only that." Momma walked over and grabbed Gemma's hands, holding them out so she could get a good look at her. "Just look at my girl. All grown-up and gettin' married. I never thought I'd see the day."

"Why?" I gave Gemma a playful nudge. "You think she wouldn't never find someone that'd have her?"

"Jessilyn, I didn't mean any such thing."

"Oh, she's only teasin'," Gemma said. "You ought to know her well enough for that." She left us and went digging around in the chest of drawers she and I had shared up to this day. Then she turned and handed us both small packages. "These are for you."

Momma shook her head. "It's the bride supposed to get gifts on her weddin' day, not the momma."

"But I wouldn't have had no momma if it weren't for you."

Gemma's words cut through the heavy atmosphere like a knife, and I thought my poor momma would burst out in a daylong cry any second. But she bolstered herself up stronger than I'd thought her capable, took a deep breath, and untied the bow. Inside was the prettiest little prayer book anybody'd ever seen. Each page was pressed with dried flowers and had a psalm written in Gemma's best handwriting. Momma turned the pages so carefully, you would have thought she was holding a baby in her palm, and by the time she got to the last page, all that valiant work she'd put in to keep from crying just a minute earlier went to waste.

Daddy heard her sob from the hallway and came into the room with a roll of his eyes. "Here she goes!" He put his arm around her like she was a mental patient. "Come on, Sadie, honey. Let's go get you some ice water."

It didn't help much that he'd taken her away, though. Gemma and I were still left there together in a room that was permeated with sadness on a day that was supposed to be nothing but joyful. I fingered the bow on my package, and Gemma gave me a nudge.

"May as well get it over with," she said with a sniff. "Let's get the cryin' all out before your daddy gives me away."

"Don't say it like that."

"That's the way they always say it."

"We ain't never givin' you away, Gemma Teague."

She crossed her arms and shook her head at me. "Then what exactly should we call it?"

"I don't know." My knees were suddenly too shaky to hold me straight, and I slid down to my bed in a heap, sure to put a wrinkle in the dress Momma had finished making me only last night. "I mean, it ain't like we're givin' you up at all. It's more like we're loanin' you out."

She stared at me for a second and then tipped her head back to laugh at me. "Okay, Jessie, I'll let the preacher know he's to ask, 'Who loans this woman to be his wife?'" She must have found herself pretty funny then because she slid down next to me and laughed like she'd never be able to stop, and I couldn't help but join in. When Daddy came in a minute later, he stood at the doorway looking at us with wide eyes.

"You girls done lost your minds?"

I stopped giggling long enough to say, "Maybe."

There's no way of keeping a straight face when you're around laughter like we were having just then, and Daddy was no exception to that rule. A smile raised one side of his mouth, making his dimple stand out. "Well, the preacher's here and guests are all spillin' in, so you best try and get yourselves ready so's you don't laugh yourselves down that aisle."

"Yes'r."

I lay back on the bed with the sort of long sigh that follows a good laugh and reached out to take Gemma's hand in my own, holding it up in the air. "Brown and white. We're two of the oddest sisters a body's ever seen." I brought her hand down and rested it on my cheek. "Two of the best kind there ever was."

She stared at me for a second with all kinds of emotions running through her eyes in ways that said everything words couldn't; then she stood and hauled me to my feet. "Just look at us. We're a mess. Your momma's gonna have a fit."

"Oh, we're fine." I gave the back of her dress a few swats with my hand to beat out the wrinkles and then straightened her veil. "You make a beautiful bride, Miss Gemma Teague."

Gemma nodded at the bed, where her gift to me lay still untouched. "You didn't open yours."

Momma stuck her head in, recovered from her crying jag. "Gemma, honey, I think we're about ready for you."

"I'll open it later, okay?"

She nodded, then took one long look around our bedroom. "I spent a lot of good years here, Jessilyn."

I swallowed hard, hoping those tears would stop tickling the back of my throat. "I know."

"I sure have been blessed."

"What God in all the world wouldn't bless someone like you, Gemma? There ain't nothin' about you ain't worth blessin'. Tal Pritchett's a lucky man."

She waved me off with one hand. "Ain't nobody on this earth that's perfect. Sure enough, you ain't always felt like blessin' me. Maybe more like blessin' me out!"

"Well . . . you do snore like a band saw. I reckon maybe I should warn Tal about that."

Gemma glared at me and tossed my pillow into my face.

"Momma's gonna get at you for messin' up my hair."

"Oh no, she ain't. It's my weddin' day, after all." She

hooked her arm through mine and looked at our reflection in the mirror.

There had been a time not so long ago when our reflection would have shown two girls in pigtails and braids. I remembered the day we'd first moved her into my room, that day I'd given up my bed to her and slept next to hers, waking up every hour to check on my best friend, who had just lost her momma and daddy. And now here we were, grown women, facing a whole new life ahead. I wondered where it would take us.

She must have been thinking the same thing because she shook her head with a sigh. "Jessilyn, where'd the time go?"

I had nothing to say in response. I only turned to smile at her and squeezed her arm tight. "Guess we'd better get goin'." After all, I figured if we didn't, we'd be a soggy mess before Gemma Teague ever had the chance to become Gemma Pritchett.

The second we walked outside and Tal caught sight of Gemma, his eyes lit up so bright, it was like his very soul was shining out through them, and I was glad to see it.

Gemma deserved to be loved that way.

As I stood in the front yard at Gemma's side, listening to her preacher talk about marriage and how God sees the vows two people make to each other, I looked around at those gathered at our home to witness the occasion.

Most of the people that stood on the front lawn of this white folks' home were much darker than those who lived here. Outside of us Lassiters, the only white people were Luke, Miss Cleta, Buddy and Dolly, Mrs. Tinker and her children, Mr. Poppleberry from the pharmacy, and Mr. Hanley, the grocer, with his wife.

Fact was, we hadn't made too many friends in this town by taking Gemma in. Oh, some folks didn't mind so much as others, but then it takes a strong constitution to actually admit it to other white folks, so most of them never did. Plenty of the colored folk kept away too. It was no secret we had our detractors on both sides of the rainbow, but just now I didn't care so much. We had those nearest and dearest on hand to watch Gemma wed, and that was all we'd ever needed.

Luke was standing up for Tal. I glanced at him only to find him staring at me. He smiled in such a way as to say, *Don't worry, Jessilyn. It'll all come out right.*

I wasn't so sure I agreed, but I smiled back at him anyway. I couldn't help but think that maybe someday soon I'd be standing up in front of a preacher with him again. There was no restraining a smile from my face with a thought like that lighting up my heart.

By the time Gemma had been renamed Gemma

Pritchett and every stomach had been filled up by Momma's food and Miss Cleta's wedding cake, I was worn to a frazzle. And the way those women at the wedding rushed the newlyweds off, you'd have thought they had only two days to be married. I barely had more than two seconds to tell Gemma good-bye, and to make matters worse, it felt like I was saying good-bye forever, even though she was just going down the road a few miles.

The women started cleaning up outside the second the bride and groom drove off. Whenever women clean together, they chatter, and I was in no mood for woman talk after I watched my best friend ride away from our home. I went inside to the kitchen and drowned my sorrows in a sink full of dirty dishes.

Luke came in midway through and put his hand on the small of my back. "You okay?"

"I'm fine," I lied. "It's only part of life, after all. She couldn't stay here forever."

His hand dropped from my back. "No. Ain't many people that can stay in the same place forever."

His words hung in the air during the silence that followed. Our relationship had been full of silent moments, but they'd always been comfortable ones, nothing like what we were having now. He might have forgiven me for my outburst the day of Noah's funeral, but I still carried the bitterness that had erected a barrier between us, and things just hadn't been the same since.

He stood behind me for a few somber moments. All I could hear was his breathing. Then he ran his hand down the side of my arm in a way that left a chill behind. "If you're sure you're okay, I'll be goin', Jessie. I got mounds of work to do."

"I'll be fine."

He kissed my hair and then left me alone with an ache in the pit of my stomach. I washed every spoon and fork that had fed the mouths of all those people who had celebrated Gemma's marriage without having any idea the hole her going away would leave behind, and I did it all with a lump in my throat the size of a watermelon. After rinsing, I had put each dish on the kitchen table to air-dry, and by the time I placed the last serving bowl there, I was a weary mess of self-pity. The voices outside the window had subsided to only a few, and I could hear my momma giving Mrs. Tinker her recipe for bean salad.

But I didn't care a bit about bean salad. I only wanted to be alone. I slid my apron off and headed on upstairs to my room. I unbuttoned my dress and let it slide to the floor, standing there in my slip while I pulled the pins from my hair. My shoes were next to hit the floor, doing so with a thud, and then I slid down onto my bed with a long sigh.

And there was Gemma's gift, wrapped all tidy and neat.

I toyed with it awhile, uneager to open it. It was as though that gift were the last thing that held her here and opening it would take her away again. But I couldn't resist the temptation to see what was inside, so I undid the bow, letting it slither down my hand onto my lap. Carefully, I pried the top off the box to find her ragged old Bible staring at me. It was in the worst shape you've ever seen, all ripped and creased so that the covering broke off into tiny crumbles when you held it. Inside, she'd written all sorts of things in the margins, thoughts that must have come to her right off when she was reading.

I'd always thought the Bible was supposed to be the kind of sacred book that you didn't put pen to, like God would send a bolt of lightning down on you if you put a crease or dent in it. But there was nothing disrespectful about the way Gemma had eaten up every word she'd seen in this book. It may have been well-worn, but it was well-loved. I flipped through the pages and then let it flutter shut in my hands, as I sat on the bed my best friend had once slept in beside mine.

And I wished I knew the treasure she'd found inside that worn-out book.

Chapter 18

The next time I showed up for work at Miss Cleta's, I walked in the door with my tail between my legs. She'd given me some days off to help with Gemma's wedding, but I wondered if it was out of kindness or if she was just plain old mad at me. Last time I'd been there, she'd set me firmly in my place, and even though I didn't share her belief in her words, I had felt the full sting of them. I peered over at her favorite chair, where she sat, her morning cup of tea on the table beside her.

She was fanning herself with a piece of paper she'd folded into an accordion. "You plannin' on comin' in, Jessilyn," she said without looking at me, "or are you goin' to stand there gazin' at me all mornin'?"

"I wasn't so sure you wanted me to come today."

She stopped fanning and brought her teacup to her

lips for a sip. This time her milky eyes met mine. "Child, I ain't a woman to harbor ill against you; you should know that. We had a quarrel. Life's full of 'em. Way I figure it, you've got a whole lot of thinkin' to do and sometimes too much thinkin' gets us all muddled up." She set her cup down and held her arms out to me. "Come and give an old lady a hug."

I crossed the room with long steps and sank into her embrace. "I'm sorry, Miss Cleta."

"Well then, that makes two of us. I can be a cranky woman some days."

"You weren't cranky. You were just worried."

She pushed me away so she could look me in the face. "It takes good wisdom to see that."

"If I ain't got some of that in me after all life's brought, then I guess I shouldn't ever expect to get any."

"You got more'n you think, honey. You just got to use it, is all." She waved her makeshift fan at me to make her point, and it slipped out of her hand and onto the floor. I reached for it, but she bent over at the same time and ripped it away from me. Only she didn't get it back before I saw what that paper was.

"You gettin' threatenin' letters from Klan now, Miss Cleta? Somebody let it out about Tal treatin' you; is that it?"

I tried to get a better look at the words scrawled

across the page, but she balled it up and tucked it into her apron pocket. "It ain't nothin' but big talk from little people. Made me a right fine fan for a hot mornin'."

"I've seen what these men can do. They're angry because you let a colored man tend to you, and they'll do whatever they feel like doin' to you to make a point. This town's about to erupt right now."

"Jessilyn, I got my God here with me, with His angels guardin' my house. Those men—no matter how big they are, no matter how many guns they got—can't do a thing He won't let them do."

"And what if He lets them hurt you like He let them hurt Noah Jarvis?"

"Then I'll go to heaven and kneel at my Savior's feet. Can't find me a better place." She fanned her face with her hand. "Won't have to deal with this infernal heat in paradise, I can tell you that."

I opened my mouth to retort, but she reached out to grip my chin with a firmness that belied her age. "Don't you ever think you know how everythin's got to be done, Jessilyn. Only God has all the answers. Don't go thinkin' you know all you need to."

My lungs were filled up with all sorts of words I wanted to say about that wrinkled-up note in Miss Cleta's pocket. But I knew she'd sooner box my ears than listen to them, so I swallowed hard to keep them back. I just nodded and said, "Yes, ma'am," as best I could. As it was, the phrase came out sharply and cut off at the end, like a hiccup.

Her teacup clattered against the saucer as she retrieved it, and I sat back on my heels while she took two long gulps to finish it off. Then she declared, "We need to go shoppin'."

Her sudden declaration almost managed to bring a smile to my face. "Well, we sure can someday. Soon as you're feelin' up to it."

She put her cup down and planted her hands on the arms of the chair for leverage. "No, I mean today."

"Miss Cleta, did you ask Tal about goin' into town? Maybe he figures you ain't in no shape for that."

"For heaven's sake, that was days ago. And there weren't nothin' wrong in the first place." I began to argue, but she puckered her lips into a tight circle and eased herself out of the chair. "Don't you go tellin' me what I can and cannot do, Jessilyn Lassiter. I may be old, but I ain't feebleminded."

"It ain't your taxi day."

"So? You think there's only one day for taxi hirin'? You can run next door and use Nate's phone to call Lionel Stokes so he can bring his taxi on over." She picked up her teacup and shuffled off to the kitchen. "Besides," she called over her shoulder, "I ain't got you your birthday gift yet. We'll get you a nice dress or two, maybe."

I rushed off to join her in the kitchen. "Miss Cleta, what in tarnation are you talkin' about? You ain't supposed to spend so much on my birthdays."

"It's your nineteenth. That's an important one."

"Ain't nothin' more special about nineteen than there is eighteen, and you know it."

Miss Cleta gave me one of her belligerent looks. "Listen here, miss. I ain't in no mind to be bossed about by no sassy girl. If I say I'm buyin' you clothes for your birthday, then I'm buyin' you clothes. A woman pretty as you should have some smart things to wear." She picked up a magazine from the table and flipped through it, frowning. "'Course, Lord only knows if they'll have any in this backward old town." About a dozen pages whispered through her fingers before she stopped and turned her attention back to me. She laid the magazine down with a sigh. "Jessilyn, you've had yourself a tough time of things of late, what with Gemma marryin' and Noah . . ." His name stuck in her throat, and she closed her eyes to push back the tears that stung at them. "It's just, things have been hard, and I figure it can't but do us good to get out and have a little fun at somethin'. I'm an old woman, child; I've got to take my enjoyment while I can."

I stood in front of her for a long moment, arms crossed,

fighting back my own bout of tears. There we were, two of the most stubborn people in Calloway, locked in a sort of duel until I finally relented and let my arms fall to my sides. "Miss Cleta, there ain't no one in this whole world like you."

She smiled and patted my cheek. "And you best thank your lucky stars for it. Now," she cried with a clap of determined hands, "let's get down to business."

The morning went by in a busy blur, and we were in Mr. Stokes's cab by ten o'clock. There was really only one place to hunt for fancy, ready-made clothes in Calloway, so there wasn't anything to discuss on that front. The store window held things I didn't see much on everyday Calloway residents.

"That yellow thing there's like somethin' off of Ginger Rogers." Miss Cleta pressed her face close to the glass to accommodate her failing eyes. "You'd look like a real city girl in that frock."

"Luke says I don't need city-girl clothes to be pretty."

"Boy's got good sense. But I still say every girl likes to feel fancified every now and again." She went back to her window gazing and squinted at the price tag. "Wonder how much it is. . . ."

"Oh no, you don't. You had to twist my arm as it was to convince me to get anythin' at all. There ain't no talk about city dresses."

Miss Cleta sighed loudly. "Stubborn as the day is long. All right! Let's get on in there and find some boring ol' dress."

"You were the one who suggested a dress."

"Don't mean I meant a boring one."

I took her hand and ushered her inside. "I figure you'll manage to be happy with some borin' dress shoppin' somehow, Miss Cleta."

There was a coldness inside that shop the minute we walked in, and I wondered as I always did how shop-workers in Calloway could think themselves so far above a farm girl. After all, it wasn't like they were rich and famous just because they sold clothes in a small town like ours. But I was used to it and so was Miss Cleta. She just nodded a hello to the shopgirl and pointed toward a display. "There we are. Somethin' like that should work fine."

The clerk stalked us from a distance like we'd come into the store to rob her blind, and Miss Cleta remarked in my ear, "You'd think she'd have better things to do with her time."

"Guess all country folk make her suspicious." I pulled a pair of trousers from the rack and held them to me. "These should do nice, Miss Cleta. Don't you think so?"

She took them from me and held them up so she could see them better. "Jessilyn, I didn't say *trousers*; I said a *dress.* Lord knows you got enough trousers." Miss Cleta looked over her shoulder. "You best put them trousers down before she calls the sheriff in." She waved a hand at the salesgirl to get her attention, then said to me, "I want to see you in that yellow thing in the window."

"Miss Cleta—"

"Don't talk back to me, girl. I get ornery when you do that." She snapped her fingers in the air twice, matching the uppity manners of the salesclerk. "I'd like this here lady to try on that yellow frock in the window."

The salesgirl's eyebrows shot up like bread popping out of a toaster. "It's not on sale, you know."

Miss Cleta narrowed her eyes at her. "I didn't ask if it was on sale. And don't you worry about money. I could pay for a dozen of 'em if I wanted." I made to argue, but she stopped me short with a finger across my lips. "Don't you go spoilin' my day, Jessilyn. This makes me happy, and there ain't much an old lady can say does. So keep that mouth of yours closed for a change and try on the darn dress!"

"Miss Cleta, you're startin' to talk like a sailor." I shook my head at her but couldn't help a smile. The salesgirl returned and reluctantly motioned me to a changing room. I gave Miss Cleta one last shake of the head before following. "Stubborn as a mule," I murmured.

I changed into the dress knowing full well I shouldn't

accept it while knowing full well I'd have to. But as soon as I felt that fabric swirling about my legs like a cloud, I knew I wanted to accept it. In fact, I figured I'd likely never want to take it off.

Miss Cleta's hand shot up to her mouth when I stepped out. "Child, you are a sight for sore eyes. Would you look at yourself?" She pointed me toward a mirror. "Just look at that. You'd give Ginger a run for her money in that thing."

"You're talkin' nonsense."

"No, I am not, and don't never accuse me of it. If there's one thing I pride myself in, it's that I always speak the truth." She pulled my hair up and twisted it to the side of my head. "You need a hat."

"A hat? No, ma'am. I got me a serviceable hat."

"When did you ever see Ginger Rogers wear anythin' *serviceable*?"

I grabbed her arm and pulled her aside, whispering, "Miss Cleta, now you best stop thinkin' of spendin' all your money on me. I just won't have it."

For once she didn't smart-mouth me or order me about. This time she took my face in her two trembling hands and looked me square in the eye. "Jessilyn, my Sully left me off just fine. Most people don't know it since we ain't lived uppity and whatnot. But I got me enough to live another twenty years, and you know sure and simple the good Lord's goin' to take me home before then." She looked to the sky and murmured, "Least I pray You do, Lord." Then she eyed me again and said, "I figure I may as well enjoy spendin' some of it while I can."

I just looked at her for a few moments, thinking all sorts of things but only coming up with the idea that Miss Cleta had lived long enough to earn the right to spend whatever she wanted wherever she wanted. My hands went up over hers, and I smiled. "You sure are a spitfire, Miss Cleta."

"And don't you forget it." She returned my smile and kissed me soundly on the cheek. "Now slip out of that thing so we can pay the girl. She's about to keel over dead from fearin' we'll hightail it out of here with these things like a regular Bonnie and Clyde."

The bell on the shop's door jingled the arrival of another customer, and Miss Cleta came as near to swearing as I'd ever heard before. "Blast it all," she whispered. "Imogene Packard! Ain't never a day I seen that woman when she ain't had nonsense pourin' from that big mouth of hers." Then her eyes flitted to me with a bit of shame in them. "Don't go copyin' my words, Jessilyn. They ain't fittin'."

I didn't get out more than a "Yes'm" before Mrs. Packard caught sight of us and screeched out, "Cleta Terhune! What on God's green earth are you doin' in *this* store?"

Miss Cleta's hands hopped up to her hips and dug into them like moles in a garden. "Any reason why I shouldn't be here?"

Mrs. Packard glanced from me to Miss Cleta and then back to me. "I see. You're shoppin' for the Lassiter girl, not yourself." Her mouth spread into a wry grin for the benefit of Miss Cleta. "I was wonderin' what you'd expect to find in here for a lady of your . . . generation."

"We are of the same generation, Imogene," Miss Cleta answered haughtily. "Lest you forget, you only appeared on this earth eight years after I did."

Mrs. Packard breathed out a disgusted "Well!" but she must not have had any sort of effective rebuttal because she turned her attention to an entirely different subject. She grabbed Miss Cleta's arm and dragged her into a confidential huddle without so much as a nod of agreement from her. "Cleta, I feel it my duty to tell you there is a wretched rumor goin' about town that involves you."

"And I can see it pains you to tell it to me."

Mrs. Packard either ignored the sarcasm in Miss Cleta's voice or didn't make the effort to even notice. Her face took on a forced sort of sympathy. "Oh yes, of course. But I feel it only right you should know."

"Well then, spit it out, Imogene. We ain't got all day."

"Well, I'll tell you. There's talk goin' about that . . .

now, I know this is pure rubbish . . . but the talk is that you had that colored doc tend to you. Now, I know you well enough to know better. When I heard Thelma Polk talkin' about it, I laughed my head off. 'Why, Cleta Terhune would no sooner let a colored man tend to her than she would take tea with a badger,' I told them. 'You ladies ought not to go around sayin' such poppycock.'"

Miss Cleta's old bones were most times shaky, and I usually did the best I could to stay nearby in case she started to lose her balance, but she didn't need me anywhere near her at that moment. It was as though she'd stored up bits of energy over the years for such a moment as this. She stood up as tall as her little frame would allow, pulled her muscles taut, and with pride lifting her chin in the air, she said, "Well then, Imogene, I guess I may as well invite you to my place for tea so you can meet that badger."

Question marks danced across Mrs. Packard's face for a good twenty seconds before Miss Cleta's response found a home in her brain, and a look of horror began to fill her expression. "Cleta, what are you sayin'? You sayin' you let that colored boy . . . touch you?"

"I'm sayin' I let a fine, educated man treat my ailin' like I always let fine, educated men treat my ailin'."

"But he's a . . . a Negro!"

"And you're a buffoon, but what does that have to

do with the price of tea in China?" Miss Cleta's posture never faltered; her voice never rose. "Now, if you'll excuse us, we got us some shoppin' to finish."

"But you can't be serious."

"Oh, I ain't never been more serious. I choose to be cared for by only the finest of people, no matter if they be white, black, red, or chartreuse. Now I'll beg your pardon so's me and Miss Jessilyn can finish shoppin' for her birthday."

For the first time in the many years I'd known her, Mrs. Imogene Packard was dumbstruck. Miss Cleta gave me a push to get me changed back into my own things, and I reluctantly left for the dressing room. Mrs. Packard had the appearance of someone who had been cow-kicked, and when I came out of the dressing room, she was still in the same spot with the same expression on her face. I would have laughed had the subject matter been less serious.

Miss Cleta took the dress from my hand and laid it on the table. "We'd like to look at that fine white hat right there." She pointed to a stand where a faceless head sat holding a pert little hat with two feathers pointing off to the side.

"Miss Cleta, I can't get away with wearin' feathers," I whispered.

"All right then." She answered quickly like she'd

already figured it would be ridiculous. "How about that plain little thing right next to it? Least it's made of fine fabric. And it only has just that little bit of netting for decoration."

"I really don't think it's necessary. . . ."

"'Course it ain't necessary, child. It don't have to be necessary."

The salesgirl walked over to the hat but paused with her hands in midair as though the hat would send electric shocks into her if she touched it.

"I can pay for it," Miss Cleta said sharply, opening her coin purse to display a small cache of bills. "If that's what you're worryin' about."

Apparently it was, and the salesgirl's face relaxed so much, it made her appear ten years younger. "Let's put this on you." Her smile fairly lit the room now that she knew she had a viable customer, and she oozed all over me. "Look at that. You look the perfect lady."

"She ain't no lady; she's a farm girl. And where in tarnation is a farm girl goin' to wear a confection like that?"

Mrs. Packard had finally found her tongue, and Miss Cleta's eyes narrowed at the sound of it. She whipped around and shook her handbag at Mrs. Packard. "What makes a woman a lady is what's inside, not where she comes from. You're the perfect example of that. Born and bred in the best part of town, but what comes out of that mouth of yours is nothin' close to ladylike."

For the first time, that salesgirl and I had something in common. We both stood there like wide-mouthed frogs, watching the two women square off.

Mrs. Packard's face turned red, and a vein in her temple stood out like a big blue log. "Cleta Terhune, you are a hag."

"Better a hag than a two-faced, lyin' gossip."

Mrs. Packard lifted her handbag suddenly like she had every intention of whacking Miss Cleta over the head with it but thought better of damaging the bead-work. Instead, she came back with a verbal assault that reached out to pull me into the argument. She eyed my reflection in the mirror and smirked. "Do what you will, Cleta, but you can't take the farm out of the farm girl. That hat looks ridiculous on her. Like lipstick on a pig."

Miss Cleta stood on her toes and opened her mouth to retort, but I put my hand on her arm in warning. "Don't even bother, Miss Cleta. She ain't worth it."

Poor Miss Cleta sputtered and choked on every word that must have been sitting on that tongue of hers, but she held herself back and considered my words for a full half minute before settling down on her heels. "You're right, Jessilyn. She ain't worth it."

But I knew Miss Cleta well enough to know this battle

wasn't over until she planted her flag in the dirt, and I watched as she whipped that hat off my head and handed it to the salesgirl. "We'll take it."

"For all the good it'll do the girl," Mrs. Packard muttered. "You're throwin' your money away."

"And I'll take that bottle of fine rosewater, too."

"Miss Cleta!" I whispered sharply.

"Hush, girl!"

"But I don't need no rosewater."

"'Course not, Cleta." Mrs. Packard came up beside me and turned her nose up. "She'll always smell of horse no matter what you put on her."

Miss Cleta's face looked ready to explode, but I touched her arm again and shook my head. "Don't give her the satisfaction."

She nodded slowly with all the determination she had left in her body, but if she wasn't going to talk back, she was bound to do something. "Give me a pair of nice white gloves." She waved the salesgirl about with her hand like it was a magic wand. "And a pair of nylons, too."

I had never seen the likes of it before. Right before my very eyes, Miss Cleta was engaged in fiscal warfare, buying another item for every bullet she wanted to unload on Mrs. Packard. I gripped her arm hard as I dared. "Miss Cleta, we best get goin'. I got me things to do at home."

The salesgirl was wrapping up purchases rapid-fire,

short of breath and agitated, though who could blame her, what with the battle of the Southern belles playing out in front of her. Meanwhile, Mrs. Packard and Miss Cleta were locked in a stare-down, so I wrenched Miss Cleta's change purse from her angry grasp and paid for the purchases before she had the chance to wave her magic wand again.

The salesgirl's hand was shaky when she set the boxes in my arms, and I had to steady them myself, then grab Miss Cleta's arm to steer her toward the front. All I wanted to do was get out of there, but it took Miss Cleta a full minute to shuffle through the jingly door, what with all the staring she was doing.

"Can't you take your eyes off her now?" I whispered on our way out. "You're nearly walkin' backward."

"Can't. It's like takin' your eyes off a rattler. The second you look away, it might strike."

"Oh, for heaven's sake. She ain't no snake."

"You sure about that?"

By the time we made it to the sidewalk, I was a bundle of nerves. My eyes darted all over the roadway looking for Mr. Stokes's taxicab. "There he is." I hoisted the boxes up for a better grip and then locked my other arm around Miss Cleta's. "Let's get on out of here before we see any of the other town ladies and you end up buyin' out every store from here to Richmond."

Miss Cleta dug her bony elbow into my side and gave one of her hoot-owl laughs. "You sure beat all, Jessilyn."

"Me? I ain't the one lettin' a harpy like Mrs. Packard whittle away my life savin's."

Mr. Stokes hopped out of the car and opened the door for us. "Sakes alive, you sure done found some treasures." Once Miss Cleta was inside, he took my packages and loaded them into the car for me. "I ain't seen Miss Cleta come away with this kind of shoppin' since Mr. Sully was with us."

I hopped in beside her and patted her knee. "That so, Miss Cleta?"

Her eyes took on that distant, watery look they always did when she thought about her late husband. "Those were the good ol' days, no doubt. My Sully, he liked to spoil me sometimes, and he'd take me into town on a whim and say, 'Cleta, angel, this here day's all about you.' And when I'd protest, he'd hold up his hand and say, 'I want to. It makes me happy to see you happy.' And he'd up and buy me some of the silliest things just 'cause he liked it." She pulled her hankie from her purse and wiped her nose twice; then she turned those shimmering eyes on me. "That's what we done today, child. Today I get to be happy because you're happy."

I smiled at her and took her free hand. "You sayin'

you still had a nice time even after that nastiness with Mrs. Packard?"

Miss Cleta folded her hankie back up and replaced it in her purse, snapping it closed with one loud pop. She shielded her mouth with her hand and said softly, "Honey, I liked it all the more for it." A smirk lit up her pale, wrinkled face, and she raised her eyes to the heavens. "May the good Lord forgive me for it."

"Miss Cleta—"

"Don't scold me, girl. Seems to me a woman like Imogene Packard needs taken down a peg or two, and I ain't averse to bein' the one to do it. Besides, it taught you good character, didn't it?"

"How's that?"

"By makin' you be the bigger person. Ain't you the one who advised me to keep my mouth shut? Way I see it, this whole thing made you realize you're growin' up and losin' some of your impulsive ways."

I raised one eyebrow in a question that I didn't mean to have answered, and she leaned in for another secret. "Least that's what we'll say happened, right?" She winked at me and let out another one of her high-pitched laughs.

Mr. Stokes looked at us in his rearview mirror, flashed a grin, and shook his head wordlessly. I did the same. After all, Miss Cleta was a woman well set in her ways.

And I loved her for it.

Chapter 19

I grabbed the last dish from Gemma and gave it a quick drying off, but she tugged it back from me. "You best get on home before dark," she argued. "You've stayed long enough."

"I ain't never stayed long enough, and you know it."

Gemma settled the plate on the stack on the counter-top where all her dishes and pots sat. We'd spent the entire afternoon painting her kitchen cabinets green, and while they were drying, the kitchen looked like a general store.

Gemma called to Tal and then slipped out of her apron. "Well, that may well be true," she murmured, "but that don't mean it ain't gettin' late. I'll have Tal run you home in the truck."

"I don't need a ride home." I stuck my face up to the

open window. "I want some fresh air. Been stuck inside with paint smells all day."

"It's too late for you to walk home."

I closed my eyes and took one more long breath of the outdoor scent that floated in on a stiff breeze. "Gemma, I've walked the fields in pitch-blackness. It ain't goin' to hurt me none to walk home at sunset." I stepped away from the window and waved Tal off as he walked into the kitchen with an expectant look on his face. "Never mind," I said. "She didn't need anythin' after all."

He looked at Gemma. "You sure about that?"

"I was just goin' to say you could run Jessie home in the truck, but she says she wants to walk."

"Ain't no trouble to do it, Jessie," he said. "Take me just a few minutes to get my things together."

"Thank you, Tal, but no. I'll be fine. I like to walk; you know that." I kissed Gemma's cheek and slipped my arm through hers so we could head out together. "Next time you need help paintin', you just call." I looked down at my green-spattered clothes and grimaced. "And I'll call Luke and tell him to come by and do it for you."

Her elbow dug into my ribs at that familiar spot it had found its way to so many times. "Hard work's good for you."

"That's just what folks say to convince other folks to

do work for them." I stepped outside and lifted my face to the wind. "See? It's a perfect night for a stroll."

"Perfect night for you to ring me up when you get home so I know you're okay, too."

I ambled down the steps and then turned toward her. "You worry too much."

"And you don't worry enough. We're even."

I smiled and hopped over the ditch and into the road. I was tired and stiff, and the fresh evening air gave me a little life. "I'll call you," I hollered over the wind. I waved to her and then sauntered across the street into the woods. The area where Gemma lived was fine, but following the road all the way home would take me through some parts a girl didn't want to travel alone in the daytime, much less at night. I rounded the corner and slipped onto the now-familiar path through the trees that would eventually lead to the meadow I would cross to get home.

Pink light filtered through the leaves, taking the edge off the dimness that had settled there, and my mind flitted to thoughts of Luke, as it so often did without my even prompting it to. Three days after Gemma's wedding, Luke had announced he was leaving town for deliveries. It was no surprise—he'd done enough traveling in the past two years for me to be used to it—but this was the first time he'd left since we'd come to an understanding. It already seemed like he'd been gone for a year, and every time I got that ache inside that longed for his presence, I clung to memories of him holding my hand or smiling at me or kissing my lips.

I closed my eyes at the thought of him close to me and blindly made my way down the path. The leaves on the trees were stirred into a frenzy by the wind, rustling in unison so that the air was filled with a sound like waves crashing to shore, softening as the breeze relented and then reaching a crescendo as it rose again. Every now and then, as the trees quieted, I could hear a forest creature bounding through the brush. With every few steps, I would peek out between my eyelashes to make sure I was still on the path, and then I would seal my eyes shut, letting my surroundings sink into my soul.

And then I drew to a sudden stop.

The crackling of underbrush is a curse to some and a savior to others. For a follower, it steals away anonymity and alerts their prey. For the followed, it warns of danger, but that warning is the sort that breeds terror. As I stood silently, listening, I felt that sort of terror well up inside me. I gave in to it for all of ten seconds before I chastised myself for letting Gemma get me worked up, then stepped ahead again, closing my eyes, seeking out the comfort the dim, windswept woods had lent me only moments before.

But it was useless. The sensations around me now seemed ominous, and I flicked my eyelids open and glanced around, over my shoulders, behind trees and shrubs.

Something wasn't right.

I continued to walk, but now every crackle and crunch within the darkened stand of trees filled me with foreboding, making each footfall heavy with fear. Every time the wind would wane, I listened, straining my ears to pick through the woodland noises to the ones that didn't belong. And each time the wind grew strong, blocking out the sounds around me, I knew with even more certainty that I had been right.

I was not alone.

I had come to the shallow creek that wound its way through the woods, and though I struggled against the force of the wind and the grip of fear, I scurried across without taking time to seek out a dry path. Despite the water that dampened my shoes, my steps grew more urgent, picking up speed in a desperate attempt to reach the clearing. My eyes darted about like a humming-bird, never staying in one place for long but whipping to and fro with jagged, anxious movements. About a hundred yards ahead, I could make out the opening to the meadow, a place that in no way offered rescue but would at least steal away the anonymity of my stalker.

But as my eyes darted sideways, a sudden flash of white crossed between two trees so quickly I wondered if I'd imagined it. I slowed my steps and furtively glanced around me.

And there it was again.

A flash of white and then gone, like a ghostly apparition playing a game of hide-and-seek. I had come to a full stop without noticing and was studying the trees behind me when a twig snapped in front of me with just enough warning to make my blood turn ice-cold. I whipped around to see someone standing there, bathed in the glow of the fading pink sky. His ghostly robe fluttered, but his eyes never wavered, and somewhere in the darkness within that hood, I could see his eyes watching, waiting for any move I would make.

A gust of wind blew strands of hair across my face, but I couldn't move to swat them away. I was frozen in place, in time, transfixed by the gaze of the man before me.

And overwhelmed by the deepest sense of hatred I had ever known.

I stood my ground and let my eyes lock with his, focusing all my concentration on those moments as though my revulsion could travel the space between us and burrow into his skull. In an instant I felt no fear, only rage. I was face-to-face with the very symbol of all that had haunted me for years, and I challenged him boldly, daring him with my very countenance. For some time we stood there, a wordless battle being fought between us.

And then his eyes changed.

Where once they had been intense, sparkling with hatred, suddenly they narrowed, a light cast behind them.

He was smiling.

The fear I had felt at the start struck me again with such ferocity, my legs felt as though they would give way, but before they could, I turned and ran. Despite the terror that filled my body, my feet moved deftly across the underbrush, almost as if they had a mind of their own. I could hear my stalker thrashing through the brush behind me, and even though he grunted from exertion, I knew he was gaining ground. The air that pushed in and out of my lungs did so audibly, and I focused on the rhythm of it to help keep my pace. Weeds and shrubs smacked at my legs, ripping at my pants, scraping my skin. But I kept moving, my eyes pasted to the scene in front of me, fearing with every stride that if I allowed myself a moment's distraction, I would be caught.

Tree branches whipped at my face and grabbed at my hair, working against me as violently as if they had been wearing a robe and hood themselves. A prickly bush snapped at my face, digging its claws into my temple, causing me to stumble. I regained my balance, and for that split second before I again began to run, I found myself compelled to look behind me.

And there he was, no more than ten yards away, cutting a path toward me with the determination of a man consumed by vengeance. Slipping briefly in the dirt, I took flight again, but I knew I'd never outrun him. His footfalls grew louder and louder until I could hear them over the wind, the crunch of his boots echoing in my ears. Twigs snapped and dry leaves crackled as they split apart and crumbled beneath him. The sound of his approach was deafening to me.

Suddenly I heard a scream so violent, so agonizing, I skidded to a halt in spite of my fear. I turned to see the ghostly man lying on the ground in convulsions, his white robe turning crimson so quickly, it seemed an illusion.

I walked toward him slowly, cautiously, squinting against the growing darkness. When I came within several yards of him, I stopped and stared at the bear trap that had ensnared his calf, crunching into flesh and bone so deeply, it seemed if he moved, it would split in two. Blood oozed from his leg, covering his robe and turning the summer greenery a deep scarlet.

And I felt nothing.

No compassion, no compulsion to duty. This man lay there, bleeding to death in front of my eyes, and not only was I helpless, I was happy to be so. In my mind, at that moment, he deserved nothing better than to die out here, caught in the very device I had once heard someone call a nigger trap.

It was perfect justice.

As I stared at him, his breathing became ragged, raspy, as though there were holes in his lungs. All struggling ceased, and he dropped to his side. He looked up at me through those ghostly slits in his hood and spoke two words.

"Help me."

I knew that voice. No muffling hood or ragged breaths could disguise it. I knelt beside him so I could look deep into those desperate eyes. "Help you, Delmar Custis? You want me to help you?" I ignored the blood that turned my blue trousers brown and ripped his hood off, looked into a face so pale, it seemed the same as the white hood that hung from my fingertips. "Like you *helped* Noah Jarvis?"

"Jessilyn, please. Help me."

I didn't always do what my daddy would say was the Christian thing to do, but in this case, I knew that getting help was at the very least the *human* thing to do. Only I didn't feel human just then. I felt outside of myself, so consumed by rage and hatred that all rational thought seemed to have spilled out onto the grass along with Delmar's blood. I dropped the filthy hood to the ground, took one more look at that pale, drawn face that seemed to foretell of death.

And then I walked away.

I didn't run for help. I didn't even intend to tell a soul what I'd seen. I pasted my vision squarely on that meadow ahead of me, and I didn't look back. For all I cared, Delmar Custis could die alone and rot away in these woods without a soul to ever know what came of him. I walked the slow, easy gait of one who hasn't a worry in the world. I wanted nothing more than to show this man I hated him so vehemently that I could saunter away from his dying body without one ounce of conviction, without a bit of shame.

The first several steps were so simple. It all seemed to make perfect sense. These men had terrorized me from the day Gemma had come to live with us. And even when they had let us be, the nightmares of burning crosses—and now of bodies hanging from trees—haunted me at every turn.

But with the next set of steps something began to scrape at my insides—some small, nagging doubt. The wind picked up again and ran crisply past my ears, calling my attention to the whispers Miss Cleta had told me of, whispers that remind us of wise words from loved ones.

But this whisper was nothing like what I'd imagined I'd heard before. This whisper didn't go from my mind to my heart. This whisper went from my heart to my mind. It was an inner voice.

It began as a murmur, but with each step it became more and more of a roar. My cheeks began to burn with a hot shame that seared from within. I slowed my steps until my whole body was so racked with despair, I could no longer move. Compelled to see the depths of my depravity, I turned to look at the human being I had left to die, and my world came crashing in.

Just like Miss Cleta had threatened, I had become like him. Like all of them.

Only I didn't have the hood.

These men were willing to kill because of their hate, and though I had not created the wound that drained this man's blood, I was willing to kill by my very inaction.

The realization of what I had become made me nauseous, and I leaned over and retched into the grass.

Delmar heard me and managed to lift his hand toward me.

"Jessilyn," he whispered again. "*Help* me."

From my place on the leafy ground, I peered at his limp, bloodstained body, and I knew what I had to do.

I wiped one arm across my mouth, stood up slowly to steady my trembling legs, and walked back to where he lay. I passed him without a word, but our eyes met, and I saw his mouth move without producing any sounds. I went past him, past his bloody robe, past his wordless pleas for help.

And I ran.

But this time as I left him behind, I didn't plan to leave him to die there. This time I knew what had to be done, and I ran toward Gemma's house with tears streaming down my face.

All I could hope was that I would be in time, that I could get Tal to Delmar before he died. It was a stunning notion to one who only minutes earlier had wished the man dead with all her heart, but now it was my deepest desire to bring Tal to that spot in the woods and hear him say that Delmar would live.

And as I ran, my lips kept forming the same words over and over: *Please don't let him die. Please don't let him die.*

My retreat through the woods seemed endless, marked by shame and guilt of a kind I'd never known before. Inner turmoil can be more devastating than outer. There are things in this world that wound the body, but when the spirit is spared, it has a way of overcoming. When the spirit is wounded, it affects the whole of a person, racking the mind and body with unceasing, unbearable pain.

And if Delmar Custis died that day with the help of my hatred, then I knew with absolute certainty that my spirit would die as well.

With a heart and conscience as heavy as mine at that moment, I struggled even to lift my feet, but the wind was at my back and fear pushed me onward. Once again, as had happened so many times in my life, I ached to be where Gemma was.

But if I had thought Gemma's home to be a refuge that night, I was desperately, terribly deceived.

There are some moments in time that sear your consciousness so deeply they never leave you. They're recalled by sensations that trigger a memory and transport you back in time so quickly, it's as though it's happening all over again. That night, as I rounded the corner to Gemma's house, the flicker of light that colored the night sky sent me reeling back to a time six years earlier. I remembered standing on my momma and daddy's porch with a rifle, Gemma at the screen door behind me, shaking in fear. I remembered the howls of wicked laughter, the haunting calls of face-less men. And I remembered the way the fire from that burning cross singed Momma's flowers and flecked the darkness with sparks.

When I came to a stop in front of Gemma's house, with darkness all around me—and in my heart—the horrors of that long-ago night were playing out again before my eyes. As I watched that cross burning in Gemma and Tal's front yard, I knew this was no mere memory.

This was now.

Gemma's screams pierced the darkness, snapping me out of my reverie, and I realized with a sudden force that my chance meeting with Delmar Custis hadn't been chance at all. There was a reason he was in those woods, and it had nothing to do with me. I was a happy accident, an opportunity to take care of two birds with one stone.

I watched in horror as two men kept Tal's arms pinned behind him while another taunted him, slapping him like he was an insolent child. Several others stood around, torches in hand, hurling insults, urging the aggressor on. Gemma continued to cry out in agony, struggling against the man who was holding her back.

The Klansman put his face right up close to Tal's so that his spit flecked Tal as he spoke. "Come on, nigger, ain't you got enough man in you to fight back? You want your woman here to think you ain't got it in you?" He gave Tal a slap to both ears twice in a row. "Look at this here boy," he sneered. "Yellow as the day is long." He

howled with laughter, and I knew him right off to be
Bobby Ray Custis.

I cried out just as he raised his fist. "You hurt him,
Bobby Ray, you kill your daddy!"

Bobby Ray's fist stopped two inches from Tal's gut,
and he whipped his head around. The rest of the men
did the same.

I stepped forward so they could all see who I was.

Bobby Ray lifted his hand to point at me with a finger
that shook violently. "You stay out of this or I'll get to
you next." His voice came out filled with a ferocity I had
never heard from him before.

Hooded cowards don't like to be unmasked.

I took a few more steps forward into the firelight
that spilled across the lawn and met his gaze. "I'm
only tellin' you the truth. You'll be sorry if you hurt
this man."

"This *boy*," he corrected, "ain't done nothin' but open
himself up to trouble. Any nigger that goes around this
town puttin' his hands on a white woman like he did
knows he won't last for long."

"A doctor cares for a patient; don't matter what color
that patient is."

He shook his head. "Matters to me."

Tears streamed down my face, my stomach felt like
I'd been pitched about, and I was scared to death, but I

did everything to keep my voice clear and steady. "Fine, then. Let your daddy die."

He'd cocked his hand back for another try at Tal's stomach, but I must have caught his curiosity because he paused in midair and turned to look at me. "What the heck are you spoutin' off about?"

"Only that your daddy's lyin' out there in the woods bleedin' to death in a bear trap." I pointed my own finger toward Tal. "And this here man's the only one near enough who can try and save him."

Bobby Ray's fist loosened; his hand dropped to his side. "You're lyin'." His words came out flat, the words of a man who is trying to convince himself of something he doesn't believe.

I stepped farther into the firelight and swept a hand in front of me, displaying the blood that covered my clothes. "Then where d'you think this came from?"

Bobby Ray stepped two paces closer to me and ripped his hood off for a better look. That was when I saw fear in the eyes of Bobby Ray Custis. Nobody looks at the amount of blood that was on my clothes without feeling terror prick at their insides.

I held my palms out to him so he could see the red stains. "This here's your daddy's blood. He near about got his leg cut off clean through, and he ain't got much time left, I figure. You best make up your mind good and quick. Who dies? Doctor Pritchett or your daddy? Because this *colored man* is the only one here who can keep your daddy from bleedin' to death in them woods." I tipped my head in Tal's direction. "Ain't you lucky you didn't kill him yet?"

Bobby Ray didn't respond. He just stood there, staring at nothing.

One of the men who had his grip on Tal released him and reached up to remove his hood. Cole Mundy narrowed his eyes at Bobby Ray. "What're you waitin' for?"

Bobby Ray shook his head. "Stay out of this."

"What's to stay out of? It's clear the girl's tellin' the truth. Your daddy ain't here, and there's blood all over her."

Bobby Ray snapped his head around toward Cole and roared, "I said stay out of this!"

But Cole didn't back down. He stepped closer to Delmar's son and spoke in a low growl. "You willin' to let your daddy die over this? That what you're sayin'?"

Bobby Ray turned so that his toes touched Cole's. "I ain't lettin' no nigger touch my daddy."

"You're insane!"

Bobby Ray shoved Cole in the chest, but Cole recovered quickly and came at him, tossing him to the ground. "I don't care what you say. I ain't standin' by while your daddy dies."

The other man who held Tal didn't budge, and Cole whipped a pistol from his waistband and pointed it at his head. "Let him go. Now!"

The man at the end of the gun barrel didn't flinch, but his voice came out in quiet shock. "You crazy, son?"

"I'm the only one who ain't."

"You can get into a lot of trouble in these parts for wavin' a gun around at people."

"What're you goin' to do, Sheriff? Arrest me?" Cole pushed him aside, grabbed Tal by the arm, and waved his gun around to warn everyone off. "I'm takin' him with me, and if anyone tries to stop me, I'll put a bullet through your gut." He pushed Tal forward and then nodded at me to get moving. "Show me where Delmar is."

Tal stumbled forward, bruised but able to walk without difficulty. "Gemma!" he called. "Get my bag."

I ran to Gemma and took her hand in mine. "She's comin' with us," I announced. There was no protest from her captor. He let her go and waited while she ran into the house for Tal's things; then he followed along behind us. The rest followed in their truck, and by the time we reached Delmar, I noticed Bobby Ray straggling at the back of the crowd.

The instant he saw his daddy lying there like that, he ran past everyone and fell to his knees, directing pleading eyes at the colored man he had been torturing only minutes earlier. "Well? Help him! What're you waitin' for?"

Tal knelt on the bloody ground and started shouting orders. Cole Mundy slid to the ground by Delmar's head and held his shoulders still, but it was clear that he was overwhelmed by the sight before him. He dropped his head and moaned.

I leaned down and put my mouth to his ear. "Too much blood for you, Mundy? If Noah Jarvis had bled out like this, would that have kept you from breakin' his neck?"

He snapped his head up to look at me, and I was so startled by the anguish I saw in those eyes, it took my breath away. I had never before seen eyes like that in any living soul, and they will haunt me until the day I die. I backed away from him, leaving him alone in his grief.

After all, who was I to convict a man of bloodguilt? I had some of my own.

"Hold him still!" Tal ordered. "We've got to get this trap off. He's mostly unconscious, but he's bound to fight at some point."

Gemma called to me, and I ran to her side to help her, but my hands were shaky and useless. It took every bit of manpower in perfect harmony to free him, and as everyone worked, Delmar's intermittent screams spurred us on.

By the time Delmar was free and the men had loaded him onto the truck, we were all covered in blood and sweat. Gemma and I stayed behind and watched them drive away, leaving me with an empty ache in my soul. For all I knew, he would be dead before they even turned the bend.

Gemma and I trudged back to her house without a word. I didn't know what to say to her. There was nothing in me that knew how to confess a sin like mine to someone I loved so much.

When we reached her house, Gemma took my hand. "You can stay with me tonight. We'll call your momma and daddy to let them know."

But I shook my head. "I can't."

"Jessilyn, you need to get out of those clothes and into bed, you hear? Now come on, let's get inside."

I let go of her hand and backed away slowly. "I can't, Gemma. Not now." I looked down at the bloody patches on my clothes. "You don't know what I've done. You'd be so ashamed."

She reached out and snatched my hand back. "You ain't done nothin' but save me and Tal and get help for a dyin' man," she said with ferocity. "That ain't nothin' I'd ever be ashamed of, Jessilyn. Not ever!"

Sobs began to escape my throat and I could only fit my words in between them, but I lifted my head, forcing myself to meet her gaze. "I walked away from him, Gemma. I walked away."

She tipped her head sideways, desperation in her eyes. "What d'you mean? You came for help."

"No. I walked away. I looked at him there on the ground with blood pourin' out of him, and I didn't feel a thing. And when he called out for help, I just walked away."

She watched me for several seconds and then squeezed my hand tight. "But you did the right thing in the end, and he's goin' to be fine. I'm sure he will."

I stole my hand away in shame, wishing I could believe it would all be okay like she said. "Tell Momma and Daddy I'll be safe. I just need to be alone right now."

She stepped forward defiantly. "I'll go with you."

"No! I need to go alone."

"Go where?"

"I don't know, but I can't stay here and I can't go home. I promise, I'll go home sometime soon, but I just can't right now." This time I reached out for her, taking both her hands in mine, willing her to understand. "Just now, Gemma, I've got to be somewhere alone."

She studied my eyes, and I knew she could see I meant what I said. "You'll be okay, Jessie," she whispered.

"I know you will." She stared at me hard through her tears and then hesitantly let me go. "I'll tell your momma and daddy the same thing," she called over her shoulder. Then she turned around in fine Gemma fashion and pointed into the darkness. "You just make sure you don't make them worry for long, you hear?"

As I watched her walk away, it felt like my heart was made out of a string that had gotten caught on her shoe and unraveled with each step she took. Out in the middle of the darkness, with a man's blood on my hands, I felt the ache of loneliness.

And I knew for certain that this was only the beginning.

Chapter 20

Sometimes there's a place in your heart you know is there, but you don't know all the colors of it. You see it in black and white, but then one day it comes to life like a rainbow, all clearly painted in colors so vivid, there's no way to avoid the truth of it.

That's what happened that night when I watched Delmar Custis bleeding his very life out onto the grass and then turned and walked away. I'd known the feeling of hate. I'd had plenty of it poured out on me and my loved ones over the years. I knew how hate kills the senses and traps conscience in a net. And I'd wondered time and again what could make a body hate so much that he'd want to kill.

Now I knew.

I stumbled across the fields slowly, taking furtive

glances at the blood that stained my clothes, even though I hated the sight of it. It was like I was compelled to look at it, as though facing up to the bloodstains would make me face up to the blackness of my heart. For all I knew, Delmar Custis had bled to death by now and I was a full-blown murderer.

By the time I reached the gazebo on our property, I was nauseated and worn through. I dropped to my knees inside the shelter. There I was, in the place my daddy had made out of his love for my momma, coming to terms with the fact that I was living for hate. And I remembered that day years ago when I'd questioned my daddy about the evil things that had been done to us the summer we took Gemma in. I remembered how my daddy looked when he emerged from the woods that day, with the weight of all the rage and betrayal of our neighbors making his gait slow and uneven. I remembered the way he lifted me up so that my toes skimmed the ground, cradling me in arms that gave as much love as they searched for.

But most of all I remembered how his words had come out of his mouth with an emotion that burned them into my soul.

"I ain't capable of hatin' like that," I'd said about those men who had haunted our summer.

But Daddy had looked at me with eyes that held all

the feelings in his heart at once and made his voice stern so I couldn't avoid knowing how serious his words were. "Jessilyn," he'd said, "ain't no man can't get someplace he never thought he'd get to. You let enough bad thoughts into your head, you can end up doin' all sorts of things you never thought possible."

The recollection of those words made my whole body ache and shiver, and I lowered my head so I was almost folded in two. That was me. Those words described me. I had become one of those people I had said I could never be like.

"Daddy," I whispered, "you were right." My face touched the knees of my bloodstained pants, and the terror of that night poured out of my heart into salty tears that soaked the crimson splotches. "I'm so sorry." The words spilled out in tandem with my sobs and joined the chorus of night creatures in a mournful wail.

I lay there until I didn't have any tears left, and even then I stayed on the floor of the gazebo hiccuping air that I didn't feel I deserved to breathe. There in the middle of the thick, hot air of that summer's night, I felt claustrophobic, closed in by my sins and failures so tightly, I didn't think I'd ever escape. How could I go home again? How could I face my mother and father? Gemma? Luke? Miss Cleta? How could I face those who had loved me and cared for me, only for me to grow into a person so blackened by hate and rage she'd been capable of murder?

Most of all I wondered where I could go to get away from the agony of what was inside of me. Where do you go to escape your mind? There is no place on this earth where your thoughts can't plague you. I would forever be trapped in this nightmare where my own mind accused me every second of every day for the rest of my life. And deservedly so.

Somehow, though, those breaths that I hadn't earned calmed down and led me to a sleep so thick, it was like I'd been drugged. My body had finally given out from the strain, and when I opened my eyes again, it was to find what I thought was sunlight streaming across my face, only it wasn't the daylight that so often made the cares of the nighttime seem distant. It was moonlight—soft, brilliant moonlight that bathed the wood of the gazebo in a shadow-strewn glow. For a few blissful seconds my mind was blurry, uncertain of where I was or why I was there, but then it all came rushing back to me in a flood of memory. A sick feeling immediately grabbed at my insides, and I struggled to lift my top half off the floor for a look at my surroundings.

The world seemed much the same as it always had, the scene around me one that I had known since childhood. But something had changed, something inside of me, and once the cobwebs of sudden but short-lived sleep slipped from my eyes, that change gripped me anew. My movements were those of someone who was ill or worn with age, but even still I managed to get to my feet and stumble to one of the pillars and peer at the moon. Dark, bold clouds surrounded it, threatening to steal the light away.

The wind whipped up something fierce, and I stepped down from my perch on the gazebo and tipped my face up to catch it. I had allowed myself to be dirtied by bitterness, cut into by the claws of evil that I'd learned about all my life but had chosen to ignore. And now, as I watched my soul slip away into darkness, I wanted nothing more than to get it into the light.

Sometimes, as a child, I would help Momma wash the windows, and she'd tell me that window washing was like what God did to our hearts. "See how hard it is to get the sunlight in the house when these windows get so filthy, Jessilyn?" she'd say. "But once we wash them up, that sunlight will just stream on through. Baby, that's what God does with our hearts when we ask Jesus in. He cleans all those dirty spots off so His light can shine on in. And then, once His light's in our hearts, it'll shine right back out for all the world to see."

And you know what? I'd seen that light. I'd seen it all my life in my momma and daddy, in Gemma and her momma and daddy. I'd seen it in Miss Cleta and Mr. Poe. And even Luke. But I'd never once appreciated it. Not once. I'd loved who they were and what they were to me, but it never occurred to me until just now that they might not have been the people I loved if God hadn't lit them from the inside out. Maybe they wouldn't have let their hearts get as dark as mine, but still they wouldn't have shined the light on me quite so much as they had.

And suddenly, for the first time, I wanted that purity Momma always talked about. But what kind of person denies something all her life until she has need of it and then expects it to just plop right into her lap? I'd been a thorn in God's side since the day I learned to speak my mind. I was always doubting Him, always resisting Him, sometimes even cursing Him. I had no right to ask Him to just up and clean house in my heart, licketysplit, mopping up the mess I'd made on purpose.

The wind blew angrily now, and I lifted my arms out at my sides, wishing it could just pick me up and carry me to a place where I wouldn't have to feel anymore.

I looked off into the distance and willed my mind to stop working, but it wouldn't turn off. The thoughts in my head haunted me, whirling over and over, images of the past and frightening imaginations of the future. When I was thirteen, I'd lived a summer possessed by the fear that I'd accidentally killed a man, and I remembered the feel of the relief that consumed me once I'd found out I hadn't. But now here I was, six years later, realizing that I had almost willingly left a man to die. And for all I knew, he was dead at this very minute, dead because I had let him bleed for those moments of my indecision.

As the wind whipped around me, I gripped my trousers in my hands where the dried patches of blood lay like the stain of sin, and I knew I couldn't live like this. Not like this. My conscience would eat me up inside until there was nothing left of me. I needed peace in my soul like I needed water, and I was afraid I'd dry up and die if I didn't find it.

In my mind, a sort of chant started. *I can't. I can't. I can't. I can't live like this. I can't.* I lifted my face to the heavens and cried out loud, "I can't!"

And then clear as a bell, I knew who could.

I'd heard it a million times before. I'd heard it from Momma and Daddy, from Miss Cleta. I'd heard it from the minister at church, especially on Easter Sunday. I'd even read about it in books. But it hadn't ever meant a single thing to me. Until this night, mired in the bleakness of my soul, with the moonlight illuminating my murky heart. That's when it all suddenly went inside me like it had sunk into my pores and found its way into my bloodstream.

I tipped my face upward and whispered one word. *"Please."*

It was the most important little word I'd ever said. It was a word I'd used a million times in my life, but it had never held so much meaning before in all my days. God must have known exactly what I meant by that one word because the second I spoke it, my heart dropped all its weight like someone had reached in and pulled all the burdens out.

I guess someone had.

Chapter 21

Two days later, Cole Mundy's momma found him hanging from the rafters of their barn.

Only this wasn't any lynching. Cole Mundy had hanged himself from those rafters because he couldn't live with what he'd done. I imagine sometimes what must have gone through his mind the days after he watched Noah Jarvis breathe his last up there in that old tree by the roadside. I imagine he saw those desperate, pleading eyes every time he closed his own, that his dreams were haunted by pictures of a young boy's body twitching until all life left it.

I had an idea of how he felt, after all. I'd come about as close as he had to having blood on my hands, and I knew what it was like to carry guilt around like heavy chains that wrap you up until you can't move or breathe without the hurt of it all.

I never thought to see the day when I'd feel sorry for Cole Mundy, but I did now. I'd walked a little bit in his shoes, and I wished he'd found the forgiveness I had. I wished his heart had been washed clean instead of beating its last there in the barn.

The day of his funeral was sunny, a day like any other. It was more a day for a picnic than a day for mourning. I stood at that graveside listening to the minister's voice like it was in the background of my mind because all I heard was Cole's momma crying her whole life out onto the dry summer dirt.

I wouldn't have thought it possible for me to cry at Cole Mundy's anything, much less his funeral. Once upon a time, I'd have thought his funeral should be a national holiday to celebrate with fireworks and gifts. But I didn't see things so much the same as I once had anymore.

With the minister's voice just a buzz in my ear, I looked around at the people standing at Cole's graveside. Klan, most of them, men who spent much of their time hating and thinking of ways to act out that hate. I didn't wonder why like I used to. I understood it more now. Even though I still wanted to see them all behind bars for what they did, I understood that the sort of hate they lived with came from all sorts of different starts but ended up looking mostly the same in the end; all it really came down to was they didn't have the benefit of knowing what I knew now. Like Gemma said, without Jesus, we don't do much but sin and mess things up.

Cole's momma reached down to pick up a handful of Virginia clay and struggled to get back up, her body was so racked with the ache of loss. And as I watched her, I wondered how many more mommas would ache from the loss of a child as long as we had our same troubles here in Calloway. Would we forever have the white folks and the colored folks living on opposite sides, just waiting for violence to erupt?

Just as always, I didn't know. No one but God did, my daddy would say if I posed that question to him, like he always did when I asked something about mankind that was beyond any man's ability to answer. I was learning more and more every day that part of knowing who God was had to do with remembering that we're awfully small compared to Him and there's no way on His whole green earth we'll ever know why He does things the way He does.

But sometimes He gives us a little bit of a hint. And that summer day, as we all stood at the graveside of a man who had taken his own life rather than live with who he had become, God saw fit to bring some hope our way.

It was the sudden break of the minister's endless drone that snapped me out of my reverie. I looked up to see every eye pointed toward the Mundys' field. I turned my own eyes that way and my knees nearly buckled at the sight of Noah Jarvis's momma weaving her way slowly through the tall grass, her hair done up just so, wearing what must have been her best Sunday dress.

Thoughts coursed through my mind over what might be about to take place. This wasn't only a colored woman coming upon the funeral of a Klansman attended by other Klansmen; it was the momma of the boy those Klansmen had taken away from her.

There wasn't one other colored soul even close to this place. Even Gemma had stayed behind for fear of starting up trouble. But here came this woman, weary yet determined, struggling across the field to step foot by the grave of the man who had helped kill her son. Daddy stood by my side, and I reached out to take his arm. My eyes darted around to see the reaction of the other men, but I didn't have to see it to know what it would be. They all looked murderous. But nobody made a move or said a word.

I'd learned a good thing or two about miracles of late. After all, the change in me was miracle enough for my whole lifetime. But I saw another one that day as those men stood stock-still just watching Mrs. Jarvis come the whole long way. It was like God had put chains around them and sealed their lips shut.

Mrs. Jarvis stopped at the edge of the grave, staring at Cole Mundy's momma the whole time, and then she stooped down and swept up a handful of dirt, letting it sift through her fingers onto the casket.

I didn't know what to think. I didn't know if she'd meant it as a good-riddance to men of his kind. I didn't know if she'd lost all her senses and gone stark raving mad. But I wasn't left in doubt for long.

Mrs. Jarvis walked past us with such determined strides, we all backed up to give her plenty of room so she didn't slip into the hole with Cole Mundy's body. She slowed her steps in front of Cole's momma and stood there for a few seconds that seemed to me like an hour. Then she wrapped her arms around her and gave her the kind of hug that looked like it came straight from God Himself.

Cole's momma started to sob so violently, the humid air echoed with it. Her knees buckled and she let herself fall so hard against Noah's momma, I didn't think Mrs. Jarvis would be able to stand up straight.

But stand up straight she did. And as we all stood by and watched that colored woman consoling the white woman, sharing the pain of losing their sons, there wasn't much that a body with any decency could do but join them in their tears.

As I stood watching them, my legs shook beneath me, and I was thankful that for the first time in my life I understood something of what forgiveness was. After all, I'd been given a heaping dose of it myself.

My momma stood on the other side of Daddy, gripping his hand like a vise, but she dropped it and moved to take a spot alongside the two grieving mothers, no doubt feeling deep inside what she would feel if she'd lost one of her own girls.

I'd seen a lot in my life, enough to know that people are funny to figure out. There isn't often a time they do what a body figures on them doing. And now in the smothering heat, with the finality of death staring us all in the face, I watched in awe as, one by one, the women of Calloway took up vigil with a white woman and a colored woman.

Death may be painful and final, but I discovered that day how a door closing on one life can open up new life for others. As those women all huddled there, joined by the ties of motherhood, I began to believe that Calloway might just find a way to win out over all the hate that had poisoned it for years.

The husbands of most of those women stood by solemnly, heads bowed, but a few of the men watched the scene with hard faces, gripping their wives' wrists until they wrenched away. Three of those men succeeded in keeping their women back; only two of them had no need to use force because their womenfolk were just as hard of heart as they were.

Those two couples left in disgust, holding their heads high as though their dignity was far above all those they left behind.

But it wouldn't have mattered if they'd cursed us all up one side and down the other. Because that day, in that lonely old field, life in Calloway changed for most of us, and for the first time in all my days, I saw the hand of God working . . . and knew it for what it was.

Chapter 22

It would be a fairy story to say that all things bad in Calloway up and flew off that day, just like it would be a fairy story for me to say that I became a perfect angel the day I asked Jesus for forgiveness. But I can tell you one thing that happened at that funeral: people saw forgiveness up close and personal, and there just isn't a whole lot a body can say or do to destroy that. Some things just stand too strong to be knocked down.

Maybe the raw emotion that poured out all that day didn't seep into everyone's heart, but it did enough to get rid of the Klan in our parts. I don't know if any of those men ever saw the error in their ways or if it was just that their wives threatened to get out the shotgun if they didn't stop parading around town like white-robed fools, but one way or another we didn't see hide nor hair of them in our parts again. Oh, if I ever went crazy and had a hankering to hunt down some Klan, I'd find them easy enough over in the next town. But for all the rest of my years in Calloway, I never laid eyes on one again.

There's not a soul in this world that could tell me there's no such thing as miracles.

Despite all the goodness that had flooded our town, August came in on a warm breeze, bringing uneasiness to my spirit. We hadn't seen Luke since he left that day in July, and there was an empty spot in my heart getting bigger every day. He wrote me three times each week, telling me all sorts of things about his travels, but mostly saying how much he wished he could be back in Calloway. There was a change in the way he wrote to me now that he knew I shared his faith, now that there were no barriers between us, and I read those letters ten times over each day they came. Always there was a promise he'd be home soon, but as each day passed, I grew more restless.

While I waited, I put a million more creases in the Bible Gemma gave me. Most days I found free time to wander off to the meadow in search of some quiet, and I'd settle down under Luke's oak tree to find out more about what it was that made just believing in God so different from giving my life over to Him.

Every night, Momma used the prayer book Gemma

gave her, and she wrote the names of people in special need of prayer right along the margins.

Malachi Jarvis's name was on the upper right-hand corner on the first page.

I didn't have a book for writing down who I should pray for, but if I had, there would have been one name sitting right on the top of the first page.

Delmar Custis.

Who would have ever thought I'd do any praying for Delmar Custis except to ask the Lord to open the ground and swallow him up? But I did pray for him. Fervently. He'd been in the hospital ever since I'd watched him toted away that night, and though he was expected to live, it was already a certainty he would do so without the use of one leg. Ever since the day I'd come face-to-face with my hate, I'd tried what I could to make amends for it. Delmar wasn't allowed regular visitors, so I couldn't do much but send him things like flowers and food. I'd sent some notes to him, too, but I'd never heard a thing in reply. He'd lost half his leg to that bear trap, and even though Tal assured me he would have lost it even if he'd gotten help right off, I got worked up every time I thought about the horror of him waking up to find part of his body missing.

Sometimes on my walks I would pass by his ramshackle house and stare at the rocking chair on the porch where he usually sat with his moonshine. In all the days that I'd known Delmar Custis and his filthy ways, I'd had bitterness in my heart for him, and I'd never passed by his home without thinking bad things.

These days, though, even as lingering hostility bit at my thoughts, I managed to utter a prayer for him. And mean it.

I was learning more about miracles every day.

It was the third Saturday in August when I couldn't take the dreariness of waiting for Luke anymore and fled the house in search of something to ease the restiveness inside me. Evening was settling in, bringing a coolness that belied the heat of the day. The breeze swept across the grass, lifting my hair from my neck as I stared off into the clouds without a single thought in my head except Luke Talley, and the only place I could think of to find a piece of him was his house. I walked through the fields with the winds whispering through the leaves, the absent cicadas a jarring reminder that summer was on its last legs.

When I reached his property, I saw the swing from my childhood twisting lightly in the breeze. I ran a hand along one of the ropes before sliding into the seat, digging the tips of my shoes into the dirt to set myself into a gentle glide. The past flooded back to me, reminders of childhood parties, laughter with loved ones, meeting my first—and only—love. In my head I could hear Gemma and me giggling when we were supposed to be going to sleep. I could smell Daddy's pipe smoke and picture him pulling Momma into his lap to tease her about one thing or another.

When God enters a heart, He opens the eyes. That's one thing I'd learned right off. For the first time in my life, I was really seeing what I'd been given—all those blessings Momma had told me about but I'd never fully appreciated. And as I sat there in that swing, holding on to those memories just like I held on to the ropes, I breathed in the true goodness of all I'd had and hoped there was a lifetime of that type of goodness ahead so I could enjoy it all to the fullest.

I'd strayed so far into the past that I didn't hear Luke's truck when it pulled up next to the house. I didn't hear or see a thing until he leaned against the trunk of the oak tree and spoke my name.

I jerked my head around to see him standing there, the moonlight casting golden flecks across his hair, and dug my feet into the ground, standing up slowly on legs that had gone rubbery at the sound of his voice. "What took you so long?" I whispered.

He smiled and whipped me up in his arms just like I'd hoped he would at all his other homecomings. I clung to him until I felt we'd almost made up for lost time and then leaned back to look into his eyes. "I ain't so fond of these trips of yours, you know."

"Neither am I."

"I'm gettin' tired of seein' you go."

"I'm gettin' tired of leavin'."

"Well then—" I slid from his arms and faced him straight on—"you reckon on stayin' put for a while?"

"I do."

"Good."

He took a step away from the tree so that the moonlight glimmered off a shiny silver box he was trying to conceal in his hand.

I could feel my face light up. "You brought me somethin'?"

He tucked his hand behind his back. "It ain't nothin'. Anyways, you're too nosy for your own good, Jessilyn."

"Ain't my fault you can't hide nothin'." I slid my hand around his arm and gave it a tug. "Come on, now, let me see."

"You got yourself a big head, thinkin' everythin' I ever buy's got to be for you." His tone was stern, but his eyes twinkled playfully. "Ain't everythin' always about you, Jessilyn."

"No, but this is." I gave his arm another tug so that he had to step forward. "I ain't never been any good at waitin' and you know it. It ain't right for you to tease me like this."

"You know, you're a real piece of work. It's been weeks since you seen me, and you can't even take a second to say 'How you been?'"

I smiled at him. "How you been? Now can I have my gift?"

He shook his head. "I don't think I need to be givin' any gift to a girl as selfish as you."

He started to walk away, but I caught him from behind. "Luke, quit teasin'!" He held the box in front of him now, so I stood on tiptoe to peer over his shoulder, wrapping both my arms around his waist to give myself two chances at grabbing it.

But before I could wrap my hands around it, he took hold of my left hand and slipped something onto my finger.

I stood there motionless with my arms around him, afraid to take my hand away and find anything less than what I'd suddenly hoped would be there.

But Luke didn't wait. With my hand still in his, he turned to face me, cupping my cheek with his other hand. "Jessilyn Lassiter, you're stubborn and impatient . . . and darned if I don't love you with my whole life."

I looked from his face to my hand. The diamond that decorated my finger wasn't large. It wasn't cradled in a fancy setting or surrounded by precious stones. It was a simple, small diamond set in a gold band, but to me it should have been in a museum somewhere, on display for all the world to see. It was the most beautiful thing I'd ever laid eyes on, and it didn't take two shakes for my eyes to fill up with tears.

Luke laid my hand on his chest, let his forehead settle against mine, and whispered, "Marry me."

I couldn't say a thing. From the time I was thirteen, I'd dreamed about this moment—how it would happen, what I would say. But now that it had happened, I was speechless, a rarity for me anytime, much less at a time like this.

Luke waited as long as he could stand before pulling his face away from mine. "Jessilyn? You will marry me, won't you?"

The tears that had welled up slid down my cheeks, and it was like the release of them gave me back the use of my tongue. "Ain't nobody in this world could stop me."

The look of relief on his face made me smile. I reached my jeweled left hand up, tracing a line from his temple to his mouth. When he kissed me, the whole world melted away. For just that moment it was only the two of us, our hearts beating as one just as I'd always known they should. I sank into the security of his embrace and tried to make my mind capture every touch, every feeling, every breath we shared.

When he pulled away, I looked past his shoulder at the moon and held a hand up so it seemed to sit in my palm.

Luke looked at me quizzically and then peered over his own shoulder. "What'd you find?"

I closed my hand around the ball of light and smiled at him.

"My moondrop."

Chapter 23

Luke came across Malachi Jarvis one day as the summer neared its end. Just when we were thinking we'd never see him again, there he came out of nowhere, sitting at the side of the road, staring off into nothing. The way Luke tells it, Malachi was just a shell of his former self, all thin and worn-out so he looked ten years older than when he'd left. Luke didn't get much out of him about where he'd been or how he was getting by. All Malachi would say was he didn't know how to go home, how his momma could ever forgive him.

I figured if he'd been at Cole Mundy's funeral, he wouldn't have wondered such things. I've read all about the Holy Spirit and what God can do inside of people, but from what I've seen, I reckon that some people let Him do His work better than others. Malachi's momma was one of them. To hear the story told, when Luke got Malachi home, it was a sight right out of the Scriptures, the Prodigal Son being fed the fatted calf.

Malachi came around every now and again, but he wasn't the same anymore. Gemma used to fuss and bother over his smart mouth once upon a time, but I could see by her face she wished he'd up and do something annoying like he used to. She worried sick about him. I guess we all did. But I've learned from experience that worrying sick won't make something better and that time does wonders at healing pain even if it doesn't ever take it all away.

The cool silence of autumn has a way of making summer seem like a distant remembrance, and as time marched on, my own painful memories quieted along with the crickets and cicadas. There was a normalcy that set in, a day-to-day roll call of everyday things that remind folks that life has a way of moving on to better places.

And it did.

It moved on to all sorts of good places that are tacked onto my memory so sharply, I can remember the dates and times.

On the last day of September, Malachi Jarvis smiled for the first time since he found his brother hanging from a tree. Three days after that, I picked out the fabric for my wedding dress. And on the twentieth day of October, we found out Gemma was going to have a baby.

Times were changing, all right, but times were good, and as the trees turned three shades of golden, I said good-bye to another tumultuous summer, as glad to see it go as I had been to see it come. With the passage of time comes understanding, and from my new way of thinking, I figured understanding could go a long way to making a heart feel at ease.

Many days that autumn I walked past the dying oak tree where Noah Jarvis breathed his last, and as I stood there one day in the sunlight, I watched the last brown leaf flutter to my feet. I bent over to retrieve it, holding it up to the sun, twisting it between two fingers. Rays of light bent around it, making it out to be nothing more than a shadow.

But my memory of a boy full of life and promise would never be lost in shadow. Nor would my memory of all that had brought us to where we were now, mixed up in a world where darkness and hardened hearts do their best to smudge out the light of God's goodness. Because the memories of where we were remind us of how we got to where we are, and I had no intention of letting Noah Jarvis's life go unnoticed or forgotten.

Luke stood down the road waiting for me, allowing me a moment alone to say one final good-bye, and I opened my fingers to let that leaf drift to the dirt, the last vestige of a summer of terror and grief, of hate and forgiveness, of pain and healing.

And of new beginnings.

Discussion Questions

1. In *Catching Moondrops*, racial prejudice again rears its ugly head in Calloway, and some members of the black community are increasingly unwilling to accept it. While Malachi Jarvis becomes defiant, Tal Pritchett favors a more peaceful resistance. Discuss the different approaches these men take to express their independence.

2. The Ku Klux Klan reappears six years after they terrorized the Lassiter family. How does Jessilyn's reaction differ from Gemma's?

3. When Gemma's church is burned, she and Jessilyn have opposite reactions yet again. While Gemma's main concern is the well-being of Tal and the others at the church, Jessilyn is consumed by a desire for revenge. What does this tell us about Gemma's heart? about Jessilyn's?

4. Jessilyn isn't the only one discovering love this time around. Tal Pritchett quickly turns Gemma's heart inside out, and though Jessilyn initially encourages her best friend to pursue him, she suddenly becomes burdened by their relationship. What brings about the change of heart, and how does she move past it? Have you ever been in her shoes?

5. For the first time in Jessilyn's life, she's turning to someone besides her father with her fears and worries: Luke. How has time and age begun to make Jessilyn turn to someone other than her father for security?

6. Miss Cleta again defies tradition by receiving medical

care from Tal Pritchett. Why is Gemma so concerned about her doing this, and what are the eventual repercussions of Miss Cleta's decision?

7. Like Miss Cleta's choice to be treated by Tal, how does the trouble between Delmar and Malachi at the meeting place stir the pot of racial prejudice in Calloway?

8. A horrifying experience haunts Jessilyn's dreams and saps her strength. But only one perpetrator behind the despicable act demonstrates true shame. What do you think is the cause of such depravity? How are we all susceptible to evil infiltrating our hearts, and what can we do to keep that from happening?

9. Jessilyn's own heart is at risk when she allows bitterness and hate to fill it. What happens to make her see how lost she truly is? How does that moment change her life?

10. When Jessilyn discovers the darkness of her soul, she reaches out to the God she's heard about all her life but never truly felt the need for. What's the difference between believing in God and inviting Him to be Lord of your life?

11. Mrs. Jarvis's appearance at Cole Mundy's funeral is a stunning portrayal of forgiveness and grace. How does that moment affect those present and how do you think it turned the tide for race relations in Calloway?

12. Jessilyn's new life began the day she humbled herself before the God. What changes do we see in her as *Catching Moondrops* comes to a close? Have you experienced a similar moment in your life? And if so, how did that moment affect your future?

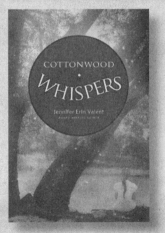
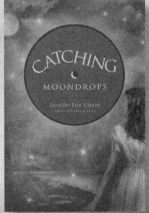

Do you love to read?

Do you want to go deeper?

Are you in a book group?

ChristianBookGuides.com

Visit today and receive

free discussion guides for

this book and many other

popular titles!

BONUS!

Sign up for the online newsletter and receive
the latest news on exciting new books.

CP0071